ONE ROTTEN APPLE

Robert Karp

ISBN 978-0-9980344-1-6

GOTCHA?

MONDAY, The Last Week in June, 1985

The final four troopers casually walked into the duty room in Waterbury. They joined four already seated among the rows of typical classroom vinyl and metal chairs with laminated half desk tops fixed to one side. It was not a big room. The Vermont State Police are a small force covering a large area, so any change of shift meetings were rare and, at best, only sparsely attended. Stephan Sears knew this wasn't a routine meeting.

Trooper Sears beamed as he turned his head and looked around the room at the seven other troopers seated with him. Five men and two women. He knew this was a special group. Trooper Sears was well regarded and those around him were either known stars or notable up and comers on the force. This was going to be special.

It was early morning, but by late June daylight was well established before most people, except farmers, were even out of bed. This was the beginning of the short warm season in Vermont. Every season in Vermont was eagerly anticipated because each was so different. The pleasures of this time of year were challenged by its brevity, black flies, and humidity. Some of those in attendance had driven a significant distance, often on country roads, to be in Waterbury at this early hour. They were pleased they were able to make the drive in daylight.

At 7:30 Chief Major Crime Investigative Officer Captain John Rondell and his deputy, Lieutenant Ted Vallan, walked in. They stood until a third person with them, Lieutenant Vallan's wife, Doctor Liza Vallan, sat and then they also sat down. Any soft chatter in the room stopped and the eight troopers all sat up, ramrod straight, facing the front.

There was a fourth chair next to the Captain. The Director of the Vermont State Police, Colonel Daniel Sawyer, walked in and sat down. As he entered heads turned but the Colonel quickly waved off the motions of several troopers to begin to stand. There was nothing reassuring or friendly about the manner or faces of those four in the back of the room.

Captain Rondell walked to the front of the room and addressed those assembled. His expression transmitted a weariness that was far from his usual demeanor. Rondell was a strict and serious senior trooper, generally known to be about as formal as a superior could be.

"Troopers. Thank you for gettin' here so early. I will not keep you here long. I know every day is a busy and challengin' day for each of you. I know you are busy.

"Every one of you knows that five weeks ago Doctor Eleanor Stanton, the Chief Medical Examiner for the state, died. She was found at the base of a hundred foot drop off the east side of the peak of Camel's Hump. Her loss is a blow to our state and a personal loss to those who knew her. Troopers, I'd like to have Doctor Liza Vallan, who many of you are aware is married to Lieutenant Vallan, come to the front of the room and speak with you. Dr. Vallan." Captain Rondell stayed up front until Liza was standing next to him at the small lectern and then walked back to his seat.

Liza Vallan looked tense and just as serious as the Captain.

"Troopers, Eleanor Stanton was a friend of mine. We were in med school together at UVM and also did our residency training in Burlington. Dr. Stanton went into pathology and after residency here did fellowships in forensic pathology to become a medical examiner. Anyone who knew her knows she was a special person. In particular, she was devoted to her profession and was very good at it. And she loved Vermont.

"After she died many of her close friends and associates were devastated. Even her teachers and colleagues were upset. I asked two of those colleagues, from out of state, to review the details of her death. A week ago Lieutenant Vallan and I sat with those nationally regarded medical examiners and reviewed every aspect of this terrible tragedy. Troopers, the conclusion of those experts and Lieutenant Vallan is that Dr. Stanton's death was not an accident. She was murdered."

No one in that room, now filled with eight startled law officers sitting rigidly at attention, allowed themselves any visible reaction or moved at all…except Trooper Sears. Sears broke out a grin and slyly leaned over and winked at the trooper next to him. Under his breath he said "puttin' together a special team, I'll bet." He oozed pride.

Liza Vallan walked to the back of the room as Ted Vallan came to the lectern. He looked very serious, but the expression on his face betrayed his anger too.

"Troopers this finding was a shock to many of us. Proof this was a homicide caused us to go back through our initial investigation and also consider much more about Dr. Stanton's personal and professional life. I'm sorry to say our early findings have raised a significant number of issues that are concerning us.

"That brings me to why you have all been told to be here this morning. Troopers, we believe that a Vermont State trooper in this room is responsible for the death of Dr. Stanton."

Almost every one of them reset or shifted in their chairs. There were enough gasps to allow a soft sound to be heard above the movement of belts filled with gear knocking on chairs. Their facial expressions remained frozen. Disbelief was as good a description of their faces as anything else. Lieutenant Vallan continued.

"The force will not end this investigation until this homicide is solved. Troopers, if one of you wishes to spare your peers and the force the turmoil this investigation will cause I encourage you to admit your guilt now and face the inevitable consequences of your terrible deed."

Trooper Sears raised his hand. He still looked much too casual for what was happening in that room. His colleagues and the brass in the back of the room all stiffened. With a look of uncertainty on his face Ted nodded in acknowledgement at Sears. There was absolute silence and maybe a few held their breath.

"Lieutenant, I'm just wondering how you want us to handle this with the media? I mean they and everyone else think this was an accident."

Ted was furious but tried to sound patient. "Sears, I will determine what we do about the media. No one in this room will say anything to any person about what you have just been told. Trooper Sears, let me be clear. None of you in this room are here to become part of this investigation. Not at all. In fact, you all have been called here because one of you is responsible for Dr. Eleanor Stanton's death."

Lieutenant Vallan stood silently at the front of the room and intentionally, slowly looked from face to face, one by one, at those sitting before him. He was somber. He also was sick at heart he had to challenge seven innocent troopers to try to root out the one who was responsible for what now appeared to be a heinous crime.

The stark, soundless room was still. No one, even Trooper Sears, dared ask how this group was determined and if, perhaps, any specific one of this group of eight was already considered most likely to be the killer. Colonel Sawyer got up and walked out without ever saying a word to anyone. He looked grim.

* * *

Ted Vallan knew he had a lot more to feel sick about than the stress on seven troopers, presumed innocent at least of homicide, whose paths had crossed Dr. Stanton's in one way or another. Try to spin it any way he could he had to accept he and his investigators missed some big clues and had not looked into her life more than casually. He now knew there was probably a lot more still to come out.

One enduring image of Ellie Stanton in Ted's mind was of a really attractive woman, more than striking in modest hiking shorts and boots highlighting her long, slim legs. He was always aware of her beauty but, for some reason, he had been clueless that sleeping around was one of her habits.

After he kissed Liza goodbye and she headed to Burlington he went to his office to meet with his junior investigator. Ted quietly cursed the commitment he made that spring to manage his son Henry's little league team. Doing community service was an important adjunct for moving up in the force. It was a little strange for Ted because he was happy in his present position as a senior investigator. Nevertheless, he took advice from others and just did it. He blamed that time commitment for dulling his skills and contributing to missing signs and facts that now others had found.

*   *   *

As he walked to his office Ted called over to Trooper Barry to follow him. Shawn Barry was sitting at his desk, one of the many small desks in the large open administrative area. Some years before it had been Ted's desk. The moment he walked into the open area Shawn's eyes caught him as Ted entered and navigated the main aisle to go to his office in the officer's corridor. Shawn was well aware Lieutenant Vallan was displeased with the events of the past week. He was sure some of the Lieutenant's dissatisfaction and anger would be directed toward him. His investigation of the death had not uncovered even a hint of what they were finding out now.

Ted picked up his phone and waved Trooper Barry to a chair and they each sat. Ted called Lieutenant James Dixon, from Internal Affairs, and asked him to alert unit commanders he wanted to be notified of any unusual trooper behavior throughout the force over the next week or so. Dixon was one of the few top brass aware of most of the details so far.

Ted was no longer so sure Trooper Shawn Barry had been such a good choice as a deputy investigative trooper in the major crime unit. He was thinking he may have misinterpreted eagerness for the intelligence, interest, and initiative he thought he saw in the trooper. So far he certainly hadn't done well in this case. Trooper Barry also had a habit of calling Ted Chief instead of Lieutenant which he found annoying. If he thought he had seen flashes of his younger and more green self in Barry now he began to wonder just how green he had really been at his own start on the unit. As unhappy as he was with himself he also did not spare his junior investigative trooper.

"Bullshit. This is bullshit." Ted leaned forward on his elbows on his desk. "Only a week since it became clear the ME was murdered and I've been able to put together a list of eight troopers who may have been closer to her than either of us would have assumed likely before. After she was found you worked this case daily for two weeks and all you told me was you thought she was sleeping around with some people and that was not a new thing for her." He was really angry. He found that easier to express than his disappointment. Ted stood up and took a few steps then sat on the edge of his desk, looking down at the Trooper.

That placed Shawn in a compromised position, forced to look up at his superior. It made him unhappy and he felt putting all the blame on him wasn't entirely fair. Shawn Barry had done consistently well in his first four years on the force and excelled at the various investigative courses he took to qualify him for his present position. Not yet thirty, he was bright, in good shape, and strongly committed to the force. Tall and lean, he had a pleasant face sitting beneath a shock of blond hair that would not be tamed in the front. Working with Lieutenant Vallan was a career defining opportunity he did not intend to mess up. Putting in long hours had not been a problem so far although recently getting more serious in his relationship with a girlfriend he was now beginning to feel some time pressures.

Early on Shawn was clear, in his own mind, both Ted and the Burlington PD had decided the Doc's death was an accident and there was very little intensity to the investigation until recently. But he did get the Lieutenant's intimation he probably should have approached the death as less certain to be an accident until he had probed the Doc's life more deeply. In retrospect there were some clues. Just to know she had many sexual partners wasn't good enough. That was obvious now.

Ted and Shawn could have had this same talk a few days earlier when Ted, investigating on his own, developed the list of the eight troopers he just confronted. But it was the recent moments, face to face with those troopers, that fueled his greater anger today. Standing in front of those eight, assuming one was involved with Ellie's murder, incensed him. The innocent were being made to feel guilty. Would they forgive the force for seeming to accuse them? Would any innocent trooper assume his career record would now be stained? And suppose he was wrong? Suppose none of these eight were involved? That was a possibility he chose to push from his thoughts.

He never considered replacing Shawn at this point. As flawed as his work had been Shawn was the one who knew the most about Ellie's death. Starting over with a new trooper wouldn't make sense just now. Ted tried to move on but his bad mood persisted.

"Shawn, wasn't Dr. Stanton's truck found near the base of the mountain?" He didn't wait for an answer. "Where is it now?"

"It's right here in Waterbury, out in the yard. You know we found it at one of the east trailhead parking access sites. I thought it was unusual that the Doc would drive almost around the mountain to approach it from so far from Burlington for a day hike. And the trail to the peak from there is probably the hardest way up. But everyone told me that was the way Doc did things; always taking the most challenging path, if she could. Thinking now about where her body was found, that access site is probably the closest to that area."

Shawn looked down and stayed quiet. He knew Ted was still angry. Ted figured a lot of new connections and probabilities would be developed with the new information.

Ted looked right at Trooper Barry. "I want that truck gone over again and I want you to tell those guys to find something this time."

"Chief. Chief. Nothing was found besides mud on the driver's floor. Doc was a mess. Whoever did this must have had another vehicle to move her and at some point brought her vehicle to that spot. Maybe there were two vehicles at the same time. Otherwise the killer would likely have left Doc's at a different access location. You think?"

Ted was wrestling with his loss of confidence in Trooper Barry. At that moment he wasn't interested in Barry's off the cuff theories. "And when they're done with her truck tell the lab folks to go back to her home again…and find something there too… Okay?"

*   *   *

It should come as no surprise that a criminal investigation is generally a messy business. It is a rare case where facts and assumptions can be easily placed in a box and neatly tied, with ribbon and bow. Long ago Vermont State Police Major Crime Unit Senior Investigative Trooper Lieutenant Ted Vallan had determined solving crimes required an ability to accept, even seek out, the unexpected. In fact, he was constantly reminding himself of the need to cast a large and sometimes ever enlarging net.

It often was necessary to consider almost everyone a suspect. It might seem counter intuitive but he had learned this approach was ultimately more efficient for solving crimes. That, and a maturing ability to remind himself to step back periodically and review an evolving case in a larger, less pre-determined context, had made a significant contribution to the successful resolution of many challenging cases; and the success of his career.

That approach made it all the more unusual and atypical for the Lieutenant to have become fixated so quickly on these eight Vermont State troopers, one of whom he seemed determined to accuse of the murder of Dr. Ellie Stanton. Hard evidence was, to say the least, truly meager. And yet, the little he did have caused a small rage in him. He knew anger was unlikely to be helpful in working through a murder; but he was angry. Was he reacting, in some way, to an odd association in his mind to his own life as a state trooper married to a physician, and the victim, a physician whose murderer, Ted believed, was likely a state trooper?

Clearly, others were skeptical of the way he quickly narrowed the investigation. His superiors were less than enthusiastic about what he had just done. But they did not challenge him…yet. Was he stubborn? Or was he so good; had unusual ability to have already looked at the large and small view and knew to commit time and resources to this path; that he knew where efforts should be directed? As in most situations in life the truth probably lay somewhere in-between. But he should have known, after all his years as a successful investigator, intuition was no good basis for structuring an investigation…That doesn't mean it didn't ever work.

* * *

THE SLEUTH AT HOME I

At home in the evening discussion about the dramatic event early that morning would have to wait. When Ted arrived Liza and the kids were ready for dinner. Liza had a longstanding hard and fast rule there would be no talk about virtually any police work in front of the kids. Ted recognized that as something of a double standard since Liza did want the kids to know about health care and the practice of medicine. She often spoke about sanitized versions of medical topics from her daily practice and health in general at dinner and elsewhere. Clearly they both, but especially Liza, wanted to encourage their kids to see the practice of a healing art in a positive light.

Ted was well aware Liza earned about twice his salary. In med school she earned nothing and in residency only a small amount. Now she was part of the faculty practice in addition to teaching responsibilities. Even working just less than full time she was earning the kind of income that doctors did. Her dramatic increase in income after residency was very welcome but, in a few ways, a difficult adjustment for Ted. Mostly he couldn't erase some anger and also even some sense of inferiority since Liza earned so much more than he did. He had spent years working very hard at his profession, studying and sharpening his skills, and couldn't imagine his job serving the public was any less important than what Liza did. They each labored in true life and death situations. They each put in long hours. And, of course, he had supported the family and Liza as she did all her medical training.

Just as he was clear, in his own mind, Liza was not overpaid for her career, he was sure he was underpaid for his work. Continually, he tried to blot out any negative thoughts or dissatisfaction that large disparity raised in him. He virtually never said anything to Liza about it. But it occasionally bothered and disappointed Ted that Liza never brought up or said anything to him about the absurdity of the difference in their incomes. This was something he supposed he had to live with; had to adjust to. Any tension this caused in their relationship was generated by him, and him alone, he guessed.

Regardless of a law officer's income Ted had some ambivalence about the idea of one of his kids going into police work. He loved what he did and found endless challenges in his work. He prized that his job was anything but routine and he enjoyed the respect his profession gave him in the community. But he also understood much of his work related to the darker side of society and human behavior. There was danger also. Or at least the constant threat of most any situation becoming dangerous. So he was okay with the approach Liza strongly championed with the kids.

They both were living busy, complicated lives. It was fortunate they each understood their equally challenging careers required time to share thoughts, problems, and of course stress to try to prevent either one of them from becoming overwhelmed from time to time. It was just Ted's issues were to be left to times when the two of them were alone.

* * *

Liza had worked hard for what the Vallans had. She didn't need to pinch herself as though it was all luck. She had to be pleased and have a strong sense of satisfaction. She had pulled it off. A loving marriage with mutual respect; Two bright and sweet kids; even the dog, George the 2nd, was a great pooch. And she loved everything about her home.

The Vallans lived about twenty minutes east of Burlington where Liza worked at the medical school and hospital and about twenty minutes west of State Police Headquarters in Waterbury where Ted was based. Their home was an endless pleasure and sanctuary to Liza. Essentially a newer tract house subdivision, there were few custom features when they moved in ten years before. It was located on a street with about a dozen others just off the main town road in the small rural hamlet of Richmond.

When the brand new house was completed and moving day arrived Liza was truly startled and overcome to find Ted had found a way to have a copy made of the small eighteen by eighteen inch leaded glass window she adored in their craftsman style rental home in Burlington. He had it installed on the wall at the landing opposite the stairs to the second floor. She often stopped to admire it as she descended the steps, especially when light reflected through the colors of the west facing window. Only recently when Henry, the eleven-year-old, started to refer to the black vertical lead strips as bars in a jail cell did some of the window's allure seem to fade.

And she loved her career. Almost fifteen years after entering medical school, every day now she was doing what she had dreamed about for most of her life. There were struggles all along the way; for all of them. But she knew it was worth it; for all of them, she thought. Liza was filled with ideas for her continuing future in medicine.

Ted, and others, did not miss the notable change in Liza's attention to her appearance the past year. She was more interested in her clothes, hair, and even often wore some make-up now. As her confidence grew with her achievements professionally and child-care became less intense and time-consuming Liza was actually blossoming a bit; becoming a more self-assured woman in different ways than in her past.

Liza wished Ted would also become more self-confident. His professional success was clearly an indication of his ability but apparently he could not resolve some of the self-doubt that seemed to continue to gnaw at him. She wondered if he would remain that way forever.

Learning about Ted's blue collar background was often a surprise to people who interacted with him. Along with his well-known dogged persistence in all his cases, his thoughtfulness, and especially creative thinking in white collar cases made him a frequently consulted member of the force. Drafted right after high school during the Vietnam war Ted wound up in the military police. Impressing some of his senior officers who, over time, became mentors, he quickly progressed from simple assignments to actual crime work. His mentors wanted him to stay in the army and go to a university, which was a good opportunity for a kid from a family where no one had ever been to college. But he missed Vermont and decided to use his GI college aid to go to a local community college and work part-time in the Essex Town police force.

Somehow, in those days before they met, they each managed to find time to volunteer on local rescue squads. Rigs parked side by side at the Burlington hospital Emergency Department the two met folding blankets and the rest, as they say, is history. Both recognized they were each a little too serious but couldn't seem to help it. They were physically attracted to each other and loved hiking and also relaxing together. Their plan was to stay in Vermont forever. He joined the Vermont State Police and she finished her undergraduate degree and worked in administration at UVM (The University of Vermont) for a year to save some money and then started medical school.

They married during her first year and by the end of her second year there was Kathy. It was an endlessly complicated time but they made it work. Generally, it was so continually busy there was rarely time for either of them to even begin to reflect on the flow of their lives during many of those years.

Few women in medicine achieved both the professional and personal success that Liza Vallan managed to accomplish at that time and she became a role model and mentor to other young women. Soon there were many who followed her. Ted's support and cooperation, which greatly aided Liza's ability to be successful, did not go unnoticed. To his great surprise, and the surprise of his close buddies, many in the state who knew of this couple heaped praise on Ted as a positive image of the modern male spouse. Mostly, he felt he did what he had to do, or needed to be done, for his wife and family. They worked it out.

Ted and Liza shared a mostly compatible life and outlook about raising their family and the world. Liza was a bit more liberal than Ted in both those areas but, of course, they worked it out.

Ted was valued and successful on the force and was advancing in his career. An eternal frustration for him all along, though, was that notable ability he seemed to have at managing and solving those white collar cases did not come nearly as directly with violent crime. Running the major crimes unit for the busiest part of the state utilized all his skills. Despite his experience and proven ability Ted knew he still longed to have the self-confidence that would let him make decisions and judgements more easily. He remained his harshest critic. He wished he could feel, especially with violent crime, he was one step ahead rather than one step behind in his investigations. He saw himself as a plodder; a tenacious plodder. For him, he thought violent crime should be easier to unravel than non-violent crime. Maybe.

Time to go running together was mostly an activity from the past for this busy couple so now they usually did that independently. With that exercise and apparent fortunate genetic gifts they both trended almost too thin as they flirted with forty. At the Burlington hospital Liza was known universally for her excellent medical skills and notably compassionate care. She was interested in everything in her specialty, internal medicine, but remained determined to continue working a little shy of full-time until the kids were a few years older. By now she had less vivid memories of Ted's struggles to support her and the family during the more than challenging years of her education and training. And Liza never really thought about the discrepancy in their incomes so it would have been a surprise to her it bothered Ted.

* * *

Around eight-thirty the kids were watching TV in the den and Liza and Ted were in their appointed chairs on the porch. Crickets and lightening bugs were very active. The day was cooling off nicely. Some of Ted's energy and concerns about the extraordinary day were less acute to him by then but it remained his main preoccupation.

"In my mind I guess I thought all of us standing up there in front of those troopers was going to go differently. As I watched them react to what we said, except for that gunner Sears, I couldn't read anything on their faces. I guess I thought one of them might show a sudden change that might actually be...."

"Oh my goodness, Ted. Really! Did you really think one of those faces was going to expose her killer just from hearing what we said?" Liza's tart response seemed a bit stronger than it needed to be to Ted. He thought she could at least hear him out.

"Ted, most of that group looked like kids, for goodness sake. They all looked blindsided to me; more glazed over than anything. But you're right, I certainly didn't notice any one of them look guilty, if that's what you mean?"

"Well, I know it wasn't too likely anyone would react like that right then. But the complete lack of really any response, maybe what you're calling 'glazed over', that did kind of surprise me. I don't know; I guess I figured there would be some differences in reactions. I don' know why."

"Truthfully Ted, I didn't think much would come from doing something like that. I think you may have put yourself in a tough spot, out on a limb, by telling everyone you're so sure one of those troopers had to be Ellie's murderer."

"Babe I don't know who killed Ellie but I'm pretty sure one of them was involved in her death. And you know what? Late this afternoon I got a call from one of those troopers that he wants to meet with me in the morning. Who knows where that might go and if any others are going to contact me?"

Liza was genuinely surprised. "That is interesting." Then she moved on. "Hey, talking about those troopers, what did you think about that female trooper, Ted?"

"I don't know. What do you mean? Which one?"

"Are you kidding, Ted? She didn't stand out to you?"

"No." Ted had an almost guilty response. What could have been so obvious to Liza and have meant nothing to him? Two young female troopers. Could have been twins for all he knew.

"Ted, who wears a rain jacket, all zipped up, to a meeting on a hot summer day?" She didn't plan to let him look clueless any longer. "I'll bet you anything she's pregnant, Ted. Looked to me like the zipper on that jacket was getting too tight to even zip."

Ted spoke but it was like he wasn't really in the room. He was dumbfounded. His voice sounded like he was in a daze.

"No…No babe, she's not married… And she isn't allowed to be pregnant and be a trooper."

* * *

LOSS OF A FRIEND

Two Weeks Earlier

Three weeks after her death those who worked in the morgue, who knew Dr. Ellie Stanton, were unhappy she was still residing on a cold slab in a refrigerated locker. There was a growing sense of mutiny in the air that a month might pass with her just left in that locker. By the third week the people who worked there began to talk more openly about their upset. Their dissatisfaction was being expressed more and more defiantly.

Liza Vallan just couldn't let go.

Liza appeared to have absolutely no good reason to be blocking final interment for her friend but she would not let Ted release her body. Dr. Harry Fowler, the Chair of the Department of Pathology, did the post and he was an excellent pathologist. But he was not a forensic pathologist. A small state like Vermont had barely enough business for one medical examiner and Eleanor Stanton was it.

You didn't need a pathologist to see that Ellie Stanton's death was the result of a tremendous amount of trauma. Her body was filled with broken bones and her head, in particular, was misshapen and a bloody mess.

Later, it was unclear if anyone from the Major Crime investigative force had been any part of the initial crime scene investigation. Dr. Stanton was spotted from the cliff she, allegedly, fell from and extricating her from the densely wooded area more than one-hundred feet below was a major challenge. The State Police Search and Rescue Squad along with the Stowe Technical Response Team were tasked with removing her body. Just getting to her was time consuming and very difficult. Removing her body was harder.

Troopers tried to document the scene with photos, measurements, and a cursory investigation of both the area where the Doctor was found and the presumed location from where she fell. The day after she was last seen it rained most of the day. From the time she went missing and several days later, when her body was found, there had been another day of drenching rain. Until days after she was removed from the scene no one from Lieutenant Vallan's group of investigators was ever at the location on top of Camel's Hump or one-hundred feet below in the dense forest where she was found. In reality, probably no one from that group ever had been at the site where she was found.

Even though there was strong feeling her death was a terrible accident of course the possibility of an intentional crime was considered. Ellie Stanton was well known to be an avid hiker. She frequently went off on her own for day hikes, especially on trails she had used for years. She was an early practitioner of what is now called speed hiking where she walked as fast as she could both up and down mountain tops and ridges. May was spring and the trails certainly were wet and slippery. Any idea she could have fallen because of a health emergency seemed very unlikely since she was extremely fit and only just forty. Besides, her autopsy revealed only the terrible consequences of trauma; no major disease was found.

Did she climb just a little too close to a slippery ledge and fall? Or was she pushed? The nature of hiking in the deep woods on the 'Long Trail' meant there were often other solitary individuals or groups of various numbers around. Any stranger to her, who was only passing through, and committed such a horrific act would be very difficult to find. Early on, a trooper spent twenty-four hours on the summit of the hump dressed as a Green Mountain Club caretaker, talking to passers-bye, trying to learn if there was any talk about the terrible accident among the many mountain travelers back in mid-May. Mostly he was amazed at how morbid curiosity seemed to compel so many to lean treacherously over the side of the mountain to look down at the site where Ellie Stanton's body was found. It was a wonder no one else fell over.

* * *

Weeks after Ellie Stanton's death Liza still often talked about her or her death. Sometimes it seemed like she suddenly interrupted her own thoughts, or a conversation with Ted, and would wind up talking about Ellie. This evening it happened again.

"You know, you think you know someone pretty well and then you hear or see something about them and sometimes a very different life is revealed to you. Ted, remember Reed Finch." A statement, not a question. "That whole thing just blew us away. And we knew him for three years. I worked with him frequently on the wards."

Ted certainly remembered Reed Finch and what happened to him. If there was ever an example of a person with a secret life, or a part of him intentionally hidden from the people around him in Burlington, Reed Finch was that. Reed was a sweet, friendly guy who even baby-sat Kathy once or twice when none of their usual cadre of nursing students was available and they had to go somewhere for a short time.

"He was such a smart guy. I think he was the first doc I ever worked with who seemed to practice what I call effortless medicine. It always seemed he was able to assess problems and decide what to do with ease while I've, like most everyone, always struggled with trying to make good decisions. We used to have him, and sometimes Henry Janus, over for dinner. We were the married couple and they were on their own. Sometimes Henry had a girlfriend around.

"We knew Reed was obsessed with Opera and Beverly Sills, in particular. Any chance he had to put two or more days off together he was on his way to New York City. When he returned he would fill me in on the opera event he attended. There didn't seem to be any reason not to believe him. He was a very smart guy and seemed quite content in the program and his life. I think I once tried to set him up with a med student I knew. It didn't work out and that was fine.

"When he finished residency he went out to San Francisco and we lost track of him. I think he did a fellowship but I'm not sure. I think back now and maybe there were some signs or indications, like the way he seemed so fastidious about decorating his tiny apartment or his obsession with orchids. But that really was not much. Till the day I die I'll never forget the moment in that auditorium in Pittsburgh last fall talking with a woman from San Fran sitting next to me at the national primary care meeting. Like all recently trained docs do we chatted about any people we might know in common.

"You've heard me talk about this before but the jolt she gave me was just unbelievable. I tossed out Reed's name and her face just drained and sank. Being told he had just died of AIDS was unbelievable to me. Oh man! A truly secret life. Nothing dark, just a secret life. He chose never to share any of that with us, or anyone around here, as best I know.

"Ted, when I think about Reed being gone I miss him but I also feel kind of guilty. Like I wasn't able to help or support him in any way. Certainly while he was dying but even as a friend when he was here. We wouldn't have cared or reacted any differently to him if we had known he was gay. Would we?"

Liza was back into her upset again. Ted had a good idea what was coming. Liza looked sad but, more than that, her face showed the uncertainty that continued to plague her about Ellie.

"Ted, I feel like I let Ellie down; a little like Reed. I had inklings she had some secrets in her life. But like the good WASP I am I never went down any path with her so that she might have shared other parts of her life with me; or us. You know what I mean? Maybe she was involved in stuff that was overwhelming her ability to control some of the things she did or happened to her in her life.

"So, maybe she slipped or even jumped. But I really doubt it. I think she had some secrets in her life and some of that got her into trouble. Somehow I think that's why she wound up in the middle of the woods."

Ted understood Reed Finch's surprising story and death had an impact on how Liza was reacting to the death of another friend. As far as Reed Finch was concerned Ted never said anything to Liza but he had thought maybe Reed was gay. Reed was an awfully nice guy and Ted guessed from the way he spoke and the way Liza talked about him he was a really sharp doc. He just wasn't the kind of guy you ever worried about time your wife spent with him at work. AIDS, and dying because he was gay, seemed unfair to Ted, just like it was for so many others. He remembered him as a good guy and dying so young with a disease that was still almost unheard of in Vermont was very sad.

Ellie Stanton was another person entirely. Energy and beauty were what flashed in your mind when her name came up. Liza and Ellie were in the same med school class and interned together. Liza completed an internal medicine residency and Ellie did pathology. They saw each other less regularly after their first year of residency, but the programs at UVM were small so they still stayed in touch, pretty frequently. Ted remembered those occasional hikes but not much else socially. Ellie was away for fellowship training for at least three years after they each completed their residencies. Since Ellie returned Ted saw her from time to time, mostly in her capacity as Chief (and the only physician) Medical Examiner for the entire state.

She was a woman whose appearance might definitely cause a wife to worry about time a husband would be with her. With what was turning up Ted was surprised he never felt uncomfortable or awkward with her. He doubted Liza ever was concerned knowing he had met with Ellie at the ME office. Actually, he had never thought about such a thing before.

Ellie was consistently friendly, helpful, and patient with him. He thought they had a good working relationship. Ellie always asked after the kids and Liza. Ted would casually ask how things were going for her but he never was seriously interested in her private life and she never, that he could recall, volunteered anything much about herself. Only in retrospect did Ted ever think maybe that was at all odd since they did know each other reasonably well.

The word he got from Liza was that Ellie did have a succession of boyfriends. Once, years before, Liza said she heard Ellie had gone out with someone from the force. At the time it didn't strike either of them as especially unusual since ME's and law enforcement crossed paths frequently. And, after all, Liza was a doctor married to a trooper.

"Ted, once someone is buried I guess it's not easy to get them exhumed for any further investigation for something like cause of death, is it?"

"No, it's difficult and, after even a short time, any ability to get good information becomes harder and harder. Except maybe for things like tox stuff. Babe, don't know if you were aware but Ellie's remains are to be cremated. So after she leaves the morgue there will never be anything to re-examine. You know, her older brother is her only living relative. He's down in Connecticut. Frankly, I'm amazed he hasn't put any pressure on us to release her remains. Did you know him at all?"

Liza looked up and to the right, a common posture for her when trying to recall things. "I met him at least once when both Ellie and I were doing our first year of residency. For pathology a year of internal medicine was still required then. I remember once he came up with her parents for some occasion and I, briefly, had coffee with them in the cafeteria. The only thing about him that struck me was that he didn't seem at all like Ellie. She was always so outgoing and lively and, even though he was older, he seemed disinterested and unusually quiet; more like a kid brother. I guessed he was just shy, although I remember he was recently back from Vietnam and maybe that affected him in some way. A year later Ellie's parents died in some kind of accident and I was unable to go to the funeral since I was getting too pregnant with Henry.

"I know he was all Ellie had left. She was so young I bet she didn't even have a will. I wonder where the idea of cremation came from?"

* * *

It was about eight in the evening. Ted and Liza had finished cleaning up the dishes and were sitting, as they often did, on the small screened porch Ted and his father, Thom, had built the previous summer. Any breeze always found its way to that porch which overlooked the fenced back yard and woods beyond. It was private and often the coolest spot in the house. Liza loved it. She felt like she was outside in the open air but away from the world; and now in the summer, free of pesky insects. For almost three seasons it was her favorite place to relax.

Liza was sipping from a tall glass of ice water. Ted was finishing a beer. Since Ellie was found Liza noticed Ted was having a beer after dinner almost nightly. She sensed a tension in him, just as she felt. Finding out, tonight, if no further investigation of Ellie's remains took place soon there would never be any more opportunity in the future upset her.

Henry was in the yard running around with George the 2nd, their two-year-old chocolate lab. Kathy was up in her room reading. Kathy, fourteen, would be asleep very soon. Helping out at the local fruit and vegetable farm nearby was exhausting her and Liza thought it might be weeks before she adjusted to the hard work. It was going to be a great summer for her. She knew Kathy was very excited to be making some money. She was a directed girl, very much like her mother. She also liked to take chances and that worried her mother. Kathy was the first of their several generation Vermont families who was becoming a downhill skier. Ted and Liza facilitated her interest and learning but Liza wasn't so sure she was happy about the obvious dangers of flying down icy mountain trails.

Sitting on the porch that evening thinking about all this Liza, in a bit of a reverie, began to conflate the lives of her friend, Ellie, and her daughter. She knew if something ever happened to Kathy she would never stop investigating until she was sure she knew every detail about what had happened. In some ways it seemed like she felt closer to Ellie since her death than the last three or four years. She didn't know why but she was suspicious about how Ellie could manage to fall off a cliff. Time was running out so it was now or never if any other explanation was to be considered.

Ted was lost in his own thoughts and found himself hoping the beer was going to help him get sleepy so he'd feel good about going to bed. All his cases seemed tough lately. The careful, deliberate, case work he was known for wasn't fitting the kinds of cases which were prominent right now. Plus, he was pissed about all the time he had to give to coaching little league. He didn't think he was even any good at it. And Henry often seemed embarrassed about the way he handled the other kids. He thought to himself 'Why the fuck did I ever agree to do this!' He was committed until at least the end of July. It was his fervent hope his team would stay crappy and he could beg off and be done with all of it before the league all-star team, likely without Henry on it, was put together for county-wide play.

Liza's voice pulled him out of his thoughts.

"I got a letter today from one of Ellie's friends from training I wrote to tell about Ellie's death. He's a Deputy Chief Medical Examiner in New York City now. Pretty big title I think. Anyway, he wrote some nice things about Ellie. He also mentioned they had a mutual acquaintance during fellowship who is now the Medical Examiner for Arapahoe County in Colorado and is building a name for himself in the kind of outdoors forensics that might be of use for a case like what happened to Ellie.

"Ted, Harold Fowler is a good guy, but I'm just not satisfied. We don't know why Ellie is dead. I don't want Ellie's remains to disappear without us trying to get every piece of information we can about why she is gone. Don't you think we can get the force to fly that medical examiner in from Colorado to give us the most complete information possible about her death?"

Ted wondered what further or new information could be developed by doing another autopsy. He also knew no one, maybe besides Liza, seemed to even care anymore about why Ellie Stanton was dead. A terrible accident was, by far, the most likely explanation. Why even consider looking at everything again? The State Police was rarely willing to pay for any outside experts for case work. He was aware though, on occasion, the Medical Examiner's office did send stuff out or bring in experts.

"Hell, babe, the ME's budget is probably not getting spent since Ellie's salary isn't being paid. That office probably can afford it. Talk to Doc Fowler. If you'd like, I'll tell him I think it's a good idea also. Hell, why not get the guy from New York up also, if you think. Let's try to put all this to rest." Ted was glad he kept his swearing mild. Liza might challenge his recent nightly beer if he let it get any rougher.

* * *

DEFINING THE CRIME

Dr. Harold Fowler was quite content with the academic parts of being a chair at the med school and directing the clinical pathology department at the hospital. Personally completing fewer, not more, post-mortems was his goal at this point in his career. He was working hard to replace Ellie Stanton as soon as possible. When Liza approached him the next day he immediately thought two visiting ME's might be helpful in his search for her replacement. He gave his okay.

The ME's office staff relaxed when they were told another autopsy was to be completed. Liza had to disrupt her own schedule to assist them in coordinating the visit of the two pathologists but the staff did most of the work. The trip came together so quickly Liza didn't have time to even forward a copy of the records she had. The men didn't mind. They felt they were coming as a courtesy to Ellie and Liza, not to second guess Dr. Fowler.

The State Police contacted Dr. Stanton's brother, advising him a second autopsy was planned. There was some surprise when, after all this time, he said he was annoyed and requested a call from Ted to explain why this was going to happen. Ted noted the resistance to the procedure by her brother. He tried but decided he couldn't know if his reaction meant he was upset about further disturbing her body or if her brother had other reasons. In any event, after Ted made it clear the state had the right to overrule any family concerns in situations like this, the brother, with more anger in his voice than Ted had ever noted previously, said he wanted the cremation to take place as soon as the second autopsy was completed.

* * *

In only a few days it was set for Dr. Harry Burns, from Boulder, Colorado to fly to New York to meet Dr. Rhaji Agarwal and they would fly together to Burlington. Liza felt a personal responsibility to the doctors, and to the ME's office budget, to arrange their time as efficiently as possible. She assumed Dr. Burns, at least, might want to hike up Camel's Hump to view the topography of that location.

It didn't turn out to be necessary. Both doctors were on their way home in forty-eight hours.

* * *

Almost predictably, Harry Burns was a tall, muscular man, with a sizable reddish beard, who looked like he spent as much time outdoors as possible. He was affable and happy to be in Burlington, telling anyone who would listen the Vermont hills looked inviting from the air, even though there still was some snow in the much taller Rockies. Rhaji Agarwal was more studious appearing and serious. When he met Liza he quickly asked if he could distribute a questionnaire he was developing to her and all Dr. Stanton's co-workers in pathology and the ME's office as a possible predictor her death was suicide.

No one liked the thought her death could have been suicide. Liza, however, understood, in all aspects of providing medical care and judgment, developing and testing hypotheses were what doctors do. There were only five questions and all staff completed what was requested. Dr. Agarwal said the results of the survey made suicide seem less likely.

While Dr. Stanton was thawing a bit, Dr.'s Burns, Agarwal, Fowler, and Vallan and Ted sat in Dr. Fowler's morgue office and reviewed what they had. The first notable sign all was not as Dr. Fowler had thought came when the post-mortem x-rays were placed on viewers along a wall behind the chairs where the out of town pathologists were seated. Initially they both turned their necks and seemed to look causally. Fairly quickly one, then the other, stood up and walked back and forth along the four x-ray viewing boxes. Then they pulled those pictures down and put up others from the folder.

"Given at least a one-hundred foot fall and the likelihood of bouncing off rocks, trees, and brush on the way down these films are a surprise." Dr. Burns kept moving and looking at different shots as he spoke. His voice reflected his surprise.

"There are several skull and facial bones fractures, and I think that's to be expected. What puzzles me are two things." Dr. Agarwal nodded in agreement, as though he thought he knew where Burns was going with this. The rest of those in the room didn't react one way or the other.

"First, I think it's odd that except for one high cervical fracture here," he pointed to a spot just below the skull, "probably C2, all the remaining fractures are in extremities; both mid femurs, and a bunch of fractures in both arms. So then, after all that trauma, there are no notable other vertebral fractures or, amazingly, any obvious rib or pelvic fractures. That's unusual, from a big fall."

Dr. Agarwal spoke up: "You know, with the number of upper extremity fractures you could assume an effort to protect her head as she was falling. But when we see this in my neighborhood we usually think of defensive injuries from trying to protect against and deflect blunt trauma."

"I see. I see." Dr. Fowler, always the gentleman, was trying to accept, with equanimity, the potential of a wildly different interpretation of his findings. Ted noted that Liza was heavily into the discussion and would likely not give even a hint of her response to all this until more was completed. For Ted this was the first inkling he was about to find out that a hell of a lot of time, too much time, had passed without his team doing a proper investigation.

This early indication the exercise might be important made it a little easier for both Liza and Ted to prepare themselves to better accept, actually stomach, what they each knew was coming next. Multiple trauma victims were never easy to look at. In the ED, twisted and torn up and bloody bodies were often also permeated with the odor of gasoline or alcohol or, sometimes, both. Anytime she smelled gasoline Liza was reminded of bodies she had to deal with in the ED during training. Ted actually had less exposure to such gruesome sights. Neither of them had watched the first post without feeling ill. Ellie's face was unrecognizable.

Dr. Fowler led the way to Dr. Stanton's body, covered by a sheet, resting on a gleaming stainless steel table. None of the pathology assistants, or dieners, were in attendance as the pathologists would assist each other. Ted and Liza stood near a wall a few feet from the prosecting table and Dr. Fowler brought a stool over and placed it near Ellie's feet. Dr. Agarwal slowly peeled back the sheet, from her head to her toes. It was clear her misshapen face was still covered with blood.

Ted and Liza were surprised Ellie hadn't been cleaned up after the last post. But Dr. Burns quickly thanked and praised Dr. Fowler for leaving Ellie in her post-morbid state. Who knew? Later Ted disagreed with the apparent traditional forensic approach of leaving a victim's body in such condition. If Ellie had been cleaned up sooner his murder investigation would have been weeks old by then.

The pathologists went about their business quietly and quickly established a routine for going through a well memorized check-list in their heads, documenting their findings via a voice-activated dictating machine. Ellie's head was saved for almost last, but the doctors had plenty to say before they got to that point. Indeed they predicted what they would find when they did examine her head.

Among terribly discolored and bruised parts of her legs and arms they believed there were linear markings suggesting at least some of her injuries were caused by a long object; most likely some sort of heavy metal rod they thought. They were even more sure of this when they saw a clear correlation of the skin findings and the location of the left and right mid femur (thigh) fractures on the x-rays.

The only way to find out if there were any indications that something like a rod-like structure could have caused or contributed to the trauma on her face was to carefully clean up the blood, especially clots, now long pasted on most of her face. Teeth and hair were stuck to the dried blood. The pathologists made sure a bucket was under the drain for the table and, patiently, worked with small amounts of warm saline (salt water) to slowly dab away and dissolve the blood. It was a gruesome process for Liza and Ted to watch.

But the doctors clearly were right. Some form of rod or heavy round object had been used, with great force, to destroy Ellie's beautiful face. Her nose and left eye were smashed. Her mouth seemed filled with dried blood. Somehow, despite initially praising Dr. Fowler for leaving all the clots the younger pathologists now seemed critical of his leaving material in her mouth. As one turned her head to the side the other poured the warm saline solution and used his gloved finger to pull loose clot out. The clot dissolved on the table in the warm solution.

"Oh my, Look at this." Dr. Agarwal crushed a clot between his gloved fingers. He went to the sink and carefully washed off an object. "It looks like a button. And there is still some thread wound in it." He placed it on the specimen table and the others came over to look. Ted's heart sank. Dr. Burns now expressed the obvious.

"Well I doubt that button wound up in the Doctor's mouth falling down a mountainside. And I'm sure you're right Raj, her upper extremity fractures could be from a defensive effort while being beaten. I wonder if she bit that button off while trying to defend herself?"

Ted was shaky on his feet. He walked the few steps back to the wall, raised one leg, placed it on a bench and leaned against the wall. His brain was racing and he felt a damp sweat. He thought about it for a little while. Then he realized Liza was looking at him and was obviously wondering what he was doing. The pathologists continued their work. Ted faced her and spoke to Liza, who was standing with the others now.

"That button…and that thread. I guess there are lots of possibilities where it came from. But, you know, everything about the uniforms in the force are distinctive and I bet that button and thread are from a Vermont State Police uniform."

Everyone stopped whatever they were doing and looked at Ted and the pained expression on his face. No one said anything…because what was there to say? No matter where the button came from Ellie Stanton was murdered and it was more than likely that button meant something about the circumstances of her death. His face fixed like stone Ted sat down on the bench and stayed there for the duration of the procedure.

The two pathologists looked closely under Ellie's fingernails for signs of any debris or material that might have been lodged there. The new and ominous findings being uncovered made it essential to search for any and all possible clues. Even if you, erroneously, believed fingernails can continue to grow for a short time after death it wouldn't have mattered with Ellie Stanton if they did. Ellie was a pathologist so she always kept her nails as short and as smooth as possible. No sense risking ever being contaminated by any of the millions of bad things that could be present on the bodies she worked with. So there was little to look for. One held a pointed probe and the other a glass slide as they scratched beneath the edge of each nail. But nothing dropped onto the slide.

To be complete, towards the end of the examination, Ellie was turned over and her anal region was inspected. Dr. Fowler had examined for vaginal trauma or penetration (and found none) but not anal. The out of town pathologists were suspicious of the appearance of the anatomy and took some swabs which later, after testing, turned out positive for semen.

The doctors chatted while they were finishing up. Dr.'s Burns and Agarwal, and now Dr. Fowler also, agreed that Ellie Stanton was murdered. Dr. Burns said her almost floppy arms and legs could have been caused by worsening of her fractures as her body was moved through the woods to the spot where she was found and also later when she was removed. Dr. Burns did not believe Ellie was thrown or fell off a cliff. He believed she was placed on the ground in a spot where it would be assumed she had fallen from the cliff.

Finally, the three pathologists and Ted moved to a corner where Ellie's clothes were displayed. They were almost in tatters, probably successively torn and ruined, from the time of her murder to the trip into and out of the dense forest and then final removal for her autopsy. A small keychain with keys to her home, office, and truck were in a pants pocket, along with tissues, a hard candy, and a few coins. There was little further information to be gleaned from examining her clothes.

Liza had walked to the metal slab where what was left of Ellie remained. A diener had been called in and he was pouring warm water on her hair trying to dissolve the last few clots. Ellie was about to be packed up to be cremated so Liza wasn't sure what the point was. She wanted to see Ellie get covered by the sheet again. She didn't regret putting Ellie through a second post, but she had very mixed feelings about the findings. Now she felt this was enough and she wanted to try to remember her as a person, not the way she looked on the slab.

Tears welled up in her eyes. Without thinking about it Liza reached out with her hand to touch Ellie's forearm, which was tucked next to her torso. As she did it she noticed, next to Ellie's arm, some debris sliding down the table with the bloody water being pulled along the slightly indented table to the hole where the bucket was. Instinctively, she reached for it and picked it up. It was another button, and it also had a piece of thread attached.

The button Dr. Agarwal found was hammered brass, commonly seen on state police uniforms. This button was a more typical bone or plastic round shape with holes in the center. It struck Liza it was notably smaller than any button she had ever seen or repaired on any of Ted's uniforms. The diener had taken no notice of Liza picking up an object. She kept it in her palm and helped the diener cover Dr. Eleanor Stanton with the sheet. She said good-bye to her friend for the last time.

Liza had responsibilities to the two out of town pathologists and her practice so she barely said good-bye to Ted as the session broke up. She didn't even really have time to consider the implications of the findings until she and Ted spoke that evening after the kids were in bed. Until then she didn't give much thought to what this all meant to Ted.

* * *

Ted politely thanked everyone for their participation and made sure he had all their contact information for likely follow-up questions or advice and started out to go to his cruiser. He, consciously, told himself to try to calm down. He felt like he was going to explode. What a colossal mess! He was angry at himself for so many things. His mind kept bouncing so quickly from one problem to another he couldn't get a handle on any of it.

He walked from the morgue corridor to the stairs to get out of the basement. When he opened the door to the main level and came out into the large open lobby he realized he was sweating despite the completely air-conditioned building. He suspected his face was still red and he hoped he wouldn't run into anyone he knew. Ted knew a lot of people but he also had become accustomed to many people who, routinely, when walking by a state trooper would make some form of nod or other sign, often of recognition or deference to his position as a law officer. So he tipped his head a few times but tried to appear riveted on his direction through the lobby to the parking area used by State Police.

Outside, in the heat, he walked to his cruiser. He noticed a bench nearby that was partially shielded from the hot sun and sat down. He put his hat and Ray-Bans on and tried to think through what he had just learned. However he tried to picture the last struggle of Ellie Stanton's life he could not escape the probability a state trooper was involved. Even if someone who killed her used that button to try to implicate a trooper where would that idea, or even such a button, come from? The implications of finding that button were enormous no matter how it wound up in her bloody mouth. There wasn't a hint of Ellie Stanton having any involvement with anyone on the force in the reports Shawn Barry had written.

Even the business about 'sleeping around' was poorly formed, reported only as a pretty frequent comment from several co-workers and colleagues. There was no investigation into who, specifically, she was involved with, especially more recently. In fact, there was nothing from anyone who wasn't known as a colleague, co-worker, or neighbor. Didn't she have anyone who was just a friend? Liza couldn't have been Ellie's only confidante since he seemed to hear about her only infrequently the last few years. At least that's what he thought. Ted would talk to Liza some more about that in the evening.

Shawn Barry had really fucked up. But he guessed maybe they all had messed up to the extent they all, right from the start, focused too much on her death being an accident or, at the worst, suicide. Through his fury and embarrassment Ted kept trying to focus now on the new task at hand. This new finding would have to remain a secret for now; as he had instructed everyone connected with the post.

Thinking about this he decided to return to the morgue and ensure all staff with access to the post and the report be clear about its confidentiality. First he opened his cruiser door and called Waterbury to advise dispatch he was remaining in Burlington, at the hospital, for a while longer and to page him if needed. As he walked back to the morgue, despite the coolness of the building, he had another flash of cold sweat. It occurred to Ted if the Docs were correct and Ellie was brought through the woods to where she was found how likely was it a single person could accomplish that?

Before entering the pathology offices he stopped for a few seconds, drew some deep breaths, and tried to relax. Inside he asked to speak with Dr. Fowler. Harold Fowler actually appeared a bit shaken also and seemed distracted sitting at his desk as Ted was shown in.

They each quickly agreed the turn of events was shocking and very disturbing. Fowler wanted to try to apologize to Ted but that wasn't why Ted had come back. Fowler's weak look, with the palms of his hands turned up, suggesting resignation and guilt, was waved off by Ted.

Ted explained, again, the need for absolute confidentiality about the post. He queried the Doctor about who would have access to the findings of the exam and also asked to sign out the hammered brass button that was found. He felt it would be safest locked up in Waterbury. He couldn't imagine why Shawn hadn't signed out all Ellie's personal effects and clothes and asked for those things to be packed up for him to take also.

* * *

THE INVESTIGATION BEGINS

Since Ted was back in the ME suite he decided he might as well go ahead and begin to do a little investigating of his own. He asked Dr. Fowler to have the office supervisor come in so he could indicate to both of them the importance of keeping the post results truly confidential and also to try to find out more about Ellie Stanton's contacts with people on the force.

From professional interactions over the years Ted had a longstanding, superficial, acquaintance with Sarah Perdy, the ME's office senior supervisor. She always struck Ted as serious and organized and appeared to be unflappable with a demeanor that helped to give the office it's solid reputation as a top-notch, no nonsense unit. She was middle-aged and thin, always dressed very neatly, with long brown hair never ever displayed in the office other than in a bun. He couldn't remember ever seeing Ms. Perdy not wearing a thin, buttoned sweater with a white collared blouse buttoned at her neck. Nor could he ever recall just shooting the breeze with her even while hanging around waiting for Ellie to finish a task. She was kind of the opposite of Ellie.

Ms. Perdy came into Dr. Fowler's office with a yellow legal pad, but Dr. Fowler, without any informal discussion, spoke his words to her so quickly she didn't sit down or write on her pad.

"Sarah, the post that was just completed, ME#3213, requires status X handling. You may have to do it all yourself. In particular, you and I each need to ensure neither of the diener's know what is going on. Lieutenant Vallan, who I'm sure you know, needs to speak with you about the post and some things related to it."

"Certainly, Dr. Fowler. Should the Lieutenant and I speak here or do you think he and I should go into my office?"

Ted spoke up. "I think it's best if we go to your office, Ms. Perdy." At that Ted got up, nodded to the Doctor, and followed Ms. Perdy around a corridor to her office, which was glassed in and offered a view of most of the administrative section. Ted was surprised to see her office was on the messy side, with reams of papers and what looked like many accounting books piled on the floor around her desk. Ms. Perdy made no comment about the apparent mess as she pointed to a chair for Ted then closed the door and sat down herself.

"Ms. Perdy, I have no idea what you know about the autopsy those out of town doctors just completed but their findings were pretty dramatic and, all of a sudden, the Doctor's death has become a definite homicide investigation. Beyond finding it was a murder some of the findings are very hard to explain and everything about the autopsy results may need to be kept absolutely confidential for some time. The Vermont State Police requires this. You are not to speak to any other agency unless I give you permission. Is this all clear to you?"

Sarah Perdy's face, usually a studied lack of expression, travelled through several emotions while the Lieutenant spoke. Initial shock and then sadness quickly gave way to an uncertain, puzzled look. Seeing her significant response to his words re-assured Ted he was speaking to the right person. The sudden death of Ellie Stanton was a huge issue for the folks in this department. He could only imagine how others would respond to his words right now and when more of this story finally did come out. Ted thought he saw some tears but she responded formally.

"Absolutely, Lieutenant Vallan. Whatever you and Dr. Fowler say." She appeared to be a consummate professional but Ted was a little concerned why she mentioned Dr. Fowler in her response. He sat back in his chair and looked directly at Sarah Perdy. But his thoughts quickly returned to the challenges of the dramatic information he had just learned.

"Ms. Perdy what kind of records does this office keep related to who comes to see the ME here? With Dr. Stanton, in particular, did she ever keep any notes about any of the professional interactions she had, day in and day out?" He intended to keep who he might be looking for as vague as possible.

"Well, Lieutenant, as you might imagine, many people pass through here every day to query the ME about many topics; the other pathologists and often pathology residents and other house staff. Also attending doctors come in from time to time with questions. Dr. Stanton always seemed to find time to speak with everyone. As I guess you've heard by now, despite what we do here, she was a very social person. I can't imagine we have any record of those kinds of interactions. Even when others, like from the community, law enforcement agencies, lawyers, or family members of some of our cases come here it's not always for strictly professional reasons."

She let her words sit for a few seconds. She could see Ted was unhappy with the way her answer was going. Then her voice seemed to add some emotion; actually become almost buoyant, which really didn't fit the situation.

"But Lieutenant, look around you at this unholy mess that has taken over my office." She smiled. "All these papers and books are what we have used for years to log visitors who come to this office for professional reasons. I wish I could tell you it's very accurate but it's what we have. The ME office received a grant from the state a few months ago to buy computers and one of the goals for that is to keep records like these on the computer going forward. Now that the program for this is up and running we're trying to go back and put the last eighteen months of handwritten entries in the system also. It's a big job and it's going slowly. Dr. Fowler and I were just talking about cutting down how far back we can go. We have some summer interns but it's still expensive."

Ted glanced, again, at the mess littering the floor. Those logs might be critical for his investigation. Computers were popping up everywhere. How helpful could these logs be if they were listed on a computer? He really didn't know. He assumed results could be viewed or printed out but he wasn't sure how that could help him find what he now thought he was after.

"Ms. Perdy, I can see that the computer will organize your visit logs so you can get rid of this stuff all around the floor. But can you get more information than that from putting the visits on the computer?"

"Well, Lieutenant, although I think this task is mostly about storing information, we're all learning about what computers can do and how they may be able to help us in other ways too. I'm by no means an expert but I think, like for this task, we should eventually be able to pull out all kinds of information about who has been here. It all depends on how much information we put in related to each visit."

"Really? Ms. Perdy, well tell me how far back you've gone getting logged visits on your new computer? And, by the way you're talking, I guess you've been putting all recent visits in the machine. Is that right?"

"Everything for the last four to six weeks has been added into the computer as it's happened by the secretary at the front desk. Maybe a month or six weeks prior to that has also been put in by now. Lieutenant, I can show you the program we are using. Basically, the way everything is entered allows us to pick out almost whatever we want from what's been entered." She relaxed her face. "Things like which funeral director usually comes in the morning for pick-ups and who usually comes late in the day, which tends to upset the assistants."

Ted leaned forward and tried to keep his best poker face. "So, Ms. Perdy, for just as an example, suppose I asked you to work the computer to break down every visit by a trooper in the State Police. What would happen?"

Ms. Perdy sat up a little straighter and Ted wasn't sure if he had pulled it off. She looked directly at Ted and started to get up. "Sure Lieutenant, follow me to the office we're using for this."

She shoed out a kid sitting at a computer who looked like he was in high school, closed the door, and sat at the terminal.

"See, here I'm querying the program to list anyone who was listed as 'State Police' when they were logged in. And here it comes." They each moved their faces close to the screen. In no time twenty-eight lines came up. Even with feigning only a cursory glance Ted could see several names, including his, were listed more than once. Almost three months' time was accounted for.

Ted was impressed. And he wanted that list. "Can I get a copy of that list, Ms. Perdy?"

It was printed in a second. He tried not to look too closely to arouse any more of Sarah Perdy's suspicions than he already had. He tried, instead, to key on how amazing it was she could answer a question like that.

"Yes, a bunch of us have been here over the last three months, haven't we? I see my deputy investigator, Trooper Barry, has, of course, also been here."

"Yes. I'm glad to see the system caught his visits since I've noticed he has been wearing a suit and not his uniform on his visits since he started investigating Dr. Stanton's death."

Ted had a jolt of awareness. "Really? Yes, you're right." Without asking him Trooper Barry started wearing a suit instead of his uniform about a month before. When Ted mentioned it Shawn said he felt more like a detective in his new job. One or two older but mostly only a few younger detective troopers were doing that, and

Ted decided he ought to try to accept the change. Recently, as he was souring on Shawn, he felt less accepting.

Handing him the printout she commented, "You know you always wear your uniform, Lieutenant."

"Yes." Ted was ready to leave and was anxious to look at the list in detail. As he was leaving he advised Ms. Perdy he might need her to get him logged visit information going back much further. At the door he reminded her about the need for absolute confidentiality. Then he stopped and stepped back in the room and closed the door.

"Ms. Perdy is there a way to make sure there is no record of the printout you've created for me?"

She appeared a little uncertain. "I believe so Lieutenant. Yes, I'm pretty sure all I have to do is click here; click erase, and there shouldn't be any record of that list being queried."

With that Ted was off. It was just after noon and he had a many things to do. His new list pre-occupied his thoughts. Like a little kid he couldn't wait to get home later and study what he had.

* * *

THE SLEUTH PERFORMS COMMUNITY SERVICE

Ted spent the afternoon beginning to formulate a plan to proceed with this case and catching up on several others he was supervising. All day, in the back of his mind, he was wrestling with how much of Ellie Stanton's homicide investigation he should manage himself. Right now he had nothing but negative feelings about Shawn Barry. But he also had a Ted Vallan moment and starkly chastised himself for leaving so much of a very high profile death investigation to a deputy. Would he have uncovered anything more working with information that was out there before the second autopsy?

When Sandy Gaynor, the secretary in the pool closest to being his assistant, reminded him at three o'clock there was a little league game at four-thirty he was crestfallen.

"You look like I said you've just been transferred to the dog catcher division, Ted. Is it really that bad?"

Ted blushed slightly, displeased how easily others always seemed to be able to read his facial expressions. He knew his red flushing face would only compound his reaction.

"Oh man! Sandy, I guess I come across as a scrooge or something. I feel like I've got some really important stuff to do but that little league cra…stuff just keeps dogging me all summer so far. Thanks for the reminder"

Part of him was equally angry with himself that he just couldn't seem to get into coaching. Working with his and other kids should be a father's delight. Both he and Henry loved baseball. How could he really think he was too busy for a once in a lifetime chance to build memories? And, in truth, no one had put pressure on him to do it, except himself. Well it wasn't working out for Ted. The whining kids and the annoying, screaming parents were real pains.

And now he was losing time he had hoped to devote to thinking through the monumental findings and problems of this day. He was desperate to look, in detail, at his list and think about how to proceed with the case. Ted was undecided what, if any, role he would give to Shawn Barry or how much of the case he would try to personally manage from here on out.

As he drove to the game at the Richmond town field he remained distracted. Shawn Barry's name was listed more than any other for the past month. That made sense. Was his name ever there before that? How abruptly had he started wearing a suit a month ago? Ted wasn't thinking kindly about Barry, but he had to admit he was pretty sure Shawn had worn a suit at least a few times before the death of Ellie Stanton.

Ted liked to wear his uniform even though he only did investigative work now. He still believed the uniform was well received in the community as a symbol of well-intentioned law and order. Besides, wearing suits was expensive…unless you did what that son-of-a-bitch treasury agent who tried to get him for a felony years before did, wearing the same suit constantly. It was wrinkled and shiny and looked like he slept in it.

Ted ate an apple as he drove into the ball field parking lot. He was happy he had talked his way out of ever being responsible for bringing the bats, balls, bases, and catcher's gear, saying he wasn't allowed to put things like that in his cruiser.

The other coach, most players, including Henry, were there and the opposing team players, the Wildcats, were arriving also. Ted was pleased to see his father, Thom, had come and was tossing a ball with Henry, mostly throwing him grounders. Rain was a possibility and Ted was hopeful. Not too many adults, which was also good. The umpire looked like he might be sixteen and Ted knew that could turn out to be a problem if the parents got going on him.

An official from the league walked over from the parking lot and called to Ted and the coach of the Wildcats to meet with him. He said they wanted to have a make-up the next day for the game rained out ten days before. The Wildcats coach thought it was a great idea; almost like playing a doubleheader. Ted struggled not to groan out loud. Didn't anybody else have a job?

His dad left him alone to work with the other coach to get the game going. Henry's Crickets were up first and Ted stood behind the chain link backstop as the first kid up stepped into the batter's box. His father walked over and talked to him while they each stared at the game.

"Teddy, you look beat. You okay?" He kept right on talking. "I know you're busy now but I need to talk with you about Ellie Stanton. You know, Liza's friend who died last month."

Ted's face stiffened and he shot a glance at his father. "What?" He almost recoiled a few steps away from him. A memory quickly flashed in his head about the last time his father was involved in a case and its terrible consequences, for all of them. "No more amateur detective and heart attacks, Pop."

"No...no Ted. But you have to hear this."

Ted immediately started to walk away. "If you want to be helpful dad go down to third base and help coach the kids about base running."

But the damage was done. Now one more loose end, or something, would have to be added to the growing list of details about a homicide he didn't know existed before that morning.

* * *

THE SLEUTH AT HOME II

Mercifully, the game wasn't close and the fans did not obstruct the game's progress. When it ended enough people pitched in for the clean-up that Ted was ready to leave quickly. His dad suggested he'd take Henry and a friend for some ice cream so Ted drove home alone.

He parked and went inside. As always, Ted first went to the closet where he had anchored the small safe he locked his revolver in and secured the firearm. Liza moved from the porch to the kitchen and spoke in the direction of the front hall.

"I'm in the kitchen. Come on in and eat. It's getting late."

Sounded like a good idea to Ted. A quick bite and then he would study his list. He walked into the kitchen.

"Where's Henry?"

"Oh, my dad was at the game. I thought that was kind of nice. After the game he took Henry and another kid for some ice cream. I expect they'll be home…"

"Ted! Henry hasn't had his dinner. Just like you, he wasn't going to eat at four and run around on a full stomach. He shouldn't be eating ice cream now. Who's the other kid? I bet his family is waiting for him to get home for his dinner also. Oh babe, how could you let your father do something like that? Who's the other kid? When his mother finds out she's gonna be mad at us; hopefully you and not me. I better call her and apologize."

He was barely in the door and he thought she was practically attacking him.

Ted looked straight ahead and thought about the other kid. "Lize, (spoken like 'lies') I'm not positive who the other kid is. I was cleaning up when they walked away with my dad. I think it was Timmy Small but, I'm sorry, I'm not positive."

Liza was angry and Ted quickly accepted he had fucked up. But he didn't agree it was as big a deal as Liza seemed to want to make it. The kids would remember the ice cream more than missing dinner. He didn't see why Liza felt so embarrassed about calling the kid's mother and explaining the foul up. Of course, it would be best if he remembered the right kid. He hoped it was Timmy.

"I'm sorry Liza, but you're not responsible so just blame me when you call Timmy's mom. You know, we keep up just fine with all the Joneses around here. It's not a major social failing that I messed up. This has been a very tough day for both of us. I don't know about you but I've been very distracted ever since that autopsy."

"Keeping up with the Joneses? Are you serious Ted? Commenting about social culture in the suburbs? Really? No Ted I'm suggesting your brain is big enough to handle a few tasks or responsibilities at the same time. We're both upset but we still ought to be able to do the things we've committed to…like raising a family responsibly. Don't put this on me babe. You messed up." She walked across the room heading for the phone on the kitchen wall. Even Liza seemed a little startled with how angry she had become. As she picked up the phone she softened.

"Okay; enough. I know today's findings are a monster problem for you. Let me call Carly Small and let's put this behind us. But you know, for a long time now we've prided ourselves in managing our careers and family. Something like Ellie's murder, even with all its implications for you, and me also, shouldn't be a reason for us to justify messing up with family."

"You're right, babe." Ted wasn't completely himself and felt some anger also. He then made a reference to continuing to "keep all those balls up in the air." He was a fountain of idiomatic expressions this night.

Henry arrived home shortly after Ted finished his dinner. His dad brought him in. As always, Thom Vallan first made his regular statement about how great and beautifully constructed Liza's porch was. Ted agreed and tried to direct his father back to the front door. Thom Vallan got the hint, but as they walked to the door he tried to talk about Ellie Stanton again.

"Ted, I need to talk to you about Dr. Stanton. When are you goin' to let me speak to you?"

"I don't know dad but not tonight. I've been waiting all day to go over some really important case information. I'll let you know." With that Thom Vallan left and Ted promptly forgot about his father's request.

* * *

Sitting on the porch as last light was fading he had to turn a lamp on. Ted appeared studious, with two pencils and the printout on the table beside him and a yellow legal pad on his lap. First he decided to list each trooper named on the printout. He left a third of a page between each name to fill in number of visits and whatever he would later decide he wanted to know about each trooper.

Shawn Barry accounted for seven visits, all but one after Ellie's death. The first was about a month before her death. Ted was listed five times and only one was before her murder. His was the last name on the printout, which was arranged so that the earlier visits followed more recent. Ted remembered that brief interaction with Ellie three months before. It was a routine follow-up related to a question he had about a body found off a ski trail at a local resort after the snow melted. No one had been reported missing (even now) and Ellie found nothing more than the consequences of hypothermia.

Ted put the pad down and tried to visualize those minutes with Ellie. She was friendly and they each said a few things in a light and joking way about the puzzles that came up in their chosen professions. Nothing different or out of the ordinary for her. She appeared relaxed and unrushed. It was clear he needed to learn if there was a different Ellie Stanton he never knew or pieces of her life or personality that led to her being murdered.

It didn't take long for Ted to sort out there were five other trooper's names listed over the three-month span of the report. Two of them were logged in three times, notably each time was about a month apart. Of the remaining three the frequency of visits suggested, on first glance, two of them had several visits over a short duration, possibly indicative of an active investigation. Ted thought he might recognize the names of one or two of the troopers. It stood out in his mind that two of the troopers were women, a scarce commodity in the state police. He wrestled with whether he could just cross them off his list. He decided he had no good reason he could be sure a female trooper could not have been involved in Ellie's death. He didn't think it likely though, especially with what he had just learned about the circumstances of her actual murder and the location of her body.

"Get a pair of black, horn-rimmed reading glasses and you'd look like a professor preparing your notes for class tomorrow." Liza plopped down into her chair separated by the table and lamp from where Ted sat. "So you're feeling pretty upset about all the time since Ellie's murder without an active investigation, huh?" Her brow was wrinkled and her face displayed futile resignation and a sadness.

Ted was pleased Liza had moved on from her anger at him from before.

"Yeah, it's a terrible mess. Doc Fowler didn't help us but I think the force should have done better anyway. There's going to be stuff out there that we will find about Ellie we should have been working on right from the start."

Liza, who had been the motivating force for the second post, now seemed truly worn out and conflicted by the most recent events. "Babe, does it really matter we now know she was killed? I mean Ellie's gone now anyway. I agree, you'll probably find out she had a relationship that went bad and she paid a terrible price. Won't likely make the world any different if you find the man who killed her or not."

Ted dropped the pad in his lap and sat forward in his chair and looked at Liza. In a way Liza was challenging the fundamental responsibility of his job. Liza got it and immediately back-tracked.

"I'm sorry, I didn't mean it the way it came out, babe."

That wasn't good enough. He wondered why she was arguing and putting him down so frequently lately? The tone of his response was resolute. He sounded like he was making an official statement.

"Anyone who has killed once is a better bet to consider killing again at some time. You know that. And you can't just kill someone because a relationship changes, no matter the emotional toll. What would the world be like if we looked at crimes of passion that way?

"I'm damn glad you pushed for that second autopsy. And I plan to find out who killed Ellie. And I guess when we find her killer we'll find out why she was killed. I hope we can accomplish that before her killer kills anyone else. Her murder was especially brutal and that should bother anyone. The idea a member of the force could be involved, or directly responsible, means finding Ellie's killer immediately becomes the highest priority for my unit."

Liza's seemingly minor comment clearly set Ted off. The intensity of his reaction conveyed how he was barely able to contain his anger at her. His words also reflected the feelings of a person thinking he was on some sort of mission rather than only doing his job working to solve a difficult case.

"Now we have lots to do and I think I'll try to handle most of it myself, using Shawn Barry to assist me. As a matter of fact I already have the names of some troopers who were known to be at Ellie's office over the last three months. That's a start. I'll need to push to get a list like this for the last year, but we will begin with what we have tomorrow."

"Yes, it sounds like a place to start. Boy, I guess I'd try to get more about her personal life. You know all those rumors about how she lived." After getting Ted upset Liza recognized she needed to reassure him of her interest. "So do you know anything about anyone on the list you have now?"

"Not really but one or two names look familiar. It's interesting that there are two female troopers on the printout. Not likely suspects." Ted relaxed, now sounding looser and maybe a bit ironic. "And I'm on the list, and so is Shawn Barry. I hope we're not likely suspects either."

Liza listened to Ted but as he was finishing she started to speak also.

"Oh, you know, I forgot. I mean I meant to tell you. This morning I found something else at the post as the diener was cleaning her up."

Ted looked incredulous.

"I mean the whole thing was done and the diener was finally dissolving the remaining blood clots from her head. I wasn't really looking at anything but I reached out and held Ellie's wrist, thinking my good-byes. My hand brushed against some water and blood running down the table and I felt something lodge between my hand and her wrist. I picked it up and kept it in my palm. The diener didn't notice and I knew you wouldn't want him to know anything. I put it in my pocket and helped him cover her and left. I think I was crying from the moment I touched her. I forgot to give it to you."

"Wow, where is it Lize? Please get it now."

"Sure… Oh, you know what? It's in my lab coat at my office. I'm sorry."

"I think I better go get it now." He was exhausted but he wanted to know what it was and secure it.

"Oh please Ted, not now. I'm sure no one will disturb that coat. My coats don't get cleaned unless I put them in a special hamper down the hall. It won't be gone, and I know what it is anyway.

"I think that may be why I just remembered it, Ted. It's another button. Not like what you found. Just a bone button with four tiny holes; but it had some thread in it, like the big button had."

"Why do you call the other button big?"

"That's the thing babe. This button is mostly brown and it's actually kind of small. You know I re-sew or replace some buttons on your uniforms from time to time. Well the button I found is much, much smaller. I didn't think about it then but now it strikes me what I found is probably a button used on a woman's clothing; likely on a sleeve. We can get it tomorrow, I'm sure."

Ted's mind was active. New possibilities and concerns were raised, but mostly, he was dismayed about the way Liza had handled her finding. At this point he knew there wasn't any real benefit in berating her about the consequences of what she did. But he did think he should at least try to explain what she did wrong.

"Babe, wherever this case goes and whatever comes out of it, I don't think we will ever be able to use the button you found as evidence. You see, we can never prove where it came from. You could tell a court what you just told me but unless you showed it sitting on the table to the pathology assistant and then gave it to me or Doc Fowler it's probably inadmissible.

"But you didn't know that. It's okay. We'll still use it as part of the investigation and that may turn out to be very important."

"I'm sorry, Ted. Please don't go to my office tonight."

"Okay." He was exhausted and agreed to get it in the morning.

* * *

THE INVESTIGATION (DEVELOPS)

Ted almost always drove fast when he was in his cruiser. Virtually any road he was on he was given deference by other drivers. Some people actually pulled off the road if he was behind them even if neither his lights or siren were on. Driving in front of a trooper made most folks nervous. Were they feeling guilty or intimidated by any (potential) interaction with law enforcement? Ted had his ideas. No one ever seemed relaxed when they noticed a trooper's cruiser behind them.

Liza loved to drive behind Ted, though. While he blazed the way she kept her speed up with his and followed him closely. They drove that way, in tandem, to the hospital in the morning. They parked in different areas and met in the lobby of the outpatient building. In Liza's office her white coat was perched on the coat rack where she left it the night before. In the large right side pocket was the notably small brownish bone button whose safety in that location had worried each of them through the night. Liza was relieved and said little, not wanting to re-kindle any discussion of her foul up the prior morning.

Ted held up the button and greenish-brown thread hanging about an inch. He showed no obvious sign of recognition.

"It is small, isn't it?"

"Yes, I think it might come from whatever that button is called that's about six inches up from the cuff and usually is always just left buttoned unless you roll your sleeve up. Mostly just ornamental, I guess.

"Who knows. Since it's so small, if I had to guess, I'd say it's something from a woman's clothes. But to know that it would be best to look at, say, some of my blouses and compare it, don't you think?"

"Yes, Sherlock. Sounds like the next step, doesn't it?"

Some of the tension of the prior evening and early morning was now relieved and they each reacted to the button's safety by relaxing their banter. They gave each other a peck and Ted went in search of the morgue.

He went to Sarah Perdy's office and asked her to go with him to Dr. Fowler's office but they found he wasn't in yet. Back in Ms. Perdy's office Ted told her he needed more information from the logs as soon as possible. He told her he was aware his request would interfere with her project and her schedule but this was a capital case and couldn't wait. Logged visits by anyone from the State Police over the previous year were necessary. She flinched, ever so slightly, at his request but made no verbal attempt to argue or, more to Ted's worry, question why he was limiting his request to state troopers.

He suggested the records be reviewed, in three month blocks, specifically culling out state troopers. The need for absolute confidentiality was stressed again. He knew this meant the task couldn't be done by anyone besides Ms. Perdy. It was a lot to ask and he had hoped to make the request in front of Dr. Fowler so any disagreement from either of them could be dealt with immediately. He already had the first three months and asked when the next list could be ready.

"Lieutenant Vallan, I will fax you the next three months by four if when I call to send it you tell me you are standing at the machine. I'll finish the rest sometime tomorrow. I want to do this for Dr. Stanton."

Ted tipped his head and thanked her for her help. In his cruiser, on the way to Waterbury, he reached Lieutenant Jim Dixon of Internal Affairs and arranged to meet with him later in the morning.

* * *

Validating the accuracy of the lists generated by Sarah Perdy would probably never be possible. Ted accepted that concern. Each time she faxed an update Ted requested she go back further until the list included the prior twelve months' worth of State Police visits. At his desk and then at night at home he kept staring at the more complete lists. The updates that kept coming were nothing like what he expected.

Law enforcement officers, certainly including the State Police, routinely had reasons to be at the ME's office. Ted was startled to find that the complete list produced for him not only identified potential suspects but aided him, additionally, in a most unexpected way. He had assumed the list would include many names, possibly challenging his ability to make any use of it at all. Accuracy aside, by some strange quirk of fate, other than Trooper Barry, himself, and the five troopers from the original list there were only five others listed for the remainder of the entire year. One of those had died (from natural causes) and one retired, both about ten months earlier.

Ted was amazed and also excited. This chance finding intensified his belief that Ellie Stanton's killer came from this list; now of only eight troopers. Ted felt a piece of the puzzle was being given to him and he should go with it.

Meeting with Shawn Barry the morning after the list was completed he could not be dissuaded from focusing practically the entire investigation on this group of eight. Trooper Barry reminded Ted there were many others who interacted with the ME, probably some from other uniformed agencies. Maybe some who even had hammered brass buttons on their uniforms also. Ted advised Shawn not to waste time investigating that. He had the names he needed.

* * *

BEFORE THE FALL

Three days before they were summoned to the meeting in Waterbury with six other troopers and Lieutenant Vallan she could no longer restrain herself.

Driving up the long, narrow, dirt road to his house, isolated in the woods, she was worried and unsure of herself. She had reached a point where her thoughts felt all jumbled and her head hurt so much she wondered if a brain could explode. Sadly, she recognized much of her immediate upset reflected how truly uncertain she was of the way he would react. She knew what should be a happy moment might not turn out that way. It was distressing to her that, despite what she knew about him and the relationship they shared, what his reaction to the news would be was unclear to her. She worried he might not share her happiness. That was upsetting, and so the whole business was more than unsettling. The timing of all this was poor. But she couldn't wait any longer.

They had not been together or had any personal contact in what seemed like more than a month. Since it all happened. She was in her own car. His cruiser was parked right at the porch steps. As she opened her door he was already out on the porch.

"Hey sweets! How are you? I figured it was getting to time we should be getting together again too. I sure have missed you."

His voice was upbeat, but she remained apprehensive and unsure.

Was it him or was it her she was reacting to?

* * *

The terrible summer cold with cough, fever, body aches, and annoying fatigue seemed to finally be improving after lasting weeks. It just continued to be one thing after another and she was beginning to wonder when she would really feel consistently better. She knew it wasn't good for her to be this way and not be getting any care. She hadn't eaten well for days. That couldn't be good. It was time to tell him and deal with this.

* * *

Suddenly so much was different. She so wanted to be happy but it was all very complicated now. At the beginning, almost two years before, her only worry was that they all had been told troopers were not to fraternize. Whatever that word really meant she knew what they were talking about. He was such a great and sweet guy and they took to each other so quickly she decided to just not worry about 'silly rules made up for no good reason,' as he said. So they lived their lives a little differently, sharing their time and experiences by themselves; alone. Which was fine for a while.

As she liked him more and more, she realized she was developing a hope their times of secretiveness were coming to an end. She knew he could figure something out. All along he seemed to have an answer for everything. Over time he told her bits and pieces of his past. He was six years older so it was no surprise he had already collected a number of experiences in his life.

He told her about his success as a soldier in Vietnam. He spoke more vaguely about his years in the army in Asia. His descriptions of his time there occasionally varied, but the idea he wanted her to have was he felt he was providing some semblance of law in a lawless land. Sometimes he talked about a small inheritance that helped to get him started with some businesses while he was over there.

He said he was able to earn good money by acting like a benevolent ruler for an ignorant people in a lawless society. How by his strength and good old USA know-how he was able to protect them. The people paid him a kind of tax to keep them safe. She didn't completely understand what he was telling her or how a soldier could do those things. He said he was very successful.

He never hid from her that he had money. The opposite. He constantly tried to lavish gifts on her. She worried how any of that would look to others on the force or even in the community. She had nothing of her own and lived strictly on her small income as a trooper. So when they drove to New Hampshire to buy her a car they argued the whole drive over. She insisted, and she won, so he bought her a used car instead of brand new. It was more than fine. She loved the car and she loved him for buying it for her. There was no precedent in her life for anyone ever doing anything like that for her.

When he told her his money was running low she understood how upsetting that was to him, even if she cared much less about the implications.

* * *

"What a business this has been, huh sweets? I've really missed you. But it's been good to think things through." He became progressively more animated as he spoke. "I have some ideas about how to keep the money-maker going. It isn't going to be easy for a while, but I think I can keep it going. It's just that this is still such a bad time. It's best we make sure our names aren't connected to any of this, in any way I guess, from here on out. Do you want me to tell you how I think we can still do it?"

He caught himself just as he was about to launch for the first time into actually speaking out loud the plans he had been working on in his head, over and over, for a few weeks. While he spoke he was pacing the room in front of her as she sat in the middle of his sofa. His eyes caught hers. Her face communicated her upset.

"Sweets. I'm sorry. I've been so caught up in trying to figure something out I didn't ask how it's been for you and how you're doing with all this. I'm sorry. Tell me how you are? Please."

He sat down next to her, put his arm around her and pulled her close. They each turned their heads and briefly kissed, in an affectionate, but not passionate, way. He then looked forward, as though his mind was already back to working on his plan.

Here goes, she thought. She spoke up, not entirely convinced of her own plan or comfortable about any of it. Her uncertainty was apparent in her voice.

"You know. So much has happened in such a short time. So much is confusing to me…"

"Sweets, please. I know you've been through a lot, but I'm hoping you will try to stay calm about it and I bet it'll all be okay after a while more. Sweets, remember about six months ago when I talked about us getting married once this deal put us flush again with cash? I was thinking then that in about a year you would be able to quit the force and we'd be good. We can still figure something out after a while. I want us together forever."

"Babe!" He wasn't making any of this easier for her. Forcefully: "Look at me." He turned, again and stared at her face. "No! No, I mean look at me sitting here. Can't you see what's happening to me?"

He looked puzzled and a hint of anger showed. He did not know what was going on or what she wanted him to understand, at all. His mind was fixed on the recent events. He assumed the recent past was still the issue.

"Look at me! It's July and I'm wearing a windbreaker. Look at what's happened to me. Dammit, I'm busting out of my clothes! I don't think I can go to work anymore."

He got it.

First he sunk back in the sofa, but he quickly stiffened and sat up ramrod straight. She could see he was already thinking about what he or, hopefully, they could do. But he made no motion to grab and hug or kiss her. There was no expression on his face of happiness or joy.

"I've been having a terrible time. I was sick to my stomach weeks ago and I've had a terrible cold the last few weeks. I seem to stay sick. It can't be good to be this way and not see a doctor. Because I'm a little chubby it took me a long time to accept what it really is. Now everyone is gonna be able to see it soon.

"And I got kicked so hard in the gut. Remember? I been really worried about that; and everything!"

He stood up and started slowly pacing in front of her again. When he spoke his tone suggested his surprise and, again, she thought she sensed some anger.

"Well, this is something to really think about. I'll need some time to figure all this out."

Now it was her turn to sink back in the sofa. His reaction was not what she hoped but neither did he appear terribly angry or react in any way to frighten her. She decided they were still a couple, even if he showed no outward sign of pleasure or affection in his reaction. Then he sat next to her again and spoke, somewhat awkwardly.

"Sweets, I guess now we share even a little more. When I saw you drive up you know I thought it's been so long since we could be together I got excited just seeing your car. Maybe if we go to the bedroom we could…"

"Babe, I'm pregnant! I don't even know what I can and cannot do. I'm not sure that's okay anymore. I'm not doing anything until I see a doctor."

* * *

THE INTERVIEWS

Eight troopers suddenly had been made aware they were under
suspicion for the murder of Dr. Ellie Stanton. Ted had no doubt
there could be significant consequences for working the case after
alerting the killer in the way he had. That made it a major priority
for him to speak with each one of them as soon as possible. In
fact, he hoped to meet with all of them over the next few days, by
the end of the week. At his present level of the investigation it was
Ted's view all he should or could do was, in effect, only informally
interview each of them. Of course, one of the sessions could turn
into something more depending on what came out at that meeting.
The first happened the very next morning.

First, early that Tuesday morning Ted had a meeting with Captain
Rondell to talk it all over and tell him how he was planning to
move ahead. Rondell was mostly hands off. But his tone and
manner should have concerned Ted. Ted could tell Rondell hadn't
fully bought into the entire direction he was actively pursuing. He
let Ted know the Colonel was not at all comfortable with what
Ted was doing. He told him the Colonel was not convinced Ted's
investigation was on the right path. Surprisingly, Ted thought little
about that.

* * *

1) TROOPER HAROLD LAUGHTON

"Trooper Laughton has arrived Lieutenant. Do you want me to send him over?"

Trooper Harold Laughton had the interesting distinction of being the only one of the group of eight from the meeting the day before to contact Ted. Later that afternoon Trooper Laughton called and asked to meet with him. Ted didn't ask the Trooper if he murdered Ellie Stanton and the Trooper didn't say why he called. It seemed they each assumed whatever needed to be said should be done in person.

Ted was glad someone called. His review of easily obtainable information about this Trooper, which included a brief chat with his direct commanding officer, led him to doubt Laughton was going to turn out to be his man. He was young and the newest on the force in that group but already had a commendable record. Ted hoped by speaking with him he could develop the pattern for questioning and hueing down on more critical aspects to seek out that would allow him to weigh responses and determine what should or should not be further pursued as he worked his way through his list of troopers. Ted saw no reason to have Shawn Barry at any initial interviews at this time.

After dramatically accusing someone in the group at the meeting yesterday, he thought he should now tread more lightly, at least at first. He would see how that tack worked with Trooper Laughton.

Laughton was at the door. Ted stayed seated and waved him to close the door and take a chair. In uniform he didn't stand out in any obvious way from a typical young trooper. At this stage in their careers most still had a military bearing and manner, since virtually all of the force spent time in some part of the military. Except for the two female troopers and Trooper Aaron Nicolaides, everyone in the group had been in the military.

Trooper Laughton walked in looking like a guilty person, with his hat in his hands, head down, and a sad, bland appearance. Something was up. It looked to Ted like Trooper Laughton might sit and stare at the floor forever if Ted didn't begin the discussion.

"I'm glad you called, Trooper Laughton. Getting to the bottom of this terrible crime is the highest priority for the force. What did you want to tell me?"

He began haltingly, spacing his words. "Lieutenant, my contact with Dr. Stanton was not something I was ever really happy about at all." He continued as only a guilty person can when determined to confess. Ted stayed motionless.

"I met Dr. Stanton about eight months ago when I was assigned to accompany the body of a drowning victim to the ME office and inform the ME about the details of the case. There was never any concern about foul play so the ME just needed to know what the circumstances were; who the guy was and so forth."

"How did you determine it was an accidental death?" Was Ted trying to relax the Trooper? Or did he want to satisfy himself an intentional act had not been missed? Trooper Laughton quickly made it clear that determination wasn't his responsibility.

"No Lieutenant, a bunch of us was at the scene. The Sergeant did the investigation. He, I mean the deceased, had some friends around and they all said the man was drunk. I guess he walked outside his camper in the dark to take a piss and fell into a drainage ditch that had froze, maybe the first freeze of the season. If any of the ice ever held him it must have cracked and he was found, frozen, face down in the icy water." Then, sounding surprisingly excited: "Doc Stanton said she'd bet his blood alcohol level would be sky high. And she turned out to be right."

Harold Laughton appeared to be a handsome young trooper but he didn't seem to be functioning, professionally, at an especially high level yet. Visualizing any involvement, beyond strictly professional, with Ellie Stanton didn't seem too likely to Ted.

"Was there anything else?"

Again, Trooper Laughton looked down and he tried to find the words he had to say.

"It was getting later in the afternoon. Doc Stanton had requested I stay for the examination. When I told her I'd never seen an autopsy before she said I should stay and she'd explain it to me. I…I thought that would be useful for me so I stayed. It took much longer than I thought. After it was over she asked me to wait while she checked the results of the blood alcohol test she had done. That's how I knew it was very high.

"By then it was dark and when I stood up in her office to leave I realized it looked like everyone else in the place was gone. Doc said she needed to get some boxes of some supplies into her vehicle and asked if I would help her. So she got her truck and drove it to a hospital exit a few steps from some stairs up from the morgue. It took me only one trip.

"All this time, Lieutenant, Doc was being awful nice to me. She was older but a beautiful girl, and I enjoyed talking with her. By the time I was bringing the boxes we was joking around and it was fun. I don't know, when she asked if I'd be willing to take a quick trip to her house and unload the boxes for her I'm not sure I wanted to say no. I mean she was kind of mysterious and her eyes kept sparkling at me. Whatever I said, and I'm not sure all I did say, she always laughed and seemed interested. It was Friday and my shift was done so I said fine. She promised to bring me back to my cruiser after.

"She stopped to pick up a pizza and beer on the way and we talked and talked. But I knew, maybe I hoped, this was going somewhere. She waited till I put the boxes into a back room at her house and it was obvious she wanted me to come on to her. So I did. We had sex, and it was okay. But Lieutenant, I have to tell you what I remember most about that day was after. A few minutes after we were done that lady seemed to change into a different type of person.

"I think it was quickly real clear to me she wanted me out of there; quick. She got real cold to me, almost like what was I doing there. She didn't say much and just got dressed so I did too. She said she'd take me back to my cruiser. I had a beer when we first got to her place but never did have any pizza.

"Back in my cruiser I started to relax. But the way she barely talked to me all that time after and in the car spooked me. By then I sure wished I hadn't ever done that. You know, when you meet someone and you get along and spend some time together like that you naturally wonder about meeting up again. But not with her for me. Ever since that day I tried to steer clear of that place. I never looked for her and I never heard she might be looking for me. She was so pretty and smart, at first she made me feel real good. But then I felt the way it all went that something was wrong. It was a mistake. Then when I read she died I didn't know what to make of it. When you talked to us yesterday I sure felt guilty and I didn't know what to do.

"Lieutenant, I never harmed Doc Stanton and I hadn't seen her in months. I don't know if anyone knew I went to her house that day but I thought I better tell you. I'm sure you're figuring it out from listening to me, but I kind of doubt I was the first or only man she ever brought to her house like that. It seemed like something she had done before."

With his last sentence Trooper Laughton raised his eyes and looked directly at Ted. Ted's picture of the private life of Ellie Stanton was still a work in progress but Trooper Laughton's story seemed to confirm a feature he kept hearing about.

Ted had been pleased to sit and only listen once Laughton began his story in earnest. But when he finished something was missing. Trooper Laughton's name was also logged in at the ME office only two months before.

"Trooper why did you tell me you never saw Dr. Stanton again after the time you just told me about? Your name is on the ME office log only a few months ago." Ted looked directly at Trooper Laughton to see how he responded physically.

Initially Laughton had no notable reaction to his comment.

"Oh, that was probably the time I dropped off some evidence Sergeant Detword sent me there with. No…I purposely stayed at the front desk until the stuff was receipted to me and I quickly left. I never saw Doc Stanton that time."

Trooper Laughton had voluntarily offered a very detailed explanation of his time with Ellie Stanton. Actually, Ted mostly just listened and never had to devise any methods to probe what happened between Ellie and the Trooper. That is, of course, if he was telling the truth.

Undoubtedly more information about Ellie's lifestyle would be easily gleaned from speaking more pointedly with her staff and even talking to her neighbors around her small home on the lake. Hopefully Shawn was accomplishing some of that right now. Ted decided to call him and make sure plenty of Shawn's questions were directly focused on the topic of her sexual activity. It just kept coming up.

The behavior Laughton told Ted about puzzled him. He assumed it might mean something about Ellie's personality. He wasn't going to try to make much of a guess though since he was well aware normal or certainly abnormal psychology was not part of his skill set. All in all, he tended to believe what the Trooper told him. Laughton, remorsefully, related his willing seduction and his greater upset at being rejected after performing. Ted wondered if Ellie had done that intentionally to try to kind of emasculate Laughton or if her actions were more a reflection of some of her own demons. He did think about whether he should talk about any of this with Liza.

* * *

A WRINKLE IN THE WORKS?

Some investigators might have felt working through a suspect pool of as many as eight would be daunting. Ted didn't feel that way. After learning what Trooper Laughton told him he was very anxious to meet with the others on his list. He no longer had any illusion a trooper was going to turn himself in.

After his session with Laughton on Tuesday morning he tried to learn more about each of the remaining seven troopers before he met with them. It was obvious if Laughton had fabricated the story he told Ted it could take a long time to prove him a liar. The whole group had to be looked at. Liars might have similar stories…or might not. It just happened that all the troopers he was tasked with considering all had good records. What would make one stand out in this setting?

Tuesday Ted worked with his staff to carefully arrange to contact the officers in charge of the work locations of each of the seven remaining troopers to get those troopers, one by one, to his office to be interviewed personally. He decided to have each trooper be told the day and time only one day before the interview. He didn't want anyone to have significant time to prepare, although, from the first day, each of them probably knew this was coming. So he planned for two on Wednesday, three more on Thursday, and the last two on Friday.

In the afternoon he reviewed what he had and worked on a list of characteristics or behaviors that might be more suspect for members of that group. Based on what was being said about Ellie and what the Trooper told him he tended to feel Ellie's sexual behavior would probably be a key to her interactions with at least some of the other troopers also. What to make of the women, and what to make of the frequency, sometimes almost like on a schedule, of some of the troopers' visits to the morgue?

* * *

Near the end of the day, close to when he was planning to leave for the make-up little league game, Ted received a call from Lieutenant Dixon, at Internal Affairs.

"Ted, glad I caught you."

"Sure, Jim."

"We've had a bit of a strange day in our unit. About late morning I was called by Sergeant Weber out of the Morrisville station. He told me a trooper, Nancy Devers, hadn't shown up for duty this morning so they sent a cruiser to her place to check on her. She wasn't there but her cruiser was. Her own vehicle wasn't there either. No one knew what to make of it so they kept looking around and checking with folks who knew her. Mid afternoon Weber said she called in. Said she was calling from the airport in Burlington. Said there was an emergency at the family home in Arizona and she had to take an immediate leave and had no idea when she would be able to return.

"Well Sergeant Weber was quite confused by her call and the plans she told him about. I guess your office contacted him earlier in the day to have him arrange for her to meet with you tomorrow morning. And he remembered I had just spoken with him late on Monday and told him I wanted to hear about any unusual goings on with any trooper. For some reason, maybe to try to delay her, he told the Trooper what she was doing was highly irregular and to call us at Internal Affairs to explain her situation before she left town.

"As soon as I heard from Weber I got in touch with Williston Barracks and asked them to get troopers to the airport to look for her. They were there within five minutes but she was nowhere to be found. No one fitting her description was reported by anyone the troopers questioned. I doubt she flew out of there, Ted. BTV is so small I doubt they would have missed her. We're getting her vehicle's plates now and will have to assume she's out of the state by now. Will need an APB for all surrounding states. We're also checking on exactly where her family is in Arizona so we can check out her story.

"But, Ted, I gotta say this is beginning to sound more and more like something for you to handle. I know she's on your list."

"Right, Jim. We should take this from here. But if she was involved in the homicide why did she call in? Why would she announce she's leaving town no matter where she's actually heading?"

* * *

"Shit!" He yelled out as he pounded his steering wheel. 'Some hot shit detective I am' he thought to himself. 'I'm heading south and the potential crime scene is north. Here I am again going to another f-ing ball game!' "Shit!" Before he left Waterbury he had called Sergeant Weber.

"Sergeant, are you sure it was Trooper Devers you were talking to on the phone? How did she sound to you?"

"Lieutenant, I know her voice pretty good. Only twelve troopers at our station. It was her. Only thing I can say is she sounded like she was in a hurry. Didn't sound good. Maybe a little scared. There was some noise in the background; like maybe in an airport? I guess could have been a bus station also; or even maybe just a payphone outside somewhere. But I don't think she was at home or anything like that…maybe. She wanted to get off the phone quick, Lieutenant. But she promised me she'd talk to Internal Affairs."

Ted decided this was not the time to query the Sergeant about why he called Internal Affairs instead of his office. Probably didn't slow anything down very much. He might look into that later, he thought.

"Oh, and Lieutenant."

"Yes?"

"After the call late yesterday I was set to contact Trooper Devers this afternoon, like your office had said, to tell her to plan to meet with you in Waterbury at ten tomorrow morning. With all the excitement I never got to saying anything about that to her, Lieutenant."

Also before he left Ted contacted Shawn Barry and asked him to get a few members of the crime investigation team together to go to Trooper Devers' apartment and at least look around this evening and mark it off as a potential crime scene. He asked him to file the needed papers to allow the state police access to her personal affairs and effects so they could check her phone, bank, and other personal records. He was convinced the Trooper's sudden disappearance was related to the murder case. But then he thought about how he would explain his rapid filings if she turned up back at her home within the next twenty-four hours. Maybe they'd get the necessary paperwork started but not do everything until they tracked her family down; wherever they were.

After he and Henry got home from the game and had a late dinner Ted called Shawn. Trooper Barry was still at the apartment Nancy Devers rented near Johnson.

"Small place, Lieutenant. Old house or duplex made into four apartments a while ago. Not in the greatest shape or best part of town. According to the other tenants the best thing about the building is that Trooper Devers lives here and parks her cruiser right in front. Tends to discourage any trouble."

"Shawn, when you talked to those neighbors did you get anything about her behavior lately?"

"Not much Chief. Everyone likes her, but all said she pretty much kept to herself. Not many visitors. Certainly no one could recall any ruckus or things like that. She actually worked on her car a lot when she was around. Guess she did basic maintenance herself.

"No. No one seems to know what's going on with us showin' up and going through her place. Nothin' different about her lately anyone noticed."

"What about inside?"

"Didn't have a dog or a pet neighbors say. Place is neat; no indication she didn't just pick up and leave. Clark pointed out, though, that a space where a suitcase might be stored is empty and stuff in her drawers and bathroom shelves are sparse. So he thinks she, at least, did some packing.

"Chief we looked around so I'm sure Devers isn't here. And there's nothing in her cruiser. You know, it almost seems like she might have intentionally left the cruiser's keys on a table near the door; like for us to find them. But we're not sure how much more we should do right now…I mean it seems like she's missing but she also could drive up any minute and could get pretty pissed at us going through her place and her things. Know what I mean? So…"

"Yeah, occurred to me also. I think you're right. We may need to back off from tearing her place apart…at least until the morning. But Shawn, can you tape her place up and stay on this until you get through to her family tonight? Where did you say her family is? in Arizona? Do we know where?

"I guess she's not really a missing person yet, but I'm worried she could be involved in Dr. Stanton's murder and that makes her a potential suspect so we are obligated to find her as quick as we can."

"Right. About an hour ago Waterbury got me a number in Tucson, Arizona. I decided to finish up here and speak with you and now I'll go to Waterbury to contact them. I hope you agree it will be lots easier to call and talk from Waterbury, Chief. We're buttoning up this place now and I'll call you from Waterbury after I track down some family."

"Sounds good Shawn. I know you will try to find out what their contact has been with her recently and whatever else they might know… Shawn, I haven't said anything about this to you, but Liza, my wife, seems pretty confident Trooper Devers may be pregnant. So you have to be careful how you try to get information from them. Wouldn't bring up anything about anything like that now… unless one of them says something about that to you."

"Wow. That would be something, huh? Another wrinkle for the white board and diagraming out the features of this case. Don't see any signs a guy livin' here, Chief. And, you know, I don't think I've ever seen a pregnant trooper…You? Man, that'd be a lot of points, eh?"

"Shawn, what do you mean?"

"Oh Chief, you know. Like points you get for seeing a nun on a motorcycle. Or how about a pregnant nun on a motorcycle? Yeah, that would be the max."

* * *

To the state police the Trooper's apparent disappearance meant involvement in the homicide case until proven otherwise. Exactly what her involvement was and why she made that phone call to the Sergeant were unknown. The wide range of possibilities, from leaving on her own to her life being at risk were all a concern.

After Shawn and Ted hung up he asked the kids to spend some time in the den and motioned to Liza to go out on the porch with him. This evening George the 2nd opted to follow Ted and Liza instead of the kids. His presence was not considered a risk to privacy.

Ted didn't want to say anything to Liza about the missing trooper until he had spoken with Shawn and confirmed she seemed to be gone and there were no other immediate surprises. Because of Liza's observation about her at the Monday meeting he was anxious to get her thoughts.

"Well, if she's pregnant, maybe more pregnant than you'd think, she may have figured it was going to come out with all the interviewing and attention to her now. My guess is she panicked and quickly packed up and got out of town. She probably had been planning to go away for a while but this business just speeded things up and made her move up her plans.

"I guess if I was pregnant and on my own and figured my career on the force was over I'd head for where my family is."

"Yeah, but leaving so suddenly like this when, rightly or wrongly, she's now considered a possible suspect in a homicide investigation...I don't know. Picking up like that pretty much will end her career, I guess. Like you say...even if she left only because she's gonna have a baby. You can't just leave like that. I guess she would be finished anyway since I doubt she's married."

"What's that got to do with it, Ted?"

'Well you can't just go and get pregnant..." Ted backtracked, knowing Liza was about to challenge him for his attitude. "You know what I mean. I mean I guess it might be hard for an unmarried state trooper to stay on the force." Best to leave it there.

* * *

Shawn's call an hour later did little to lessen Ted's concern about Trooper Devers.

"Nothing, Chief. No. Spoke to her mother, who told me they hadn't heard a word from Devers in over a month. Got the idea from talking with them that Devers and her family may not be on the best terms. But when I told them we were trying to speak with her since she told us she was going home they became real concerned. Now they're worried too.

"But they weren't much help, Chief. They didn't seem to know much about her life in Vermont. Didn't know the names of any friends here. And they had no suggestions for me who else or where else she might be heading for. I didn't get any sense from them they knew she's pregnant…if she is."

* * *

HEDGING THE INVESTIGATION?

All of a sudden Ted was nervous. He woke up Wednesday morning fixated on why he was only considering state troopers as suspects in the homicide. It was an annoying moment of second guessing that Ted recognized well. Just as there appeared to be at least circumstantial evidence one of the troopers he was already targeting had possibly implicated herself in some way with the murder he started to worry about the method he was relying on to find his suspects.

Now Trooper Nancy Devers was gone so she couldn't be interviewed and Ted had to add concerns about her whereabouts and well-being to his investigation. Something very concerning was going on with one of the eight possible suspects he had keyed on so quickly. It was plausible this might have reassured him about his direction. But, for some reason, her disappearance disturbed Ted's sense of control of the case. Maybe he took this as a possible curve occurring so early in the investigation he was plotting it shook him a little.

Even if Liza was right and Devers is pregnant, suddenly leaving town because of that wasn't as good an explanation because of the way she disappeared. But who knew. With all that's going on maybe Liza was right that she sort of panicked and left abruptly.

He mulled over his new found uncertainty as he drove to Johnson to meet up with Shawn at Trooper Devers' apartment. Shawn was waiting for him and they entered together. The first thing Ted did was walk over to the closet in the bedroom. Not much was hanging on the crossbar. Among the clothes there were only two regulation shirts. He picked up the sleeves of each of the shirts. All the buttons were intact. The very small gauntlet buttons on the forearms were all in place. Their size and configuration were identical to the button Liza found at the autopsy.

While he and Ted walked around Shawn reviewed what was noted the prior evening. She sure seemed to be living there by herself. Ted also was struck, just like Shawn, by where her cruiser's keys were sitting on the entry table; left in an obvious location, almost like turning in her keys before leaving her job. In much the same vein some personal items and clothes were gone and there were no signs of an altercation or trouble.

They locked up and restored the crime scene tape on the door. Outside in the warmth of the early morning sun they leaned on Ted's cruiser and talked. Shawn was in a suit and clearly felt the heat more than Ted.

"I can't imagine we're going to hear from Trooper Devers soon or maybe ever. I think we should give her until later today and if there's still nothing you should go ahead and get what's needed so we can examine her records."

Shawn nodded his agreement. Ted paused a few moments then continued to speak. Shawn was surprised by what he said.

"You know, Shawn, I've been thinking about when we talked last week about keeping the investigation exclusively based on the eight troopers. Maybe that is too narrow a focus at this stage. The killer could be someone other than a state policeman. Getting the ME logs for others in uniformed law enforcement might not add too many to our list."

Then he backtracked. He sounded like he was ready to discard it as quickly as he brought the idea up.

"Aw, I don' know. Probably really not worth it. We'd only be fishing and it's an awful lot to ask the ME's office, actually Sarah Perdy, to do. Dr. Fowler and Sarah Perdy will be unhappy with a task that's bound to be very time-consuming…and probably for nothing."

Ted may have felt he was thinking out loud but Shawn spoke up as soon as Ted appeared to be finished.

"No Chief, I think it's a real good idea. Who knows where it might lead the investigation? Maybe I should take some time and go over the last year's logs with her. Good chance someone or some others could become a person of interest."

Shawn's quick, whole-hearted embrace of the idea and optimism about what might show up annoyed Ted. Shawn was now another one who still doubted Ted's assumption the ME was murdered by a trooper. Ted cut short any more discussion.

"Well I'll think about it some more. I'll let you know if I talk with that office."

He headed back to Waterbury. He took his time since his planned first interview was with Trooper Devers, who was nowhere to be found. He thought things over as he drove.

No one; his superiors, his deputy, or his wife, had praised his quick production of eight suspects, one of whom he told them all was involved in or responsible for Ellie Stanton's death. When he relaxed a little and thought more about it he still felt there was no other explanation for the hammered brass button that was in her mouth. It was identical to the epaulet buttons on the Vermont State Police uniform. He was certain of it. But how well was he acquainted with the exact construction of the uniforms of other law enforcement professionals? He had to admit he wasn't.

Later in the morning, back at his office, he finally decided to go ahead and speak with the ME's office; Sarah Perdy in particular.

"Ms. Perdy, I am sorry to trouble you some more. You have been extremely cooperative and have done so much, so quickly. But I think I need more information from your logs. You may want me to speak with Dr. Fowler and I can understand that."

"What is it that you want to get from the logs now, Lieutenant?" Her tone was non-committal and bland, as usual.

"Well I think we need a list like before but this time, with names and dates of visits for all law enforcement officers over the last twelve months."

She waited to be sure he was done speaking and then responded, in the same tone.

"Lieutenant, while I was culling the logs for the information you requested I made notations on the computer of categories of visitors to our office; all law enforcement, all lawyers, and all relatives of ME cases who came to see Dr. Stanton. It was easy to do with the computer. It will not take long to do some checking and print out what I think you are asking for.

"I'm sorry I never told you this information was relatively easy to collect when I was doing the search you requested. It seemed to make sense to include other categories."

'Damn' he thought. Another one who was critical of his fixation on the state police. But he got over his initial reaction quickly and praised and thanked Sarah Perdy for her foresight and ready assistance. She told Ted she would fax a new list to an attended fax machine in his office later that afternoon.

* * *

2) TROOPER CORPORAL JOHN DAVIES

"You ready to talk to me, Lieutenant Vallan?"

Trooper Davies had managed to bypass the secretary at the front desk of the officer's corridor and walked to Ted's open door and poked his head in.

Davies was a big man; tall and lanky. He carried himself very smoothly and seemed remarkably self-assured. He had a reputation for being good-natured and people on the force liked to work with him. Ted was aware that at the academy and one time a year or so later he was criticized for using excessive force in confrontations. But he appeared to have learned and accepted more appropriate methods for handling challenging interactions with the public and maintained an exemplary record thereafter.

"Sure, come on in Corporal Davies." Ted stood and offered his hand and then directed Davies to a chair. Davies had closed the door behind him. "You have a good record, Corporal. I don't think we've run into each other before. You're working just on the fringe of where there's a lot of territory to cover for each of the troopers up north. We're glad to get members of the force who feel comfortable doing so much on their own in areas like that."

"Yessir, I enjoy the challenge of managing a big territory. I grew up in the Vermont woods and I'm glad to be back in them."

"Corporal, you know why you're here. I need to find out about any contacts and connections you had to Dr. Stanton, who was murdered."

The probably almost perpetual slight smile on Davies' face evaporated and his face became somber. He looked down at his upturned hands in his lap and barely nodded a yes. His look suggested he knew this was a serious and terrible business they would have to talk about. His actions managed to convey a sense of disgust about what had happened. Ted let the conversation die for a few moments to see if the Trooper planned to offer anything on his own. He did. Virtually all of the troopers he confronted personally were ready with something.

"Well I'm sure you already know, Lieutenant, that the Doc and I were working together on a charity project for a hospital in Thailand." He leaned back in his chair and began to tell his story. As he spoke his manner returned to the more relaxed demeanor he showed when he first entered Ted's office.

"Of course, I met Doc Stanton at her office, on police business. But we got to chatting and it turned out we both had spent some time in Thailand, years ago. I guess hers was just a vacation. I was there longer. After my year in 'nam… You over there at all Lieutenant? I can see you and me were young bucks back then."

The corporal was obviously older than most troopers at his level and it was a feature that stood out. He played his larger experience as a positive and didn't invoke any sense of superiority or impatience with those younger.

"Yes, I was drafted at eighteen."

Davies bounced his head with a grin, indicating the same with him.

Ted continued. "Never left the states though. I did military police for two years and I guess that got me started on a career with the force."

"Well I figured if they were coming for me I'd be best off with the Marines. In no time I seemed to make it right to the front lines. I did a lot of fighting."

Ted was aware that three of the five who had been in the military had spent some time overseas; two in the Marines.

"Then the war ended and I still had time to go and wound up on easy duty in Thailand; kind of like MP work, Lieutenant. I liked Thailand and used my free time to travel around.

"That's what set up my connection with the hospital on the coast we've been trying to help out. I was talking with the Doc and she noticed the pretty bad stitching job on my left hand."

He held up his left hand revealing a prominent four-inch scar and at least ten stitch cross-marking scars that suggested a rough repair.

"When I told Doc I got it in Thailand at a small coastal hospital while I was hiking the area she told me almost the same thing happened to her. She cut her thigh, real bad, on some coral in the water. And, believe it or not, she wound up at the same dinky hospital for treatment. Well, we got to talking and that's how we decided maybe we could figure a way to collect some medical supplies for that place; better stitching stuff anyway. Know what I mean?" He smiled.

"So she looked into it. It was mostly her idea and she did most of the work; coordinating the collecting and shipping the stuff over there. It has been working pretty good for a while. Not a ton of stuff but enough to make the hospital very thankful. I don't know what will happen now. I'm not sure I can handle it without her.

"You know, when we first got it all set up and working they asked one or both of us to come over and see how we were helping. Doc and I thought about going there but it never seemed to happen."

Ted didn't react visibly to those words but the way Davies said them struck him. He was openly telling him he had a relationship with Ellie; exactly what that involved was unclear. And no, Ted knew nothing about any charity this trooper and Ellie Stanton apparently were involved with.

Ted wondered if Davies had gotten carried away with his story and might have shared more than he intended. Indeed, Davies was quiet after that, apparently deciding he would not volunteer any more. Ted determined to probe further.

"Trooper, we think Dr. Stanton had sexual relations with more than a few law officers."

Before Ted asked the inevitable question the Trooper spoke up.

"Sure lieutenant, we went to her place a couple of times for the evening. I guess you know that's the way she was. I can't say I didn't want to do that stuff with her but the hospital work became more important to me. And, you know, I think Doc had to trust me so we could work together. After a while it was more the charity than anything else."

"Corporal, we have records of everyone who was at the ME office for the last year. You were there a number of times, but if you and Dr. Stanton were doing a charity together there weren't any other signs of you two working together on it. There's only two contacts listed on her phone records…"

The Trooper understood what Ted was asking. He took a breath, seemed to be considering his response, and spoke.

"Lieutenant, I don't know if you knew the Doc much, but she was different. She was very secret and a little almost mysterious about her private life. It was like she didn't want anyone to know a whole lot about her. I got to know her enough to see she had personal problems and didn't really want to get close to anyone. And, frankly, the couple of times I was with her she made me kind of nervous and it wasn't much fun."

"So what's any of that got to do with working together on that charity?"

"Well Doc didn't want me calling her. I don' know why but I guess what I just told you was part of it. So she first gave me a key to her house so I could just drop off supplies that other troopers picked up. After a while I told her Colchester, by the lake, was a long ride and she gave me a key to her truck so all I had to do was get to Burlington during regular hours and move stuff from my cruiser to her truck. I think we each thought it was fine to do it that way; and maybe for the best since getting personal with her was kind of strange."

Ted doubted he would hear exactly the same story from Ellie if she could speak, but who could say? If she really had so many relationships who was to say what was or wasn't unusual for her? For the moment he was left in little more than an information gathering mode and had sparse reasons to challenge what he was hearing. Davies maintained an earnest look on his face and was describing events in what appeared to be as matter-of-fact a way as possible for him.

"At your station you worked with Trooper Nancy Devers, is that right?"

"Sure Lieutenant, I know Nancy. We're all sick with worry about her."

"She helped with supplies for the charity?"

"Yeah, she was very helpful. But so were a bunch of other troopers around the state."

"Did she ever go with you to Dr. Stanton's house to deliver supplies?"

"No. No I never went there with anyone else, sir."

"Did you and Trooper Devers ever do anything, like get together, unrelated to the force?"

"Why no, of course not, Lieutenant. We all know the rules." He paused. But he wasn't able to leave it there. "I can't honestly say that she might not have had a little crush on me, way back. You know, she was young and was pretty green so I helped her out on the job from time to time. Experienced older guy, you know; like that. That was it. No, she was way too young for me anyway."

Ted wondered why the Trooper referred to himself as an older guy rather than just an experienced trooper. Despite what Davies said Ted thought there could be more to this. And was Davies referring to Trooper Devers in the past tense?

* * *

USEFUL INFORMATION?

Shawn Barry walked into Ted's office around five. He only had one piece of paper in his hand.

"I guess you decided to request the ME's office put together that list with the rest of the law enforcement officers to visit Doc Stanton over the past year. This is the printout."

Ted looked up from the work he was doing at his desk. He, correctly, sensed Shawn was going to go ahead and say something about the list.

"Not many other law enforcement officers, Chief. Interesting. One Plattsburgh cop from across the lake. Three Burlington PD, one Stowe City, and one Chittenden County cop… Oh, and also one Fish and Wildlife Warden, if you want to count him."

"And a partridge in a pear tree, eh?" Shawn didn't get the reference. "Well, I'm working on the troopers. I'm sorry Shawn, but you are going to have to interview each one on the new list. My suggestion is you don't need to do any bullshit with them. You can tell them we know she had a thing about sleeping with cops and we're gonna find out about them anyway even if they don't tell us. We know she did it with doctors. I want to know if she did it with any cops other than troopers."

Ted was pretty much back to assuming his murderer was a state policeman.

* * *

3) TROOPER STEPHAN SEARS

The interview with Trooper Sears went, well, mostly as Ted might have expected. Sears was more interested in helping to solve the homicide than even recognizing he might be considered a suspect. His defense was an offense. As he sat in front of Ted, frequently pulling one leg up and resting it on the seat of his chair, he also kept looking off in space, as he was thinking about things; perhaps trying to visualize scenes and his thoughts in a world of his own. Ted had to be careful about his own initial reaction to parts of the Trooper's manner. Liza, from time to time, did much the same thing; looking into space while thinking intently. No one doubted her interest or ability.

But, from the start, Ted was amazed how Sears acted as though he was there to consult on the case. Always animated, he spoke with his hands and fidgeted a bit, moving his thin, wiry body around in his chair. He was also one of the troopers who had spent time overseas in the military.

Make no mistake, Sears stood out in the few short years he was on the force. He and others knew he was headed for a good future with opportunity to rise through the ranks, concentrating mostly on white collar cases. Actually the kind of cases that Ted excelled at and often had solved quite nicely. Ted recoiled a bit at the idea Trooper Sear's manner and demeanor was, in any way, a reflection of how Ted acted when he was a beginner. Try as he could Ted was just not predisposed to like Trooper Sears.

"Lieutenant, don't you think the Medical Examiner knew her killer? I mean, I've read all the stuff in the paper, you know, and if you know a trooper did it, well that means she was pushed off that mountain top by someone who had planned to do it. That person went to all that effort to get her to go up to Camel's Hump and, I guess, push her off to make it look like an accident…well someone felt there was a reason to do that because he probably knew her. To avoid being under suspicion 'cause he knew her, and other people probably knew that. You think?"

"Trooper, I need to know what your connection with Dr. Stanton was. We know you were at the ME office in Burlington, at least once, a few months ago. What were you doing there and did you have any direct contact with the Doctor?"

Sears seemed startled out of a reverie and sat up more straight and answered right away.

"Yes sir. I went to the ME's office in early April this year to drop off clothes from that guy who got shot near Charlotte on the first day of spring hunting this year. Yeah, when his buddies found him they ripped all his clothes off his chest to give him chest compression but it didn't work. Anyway, the ME, Doc Stanton, told me she wanted to try to put the clothes back on him so's she could maybe get a better idea of the direction how the bullet went into him.

"Seemed like a fair question to me. Doc actually asked me to go into the morgue with her to help her put the clothes back on him. Man, that was a little nasty; know what I mean?"

"Sears, tell me about your personal interaction with the Doctor."

"Sure, Lieutenant." Stroked his chin and looked up and away. His body language offered no sense of a guilty bone in his body; a little kid trying to help out. "Doc explained stuff about what she did and how she determined such neat things from his body. That was about it. I helped her so she could better define the bullet's trajectory. We talked about a bunch of things: hiking, even some books she liked that I had read too. After a while it was getting late and it looked like the office was closing up. So I said I guess I better go and got my hat. She thanked me for bringing the stuff and helping her. I thanked her for the things she showed me and that was it. Never saw her again."

Finally, Ted thought…a man in uniform who Ellie didn't invite home to sleep with her.

"So you never had any personal involvement with the Doctor? Trooper we know that the Doctor had sexual relations with some members of the force. Did you have relations with her or do you know of any trooper or troopers who did?"

"Oh, gosh no sir. I told some of the guys in the Williston barracks about the time I was with Doc in the morgue and no one sniggered or said anything like that about Doc." Then Sears looked more serious than Ted had ever seen him appear. "And no sir, that Doctor and me never did anything like that. You mean she was doing things like that right there in the morgue? Man, that's kind of creepy, isn't it?"

"Trooper, do you know Trooper Nancy Devers?"

"Well I know she was at the meeting this week and then I just heard guys talking this morning that she's left the force. What's that all about, Lieutenant?"

"Did you know her personally Sears?"

"Oh, no. No sir, never met her."

As Ted stood, Sears got up also. Ted thanked him for coming in and raised his arm towards the door indicating he could leave. Just as the Trooper began to open the door Ted thought of another question.

"Trooper have you been involved in transporting medical supplies for a charity to the Burlington hospital?"

"Sure, Lieutenant, I'd be glad to help out if you think so. I've never been asked to do anything like that before."

Sears was not his man. What Sears did need was seasoning; more time to mature. Maybe he'd be okay…someday, Ted thought.

* * *

HUMAN BEHAVIOR 1

There are many ways to make love. Over time couples in committed relationships develop patterns and generally a rhythm to their lovemaking. Satisfying a partner and being satisfied usually leads to a repetition of movements with an almost logical progression through the process for each couple. Complete and reliable satisfaction for both partners may never be achieved even over a lifetime together. In a long, loving relationship acceptance and compromise allows many couples to have personally meaningful and pleasurable sex.

In a busy, complicated world the act of making love can mean or signify many things: A repeating commitment to ultimate sharing of total closeness; a sense of oneness, together, can be a way to define passion...for one couple. A recurring desire to sense a brief reversion to a quest for an almost first time excitement of melding together with another. A method for relaxation; to relieve tensions. An effort to help restore a basic commitment in a fractured (or fracturing) relationship.

There may be little else in adult life that so dramatically reflects the fundamental nature of an individual's psychological dynamics than what we bring to our lovemaking. Whatever the understood or unconscious motivations of the significance for each individual for making love, and the way each individual makes love, most of us like to do it over and over, for a very, very long time.

Making love in an uncommitted setting should be quite different. Especially in an almost random hook-up. Lack of knowledge of so much of the personality and history of your partner should mean that satisfying one another, if that is even a goal, is more difficult. Every aspect of having satisfying sex in this fashion should be a challenge. Unless, of course, the excitement and pleasure of the experience is directly connected to those features: The randomness; lack of common comfort with the partner; the newness of the interaction. Could taking the risk of less, maybe much less, attention to the satisfaction or pleasure of the partner be more permissible in that setting? Satisfying oneself the main goal? Behaving in a way with a partner that could not be envisioned with a partner who you loved?

Or maybe it could be the opposite. A repeated desire, or need, to experience pleasure by satisfying a stranger. Ellie Stanton's self-analysis over time leaned a bit in that direction. She fantasized herself almost as a canvas upon which a stranger could use her to create his own progression and pace for making love. Each time she offered herself as a blank, naked canvas to be drawn on. She enjoyed sensing the desires and rhythms of her partners and helping to create and sustain excitement.

Well, that was what she thought anyway. That was probably mostly true. But, mind games aside, Ellie was also very much into pleasure from the physical act of thrusting back and forth while penetrated. Rapid and hard. She was not in a rush to reach a crescendo or climax with that effort; it just felt spectacular. Frequent and repeated orgasms were the norm for her. Partners often reached a point where they had to hold on for dear life from the intensity of the gyrations she developed and sustained for surprisingly long periods.

Making love with a prize like Ellie Stanton was enough gratification for most of her partners. Her willingness to indulge a lover's fantasies was a bonus. Sensing the unusual way she stayed in charge of the sex, and being pushed away when they were done, was a small price to pay for most for the excitement of being with her for even a limited time.

* * *

He made it a point to conveniently run into Ellie as she was parking or getting into her truck at the hospital. If it was clear she was with someone or being followed by someone he backed off before she knew he was around. Over the weeks following their first tryst he connected with her twice. She invited him to follow her home the second time. To his surprise she had a dinner planned for him. They had a good time and he stayed most of the night.

He suggested she have a key to her truck made for him so they could leave messages for each other to plan future meetings. Ellie suggested the telephone was generally used for such purposes. Jokingly he looked around her kitchen, feigning paranoia, and told her he was planning to talk with her soon about a way for both of them to make a lot of money and connecting by phone might not be such a good idea.

For reasons she later could not figure, at the time he first brought this up, it seemed tempting and mysterious. His infectious personality and the way he related to her made her feel he was different, in an exciting but also puzzling way. She couldn't figure him out but knew she enjoyed being with him.

And besides, sex with him was different. He could perform like all the others but he also seemed to sense Ellie's pleasure from serving. He found methods that made that more exciting for her. He didn't do anything restricting or painful to her but he found ways and places to excite her that she had never previously been aware of. In doing so, over time, she began to feel her control of their love making moved from more passive to active involvement. That was new for her. And so she began to rely on their sexual relationship.

He understood and was happy to accommodate. It was only very gradually, over some months, that he began to make Ellie understand there was a price for her to pay if they were to continue their relationship.

* * *

4) TROOPER MARY MANINO

The interview of Trooper Mary Manino became more important to Ted after the only other female trooper disappeared. Word that Trooper Devers was missing was probably out by now and that raised the intensity not only of the investigation but also the concern of those troopers singled out by Ted. It was almost an affirmation that when Lieutenant Vallan had rounded them up he was on to something, for sure. Of course her disappearance might have been a relief to the other seven troopers since it naturally turned Devers into a prime suspect. But the idea that a young female trooper had brutally murdered the ME seemed difficult to accept, to Ted and most others. So her disappearance raised the guard of everyone involved just that much more. Trooper Manino seemed to Ted to have had just such a reaction.

Ted scheduled her interview for early afternoon since he knew she'd have to drive up from Brattleboro, far south in the state. He made sure he returned to Waterbury by noon from an investigation he was monitoring in Burlington so he could clear his desk and concentrate on why his only remaining female trooper might have had a connection to Ellie Stanton.

Like all the others Trooper Manino was punctual, arriving at the secretary's desk just minutes before two. She, like Trooper Devers, was notably shorter than most male troopers. Nancy Devers wore a short pony-tail but Manino kept her jet black hair short.

Sitting directly across from Trooper Manino, remembering pictures of Nancy Devers he had looked at just that morning, Ted wondered why he had ever thought of them as practically twins when Liza first told him she thought Trooper Devers might be pregnant. Maybe they were about the same height but that was about it, in many ways. Yes, they each had features of that practiced, bland expressionless face that many police officers thought a professional necessity. But Manino had a penetrating stare and her facial features were more tight and severe. Despite her professional pose Nancy Devers' eyes and lips expressed some warmth and, probably, softness.

Manino came much closer to having that military bearing of so many troopers. Her uniform was beautifully pressed with sharp creases on the arms of her shirt and her pants. She clearly worked out. She looked tough, strong, and no nonsense: what the force wanted of its troopers. Her appearance and the way her eyes followed Ted made it clear she was on guard for this interview. Ted was fixated on Nancy Devers' sudden disappearance at the moment but reminded himself it was Ellie Stanton's homicide that brought Trooper Manino to his office that afternoon. The formality of their greeting and her ramrod straight posture in her chair warned Ted.

"Trooper Manino, thank you for making it up to Waterbury so promptly today. You know I want to ask some questions relating to the homicide of Dr. Eleanor Stanton."

Trooper Manino sat still, only moving her eyes. Ted realized his words were not phrased as a question. No reply was required and she did not offer one. This Trooper did not plan to volunteer anything.

"So, we know from logs in the Medical Examiner's office that you were there on at least two occasions over the last almost twelve months. Do you remember why you went there those times?"

"Sir. Official business."

"Trooper, can you tell me what your business was and whether you had any contact with the Doctor on either of those visits or at any other time?" He wasn't sure if her curt reply was meant to be hostile or was a reflection of her professional manner. His follow-up question gave her an opportunity to make that distinction for him…he hoped.

"Sir. I was in the Medical Examiner's office three times over the time you specified. On the first occasion I only stopped by there to drop off two boxes of medical supplies a trooper had called and asked me pick up at the Bennington hospital and drop in Burlington some time when I was going to have to be in Waterbury. I was introduced to Dr. Stanton, who thanked me, and I was on my way.

"Two months later I…"

"Do you remember who the trooper was who contacted you about bringing those supplies up to Burlington?"

"Trooper Nancy Devers. Sir" She paused, possibly assuming Ted's attention would now be directed to her relationship with Nancy Devers. But Ted wasn't ready for that yet.

"Yes, go on and tell me about the other times you were at the ME office."

"Two months later I brought evidence the office had requested. From an industrial accident with death developing."

Like dental work.

"Did you see or have any contact with the Doctor at that visit?"

"Yes sir."

Beginning to get frustrated over her pattern of replies.

"Trooper Manino, I want to know all the details of your contacts with that office and Dr. Stanton. Everything, please. If you talked to her I want to know what it was about."

"Sir. First the Doctor asked me to review the details of the case; the specifics of the accident and how we found the deceased. She then requested I stay for part of the autopsy examination to be available to answer any further questions she might have as she worked on it."

'Oh my' he thought. He never considered Ellie's pattern of seduction might also apply to women. Was that where his probing of this Trooper was leading? Was that why Manino was being so terse and staying so formal; trying to bluff her way out of a true description of her contact with Ellie? Did they have a sexual interaction?

This was all so awkward. This idea was, of course, not unheard of in Ted's experience but still very foreign for his mind set. As uncomfortable as he felt questioning this woman about this he knew he had to go ahead. He would tell her what he knew about Ellie and see how she responded and what she said.

"Trooper, we have been learning a lot about Dr. Stanton; in particular, about her personal life. We know she had sexual relations with a large number of me…people; often law officers; often with people she did not know well at all. Speaking quite frankly, Trooper Manino, I need to ask you if you and Dr. Stanton ever had any sexual activity together?"

"Sir. No sir. That did not happen."

"You see, we know Dr. Stanton had a pattern of requesting troopers bring evidence and inviting troopers, and maybe others, to her autopsies. The autopsy would run late and the Doctor encouraged some of those people to go to her home with her and have sex. Do you know anything about anything like that with the Doctor?"

For the first time during the interview Trooper Manino shifted a bit in her chair and appeared slightly conflicted.

"Yes sir. I have heard rumors."

Back to dental work.

"Trooper, did you have any sexual activity with Dr. Stanton?"

"No Sir."

"Did you ever get the feeling when you were with the Doctor that she was trying to... how can I say this... make a move in that direction with you?"

"No sir."

"You said you had three contacts with the ME's office. What was the last one about?"

Less pretense this time.

"I do not know exactly why I was asked to go there then. It was several months ago. Doctor did request I stop by there late in the day to answer some questions pertaining to the industrial accident from long before. It was a big effort for me to get there. I told her I was in a hurry and declined to go to her office and talk. So I answered her questions at the desk and left."

"Was Dr. Stanton angry with you? I mean about that?"

"Sir?"

On the surface it seemed Ted had followed a false channel. But she could just as easily be lying. He thought it a good possibility. Later he would wonder if he should have tried to probe further. Maybe there was more to Trooper Manino and Ellie. But he felt it was time to move on to Trooper Devers. Was Devers' status about to become more complicated?

"Did Trooper Devers call you to ask you to pick up those supplies for a charity because you knew each other?"

"Probably."

She just wasn't going to make this any easier for either of them.

"Then tell me about how you knew each other and what you knew about Trooper Devers." Ted was getting frustrated. He was making it too easy for Manino. He was lobbing her softballs and he had no way, so far, to know if her responses were truthful.

"Lieutenant, there are very few female troopers on the force so we all have kind of kept track of each other, you know. We used to do it more, but even now most of us meet up somewhere in-between Waterbury and Rutland at a tavern, about two, three times a year, to hang out and kind of support each other. Being on the force is not always easy for a woman.

"Trooper Devers came sometimes, so I knew her, a little. Wouldn't say we were friends. I don't think I had any contact with her since she called to ask me to pick that stuff up…until we met at that meeting you had a few days ago."

"So you don't know how she's been doing lately or why she seems to have disappeared?"

A look of true concern appeared on her face.

"Sir, I don't know what you are talking about. She's disappeared?"

Ted assumed the entire force knew this by now, but maybe he was wrong. Anyway, he suspected even though they both had reason to know each other because women were such a small minority on the force, the two troopers worked in opposite parts of the state and probably were not active friends; like Manino indicated. That made him all the more interested in Manino's take on Nancy Devers' appearance at the meeting a few days before.

"I saw you were sitting next to Trooper Devers at the meeting." Manino tensed, ever so slightly. "Did she say anything to you? talk about anything going on in her life? How did she look to you?"

She exhaled and then took a deeper breath. Ted took it that she had something to report.

"Nancy, …Trooper Devers, seemed nervous, sir. But I think we all were a little worried about what was going on."

That was it? Manino was not much help.

"Did she seem distracted to you?"

"Maybe. But she was always kind of quiet. She never drank much when we all met up."

"What about the way she looked? Her physical appearance. Anything you noticed?"

For the first time during the whole challenging interview Trooper Manino cracked the slightest smile.

"Well Sir, Nancy has always had a bit of a weight problem. I told her she better get back to the gym or she was gonna pop out of her clothes, sir."

He thanked Trooper Manino for making the long drive up to Waterbury. Mary Manino had worn Ted out. He had about forty minutes before the final interview of the day on Thursday.

* * *

5) **TROOPER AARON NICOLAIDES**

He was angry and defensive from the moment he walked into the room. His language was more salty than you would expect from someone speaking to a superior he did not know. Ted's initial reaction was the Trooper, Aaron Nicolaides, in person, and the Trooper described in his official file, might have been two different people. His record was outstanding. He was a young man who demonstrated a prescient grasp of force procedure and was notably successful working with the public in a variety of challenging situations in his three years on the force.

In the flesh he was something else. Nicolaides was shorter than the two female troopers in the group of eight. Ted had to think his abilities must have played a role in him being allowed on the force since he was probably technically, by the regs, too short. His face looked like he might need to shave twice a day to keep his dense beard down. Sitting across from Nicolaides Ted had the impression he was hairy all over. His body was muscular and the angry scowl he flashed at Ted made him appear not only tough but, actually, ominous. Today, he looked like he was spoiling for a fight.

Ted finished his opening comments as he had with the others. He consciously tried to coordinate his questions through all the interviews to be similar so he could look for both patterns and, hopefully, inconsistencies in at least one of the trooper's responses.

"Lieutenant, if I didn't get the word about that crazy Doctor before I met up with her, I sure as shit learned about her the hard way. I'm telling you, that lady was some ball buster.

"She ast'd me to fuck her in the ass, Lieutenant. So I did…Wouldn't you?" This guy wasn't uncomfortable with what had happened or talking about it. "The last time she made it like she wanted me to lick her ass too. Imagine? 'No fucking way' I told her. I wasn't goin' there."

"Back up, Nicolaides. I want to know when you met the Doctor and how those things you're talking about happened."

But Ted had heard it before. Another trooper called to an autopsy and quickly seduced by Ellie. Nicolaides was listed in the logs a couple of times, but he turned out to be the second trooper who also made alternative contact, getting her calls to him patched to her from an ME secretary and then arranging to meet him at her home after dark several other evenings. This Trooper and Trooper Davies seemed to have a number of return visits.

Nicolaides looked like he was seething just below the surface. Why? What about?

"Trooper, I'm not sure why you're so hot? That Doctor was murdered and I intend to find her killer. Can't you see even if the only thing you did was sleep with her that's enough to make you a suspect? Are you gonna talk with me about this or should we start shouting at each other?"

This was the third interview of the day and Ted had less patience. He stood up and paced around his small office. He never thought about it but that was guaranteed to further upset the Trooper, who now looked even smaller, stuck in his chair.

"Look Lieutenant. It started off real good and, of course, I got excited to go to her place and all. She was some fucker. I mean, at first it was real good. For a while it was almost like she was trying to play dead, encouraging me to get all over her; do anything I wanted. Who wouldn't get excited by that?

"Then, after a few times, it was a little different, you know. That Doc was a big, tall lady and I'm not. I got to do what I wanted but then she started to seem to be playin' with me. You know, like I was a little kid or something. For a while I thought, 'whatever turns you on'. She played with the hair on my body and sometimes I'd feel like she was makin' me into a monkey. Christ, I didn't like that. She laughed at me, right in my face, and tried to hold me like some f'ing pet. Didn't want to be with her anymore. Enough!" He glared at Ted. Then he calmed but only barely.

"So I was losing interest. And besides, after we fucked her whole body and face changed and I knew it was time for me to skedaddle. So I did. Lieutenant I like to fuck as much as the next guy, but she got to be weird, from start to finish. When it got to playing with her ass I decided enough was enough."

"She made you angry because you thought she was using you?"

"Yeah…but not just to fuck. What still burns me was the way she fucking played with me like I was a kid… or a monkey. I had enough of that shit when I was little. Then, when I said no more, I wasn't coming back, she started to threaten me. Really Lieutenant, this whore was diddling the neighborhood and she was telling me she could get me in trouble; that she knew everyone who ran the force. Coming from her that was something, eh?"

Ted had stopped by the back of his desk as Nicolaides spoke his expletive laced rant. Now he leaned over the desk directly across from the Trooper and placed his hands on the desktop.

"What did you do about her threat Aaron?"

Nicolaides sat back in his chair and waited until the fire in his eyes and the red in his face began to fade.

"I just walked out, Lieutenant. What did you think I would do? That bit…Doc had someone in her office call me about a few weeks later. I was smart. I stayed polite with the secretary, but when Doc got on the phone I let her have it. I told her to leave me alone; to f'ing fuck off. And that was it. Never heard from her again."

"When was that Aaron?"

"Oh, I'd say we finished about a couple of weeks before she wound up at the bottom of that cliff. I guess she pissed someone else off too."

The Trooper's anger impressed Ted and there was nothing about his words or his manner that didn't worry Ted. If he killed Ellie in a rage he sure wasn't trying to lessen any suspicion of him doing that. That was odd. A hot-headed guy expressing pure anger. Sex, even essentially almost one-night stand sex had its complications. 'Who'd have thought,' Ted wondered. This guy accepted being an alpha male and that was it. Ellie's behavior set off a torrent of memories and upset in this Trooper. Did he kill her? Obviously Ellie never made any fuss about him because if she had she would have complained to him (Ted), the person she knew best on the force. But Nicolaides might never have known if she did or didn't say anything to someone.

"Aaron, did you ever get involved in collecting or delivering any medical supplies for a charity to Dr. Stanton or the Burlington hospital?" Ted decided that calling him Aaron had helped to defuse some of his anger.

"No sir. Never heard anything about anything like that."

"What about Trooper Nancy Devers? You may have heard she seems to be missing. Did you know her at all; ever have any contact with her? Have you heard anything from anyone about where she might be?"

"She was one of the troopers you called in that day, right Lieutenant?" Ted nodded.

"No, I don't believe she and I ever crossed paths before that day. I work Connecticut River region and I believe she's up north, right? No, don't know anything about her."

At least the Trooper had calmed down.

* * *

THE TWINS

6) Trooper Steven Tulip

7) Trooper Martin Verdon

Ted purposely scheduled the final two troopers to come in the same day, Friday. Because they were both married he lumped them together. He wasn't sure why that became the outstanding feature that made him decide to link them. Knowing they were married and there was a good chance one or both had sex with Ellie made the character of those men suspect to Ted. That was his code. He was predisposed not to like them.

They both had been in the military. Trooper Verdon spent his time overseas.

Trooper Steve Tulip and Trooper Martin Verdon turned out to be pleasant, affable men. Were they innocently sucked into the web of seduction Ellie could masterfully weave on some men? Their stories about their interactions with the Medical Examiner were very similar and took almost identical paths as the others who admitted to sex with Ellie. If any of the eight troopers he was interested in appeared to be twins it was these two.

He met separately with each of them but probably little different would have been learned interviewing them together. Not only were their stories identical but their conflicted narratives indicated both disgust with themselves and excitement about it having happened. Ted thought they behaved almost like children in front of him; looking down at the floor, sheepish, slight smiles on their faces. Ready for punishment but not especially unhappy about their actions.

Just like Ellie, they, and actually virtually all the men he knew of who slept with her, took from their interaction and sex what they wanted from it. Ellie had her needs, which fashioned the path of her seductions and then her love-making and after. Bottom line, each of the men took what they could; for better or worse. None were truly coerced into her bed.

These married men had obvious boundaries in their lives but chose to disregard them when opportunity arose. The yin and yang of all lives flowed out of them as they tried to live on with their sense of guilt and disgrace but also the remembered pleasure from their, supposedly solitary, transgressions. Honest men who had literally fucked up, Ted thought. At this point, after what happened to Ellie, their single night with her would more likely take on an aura of mystery for the remainder of their lives. As her story would, of course, eventually come out for all the world to know they would probably use her oddness to try to lessen their own feelings of guilt.

If they hated Ellie, which he doubted, it was because she was part of a moment where whatever moral compass they presumed to live by dipped in a dark direction. But Ted seriously doubted, despite the modicum of guilt and remorse they each expressed, at least in the similar way they told their stories, that either one was nearly upset enough to want to kill her, much less actually do it.

There was one thing about one of the troopers, Tulip, that did make a singular impression on Ted. He was something of a gossip. Ted's modest chauvinism made him assume those kinds of stories would have come from Trooper Devers or Manino. Tulip had some comments about several of the eight suspects Ted was evaluating. Something he said about Trooper Devers struck Ted could be important.

He said he knew Trooper Devers from a training exercise day they completed together in the winter. When he made a comment about how nice her car was she told him she and Corporal Davies had recently gone to New Hampshire together and Davies helped her pick it out.

* * *

SHOULD SEX TALKED ABOUT AT THE OFFICE STAY AT THE OFFICE?

Driving home Ted felt increasingly discouraged. Five days before he stood in front of all eight of them and thought he could shame the guilty one into confessing. What a joke. Now he had finished interviewing the seven remaining troopers and what had he gained? Not very much, and he certainly didn't feel he was closing in on a killer. Sure he had learned some things and suspicions were raised. But, truth to tell, other than Trooper Devers' sudden disappearance, and working on the uncertainty of whatever happened to her, the whole damn week he hadn't uncovered a tremendous amount of information to guide his next steps.

Definitely couldn't call what he had just completed interrogations. He never really put pressure on any of them. No conscious effort to make any one of them truly uncomfortable. Maybe that was a mistake. Maybe he was too close to these troopers since he was one also and they shared so much in their make-up and work ethic. Possibly. Never before in his career had he ever considered going outside of the force for any real support, much less to run an investigation. Colonel Sawyer was already on his back and that would not sit well with him. Sawyer wasn't happy with Ted, in general.

No, he wouldn't consider putting the integrity of the force in the hands of any other organization, even if there was a terribly bad actor in the force. It was his job. The relatively benign time he spent with those troopers didn't correlate in any way with the terrible and brutal method and facts of Ellie's murder. He better get tougher.

Moving on to the need to re-energize his efforts on the case occupied only part of his thoughts. Ted also knew he was still more than waffling in his mind about whether he would, or could emotionally, even share with Liza the stories he had learned about those lives and their intersection with Ellie Stanton's. Ted thought he might have difficulty discussing the details of the sex Ellie had with so many, especially Vermont State Troopers. He even recognized he was worried about what impact knowing those stories might have on how he would react the next time he and Liza made love.

All week long Ted listened to various versions of how Ellie Stanton made love with different people. Patterns and peculiarities of her love making had more than a casual impact on him. It was clearly not everyday stuff to Ted. He was pretty comfortable with himself, he thought, that none of that turned him on. But he would never again ever think of Ellie in any way other than as a highly sexual person. Remembering her beauty would forever on be attached to her voracious and unusual sexual behavior. He was pretty sure he had never missed any seductive come on from Ellie to him. He shuddered a little, counting his good fortune that if she had ever tried he was clueless enough he never even realized it.

But what about Liza? Why was he thinking about her while driving home? If he wanted to talk with her about the interviews this week what was he looking for or expecting from her? Would hearing about Ellie upset her? Was he unconsciously hoping it would turn her on and have an impact on their sex life? What a thought. Ted realized he generally thought little about their love-making. He just liked it and relied on it and probably wished it happened a bit more frequently than Liza did. And, therefore, it didn't. Quiet was the word for having sex when there were two growing kids sleeping nearby. Ted knew he was satisfied with their pattern but it was light years from what he heard about all week.

Closer to arriving home he thought he began to better understand why his thoughts had drifted to Liza. Yes, there was probably an element of wondering about him and Liza and more intense sex. But he didn't need to fear himself reacting to any fantasies. Their die was cast and sex would be sex for them; as it had been for a long time.

No, he thought of her because he knew she would be expecting to hear how the investigation of the death of a good friend was going. Ted was focusing on Ellie's sexcapades and Liza likely would not. But she probably would want to know about that part of Ellie's life. And, though maybe a bit embarrassed about being clearly personally conflicted in response to what he had heard all week, Ted really did want to know what Liza thought about it. She was a woman and a doctor so she often had insights coming from perspectives he never considered. Then again, did Ellie's unusual sexual behaviors and history really matter any longer since it was her homicide he was entrusted to solve? But it seemed an inescapable part of it all, he thought. Did doing that stuff get her killed?

* * *

"How's the investigation going? How many of those troopers have you been able to meet with by now?"

Of course, Liza did want to know everything Ted was learning about the death of her friend. Her brief expression, just after the second autopsy, of no longer caring who did this to Ellie occurred after an emotional moment of despair and had long since been replaced by a strong interest in the case.

The dog had been out for the last time and they were in their room getting undressed and into bed to read. The kids were finishing up a TV show and would be in their rooms for the night soon. Ted couldn't think of a more awkward time to begin to talk about details of Ellie's investigation. He thought about only telling Liza his latest information on the disappearance of Nancy Devers. But there wasn't much she didn't already know to tell her. Liza knew he was busy working through interviews with all the remaining troopers.

"Actually Lize, I just finished meeting with the last two on the list today. They were quite a pair; almost like twins the way their stories were so similar."

"What do you mean they told the same story? I don't know what that means. How could they have crossed paths with Ellie in an identical way?"

He was stuck. He was exhausted and she was wide awake…and even the few words he had spoken clearly peaked her interest. He looked to their bedroom door to make sure it was only open a crack so if they kept their voices down the kids would not hear them. Liza seemed to understand the implication of his glance and she looked more intently at Ted, waiting for his response. He wished he could say something harmless sounding, like 'Oh there's a lot up in the air; still more to find out', but he knew what any discussion with Liza should be about. He drilled right down to the heart of what he had learned.

"Babe, all week it was pretty much learning more and more details about Ellie's sex life; and it was pretty strange. An unusual pattern." Liza didn't react physically. She left her book open on her lap and looked straight ahead, waiting for Ted to continue. "Those last two troopers today are both married but they each had a one-night stand with Ellie."

There. He already introduced what was, for him, probably the most difficult idea to share with his wife as they lay, side by side, in their bed. Now all he had to do, hopefully just as briefly, is tell her about the frequency of Ellie's sex with strangers and Ellie's unusual sexual patterns. At least he thought they were unusual.

He tried to waffle.

"I'm also finding out about some kind of charity Ellie was involved in to send medical supplies to a small hospital in Thailand. Babe, did Ellie ever talk about that with you or ask you to help her?"

"No. No, she never mentioned anything about anything like that to me." She turned in bed and looked directly at Ted. "Ted, are you going to tell me what on earth you're talking about? What the hell does 'unusual sexual pattern' mean?"

Maybe telling her about marital infidelity wasn't the most difficult part for him.

"Lize, two of the seven didn't admit to having sex with Ellie but the other five did. And I guess there's a whole bunch of police and doctors at the hospital who had sex with her too. Mostly only one time for many of them. Ellie had a routine, I guess, where she got them to her autopsies, kept them there late, and talked them into going to her home with her and having sex. I guess you'd have to say she seduced each and every one of them. At least from the way they each described their time with her that's what I guess it sounds like.

"Babe, Ellie controlled or at least tried to control everything: From getting them to the morgue to how they had sex and even after."

"Really. What do you mean about the sex?" Liza's response was spoken in a more clinical way of wanting more information, not suggesting his story was lurid and she wanted more. That made it a little easier for Ted. And so he told her the pieces that he had been struck by.

"During the seductions Ellie was all interested in them and was sweet. They said the sex was weird because it sounds like she became all passive. She lay there and encouraged them to play out some fantasies on her…with her…oh I don't know; you know what I'm saying. I think it means they played with her body and she really acted like she enjoyed it, maybe. Do you know what I mean?" Ted said it but it was awkward and he felt flustered.

Ted was a cop and he had seen and heard things in his career that most people never dreamed one human could consider, much less do to another human. And yet this discussion with his wife was difficult for him. Clearly because it was about sex. Ted more than wondered what that meant about him?

Liza was far from a prude but, at least at this point in her life, her interest in sex seemed to Ted far from a motivating concern. Of all the many balls she managed to keep up in the air in her extremely busy and, he assumed satisfying life, even thinking about their sex, much less any fantasies, just wasn't happening, as best he knew. She was a lover. She appeared to overflow with love and affection for her husband, her children, her house, her marvelous career, and even George the 2nd, their dog.

Of course life always presented some problems. But Liza was an optimist. He knew she occasionally expressed imagining her life and her family living in their small home in tiny Richmond in tiny Vermont as a bright light of energy; a going concern of real people devoting their lives to each other and to helping the world. Less love of sex now, he figured.

Liza Vallan was also a physician. Physicians have the unique privilege and responsibility to be as non-judgmental as possible as they work with patients and often learn the most startling tales of human behavior anyone could imagine. So there wasn't much she hadn't heard about human sexual behavior before; even in Vermont. Liza had pegged her husband as someone who might have difficulty understanding and reacting to stories of some of the behaviors she had encountered and decided to spare Ted from most of them. Physician-patient confidentiality also required her to keep most of those things to herself anyway.

Liza could tell he had more to say, so she kept her face neutral and patiently waited for him to continue.

"They all made a point of saying how Ellie's mood and behavior changed so dramatically as soon as they were done. They said she became cold as ice. It was like she didn't even want to talk to them anymore and wanted them dressed and out of her life as quick as possible. It sure soured most of them on the whole business. It made a few regret that they had sex with her."

Ted wasn't sure how he felt about those expressions of regret. Maybe it was because they were angry? They thought Ellie treated them badly? What more did they want from her? Why did he feel stuck on that? Shouldn't they have keyed on having sex with a beautiful woman instead of regretting the whole thing because she brushed them off after?

"So, Ted…"

He gently raised his hand to indicate to Liza he wasn't finished. If he had managed to get this far he figured he should get it all out; finish by telling her the part he heard from Trooper Nicolaides.

"One Trooper told me quite a story about the sex he had with Ellie. Without me asking him any specific questions about the sex he told me she encouraged him to do it in her backside…and she wanted him to lick her there."

There, he said it. He had told her just about everything. It wasn't easy for him and, from looking straight ahead, he turned his head only a little so he could see Liza's reaction to his words.

But she didn't really move or change her expression. Ted could tell she was thinking about what he told her and the room was silent for a time. Liza's response was clinical and, although that relaxed Ted, he was shocked by what she said.

"Ted, I think Ellie's pattern of behavior and even that last bit about anal sex is pretty strong stuff. I think it suggests a need or obsession to satisfy or re-live something in her life. If Ellie had ever come to me to talk about any sexual needs or behaviors like that I think I know what I would have thought and what I might have talked about with her."

Ted was clueless about any possible explanation for behavior such as Ellie's. Admittedly he felt he was stuck more on the mechanics of what she wanted and what she did. Liza didn't expect Ted to contribute to the direction she was going in but her pause allowed him to say something if he wanted. Ted was mostly just glad he managed to get out all the main features of a story that was difficult for him to share with his wife. He wondered what Liza was about to say.

"We'll never know, but from what you said I'd be real worried Ellie was abused in her past; probably as a young child. Her need to be passive and then her coldness after makes me think of something like that. Those men probably thought she hated them after the sex, and it's likely she did; but not as much as she hated herself for any pleasure she felt during the seduction and sex."

Ted was startled by this possible new layer of sadness Liza added to the entire business. Who knew if Liza's speculation was correct but it seemed like it could make sense.

"Man, what an idea, Lize. Like a moth to a light, she had a need to keep at it, I guess. That's a possibility I doubt we could ever confirm."

"Of course you're right Ted. But you remember when we talked about Ellie's brother; how strange I thought he was? He was older too."

"And you said her parents died in some kind of accident. Wonder what that was all about?"

They looked at each other with sad faces. But as discouraging as it all seemed Ted felt more relaxed that Liza didn't plan to dwell on the details of the sex and only wanted to think about Ellie's motivations to behave the way she did.

"Sounds like Ellie's unusual lifestyle must have contributed to her being murdered. But I don't know by who. Babe, don't know if you're thinking we need to check out her brother in Connecticut but I can't see doing that right now."

"No. I don't know why Ellie did what she did. I don't know how that got her killed. I think you're going to have to push harder with the troopers you're looking at."

Liza was right. The worries he brought home with him were no longer as awkward or embarrassing. Ted's insecurities about sex hadn't hindered the discussion. Whether Liza's theory was correct or not he agreed with her: Just as he recognized when he was driving home he needed to be tougher on his suspects. He also sensed a lightening of his worries about the future sex life of Ted and Liza Vallan. At the right moment he would do fine even if Ellie's story and the stress of the case worked against any interest in making love right now and maybe for some time.

* * *

THE WRINKLE STAYS GONE

Late in the afternoon on Saturday Shawn Barry called Ted at home.

"I think our girl is definitely on the run, Chief. State Police in New York called with a hit on her vehicle's VIN. They think her car's sitting on a used car lot in Cortland, which is way southwest in the state."

Ted was irked at Shawn's light tone; almost treating this business, and Trooper Devers' disappearance, like comic relief in this terrible case. Devers' whereabouts and life were a great concern to Ted.

"Why are you sure Trooper Devers can even be linked to the location of her vehicle when there are other ways for that car to show up there?" Ted's tone reflected his annoyance and Barry got it. But he didn't assume he was supposed to apologize.

"Well, I called the dealer, Lieutenant, and his story sure sounds like he bought the vehicle from our Trooper. Said the young lady who sold it was a mess. Just short of breaking down in front of him. And he said she was wearing her clothes in a way so it was obvious to him she was knocked up. His words, Chief, not mine. She had a backpack and a suitcase with her. She gave him a registration and said she'd be back later with the title. Says he felt real bad for the girl and offered her about eight hundred in cash and another eight when she brought the title. Knew she'd never come back. She took the cash and headed towards the downtown, where the bus and train stations are located.

"Little later, when his guy went over the vehicle they realized the registration was for a different year than the car he had. Called the local police and state picked up the report. Turns out there was a registration and plates stolen from same model and color about fifty miles away. Some jerk had a habit of never locking his vehicles and this one was sitting by a county road. Easy pickin' for our trooper a night or so ago."

Nancy Devers wanted to disappear. Was it because she was pregnant and her career was over? What about the father? She could have resigned from the force and married and still stayed in the area. Unless the father was also a trooper. Ted was not sure how that would have played out in the force. But, more worrisome, suppose Trooper Devers killed Ellie Stanton or was, in some way, responsible for or part of the reason she was murdered?

Or, what if she even only knew who the murderer was and her own involvement in the killing was peripheral? Could she be running from the killer? How much was her life in danger? Where was she headed and who else might know where she planned to go? Shawn's words interrupted Ted's thoughts.

"Used car dealer was angry but understood we got to get that vehicle back here. I can go down there, maybe take my older sister's kid who just turned eighteen, and drive it back. What you say he and I stay overnight since that's a long haul to do in a day?"

Ted was in a sour mood. More, not fewer, questions and possibilities were germinating in his head, and his interviews were upsetting. He felt no need to bend to Shawn's suggested plan.

"Then I guess you two will have to get an early start Monday so you can be back before midnight." Ted didn't care how Shawn reacted and they ended their call.

Then Ted asked one of the ladies in administration to put in a call to the Arizona State Police. That call was followed by one to the Tucson Police Department.

* * *

Nancy Devers was heading to New York City; first. From there she flew to Oahu in Hawaii, home of Pearl Harbor and large military bases. She was met by an active duty Marine and an older Asian civilian with a heavy accent. They were pleasant and helpful but not especially friendly. They made it clear they were doing what he asked them to do.

She was set up in a small but comfortable, apartment just off the naval base. An appointment was already scheduled with an obstetrician for the next week. The older man gave her a generous amount of money and told her he'd come by every week with more. For the first time in many weeks she felt herself relax. The tropical weather was a treat and she no longer had to hide her pregnancy. She met some other pregnant women whose husbands or boyfriends were out at sea and found herself almost pleased with her circumstances.

Despite all the many difficult and terrible things that had happened most days there were really only two things that still weighed heavily on her. She knew her family would find out she had disappeared and she struggled to come up with a way to at least let them know she was okay. And she kept waiting to feel better. She was pretty far along by now and thought it should be time to be over feeling so ill every day.

* * *

CONSEQUENCES OF CRIMINAL BEHAVIOR IN PUBLIC

July 4th, 1985 was on a Thursday. Celebrating independence day on any of the days in the middle of the week meant losing out on a three-day weekend. Canadians are so much smarter to make sure virtually every month of the year includes one three-day weekend. In Burlington, the tradition to always have the fireworks on the third, this year a Wednesday, was continued.

A Beautiful day. Cool and dry. Most businesses started the holiday early by closing in the afternoon so many could go home and prepare for the celebration. Hordes of people worked their way to the Burlington waterfront for the evening fireworks display. This year at least twenty thousand were attending. The Burlington PD and some state troopers were there along with a smattering of officers from surrounding small towns. But police presence was always light at what remained a family event for years and rarely generated more than just a few fights and public intoxication arrests.

Diener Morty Stern sat on steps outside a small building on College street on the fringe of the crowd, more up the hill and into the city. Drinking beer with two buddies it was obvious they were not waiting with excitement or anticipation for the fireworks. He stood up and motioned he was going up the street, away from the lake and fireworks, to urinate. He walked behind a building. It was getting dark. Morty took a swig from his beer can and marveled at his ability to drink and whiz at the same time.

"Urinating and drinking in public, Morty. Not a good thing, eh? Now you know they're both against the law, don't you?"

Morty stood up straight, dropped his beer, and zipped his pants. He started to turn around but a hand on his shoulder directed him to stay as he was and then gave him a gentle shove to begin walking up the darkening street, farther away from the lake.

"Morty, we have to figure this all out. Now it's getting complicated, isn't it?" Morty said nothing. He was drunk and he was scared. It was dark now. They walked a block north, Morty directly in front. The streets were almost deserted and the fireworks had just begun, filling the area with loud booms. When he was directed to the front passenger door, not the back seat of the cruiser, Morty relaxed a little.

He got in and was never seen again.

Morty's friends knew he was due to begin a week's vacation the next day so when he didn't return decided he left to get ready to leave early in the morning. Each year he drove to an isolated lake in northern Quebec where he fished and drank by himself at a small resort. No one missed Morty until ten days later when he didn't return to work.

* * *

WHERE HAVE ALL THE DIENERS GONE?

At first, once it was clear the pathology assistant was really gone, his disappearance excited Ted. He told Shawn about a case from years before when another pathology assistant, or diener, was killed. Morty's disappearance led Ted to guess there probably was something related to the morgue involved with his vanishing and, therefore, Ellie's death also. Ted took this turn of events as a lead to follow; almost a break in the case. He never considered the man's continuing absence would be viewed in a different, very unsettling, way by some others in the force.

Later, after what developed, he wasn't sure if his upset and anger was directed more at the others or himself. Either way he felt blindsided and was angry that he was so slow to recognize the potential for Morty's disappearance to generate a preferred explanation for the homicide for some people.

It was a little over two weeks since Morty had been last seen and he was long overdue to be back at work. He was now, officially, labelled a missing person. Ted arrived at his office at the Waterbury barracks around nine a.m. His day had started with an early morning meeting in Rutland where he was supervising the investigation of a hit and run death that was getting complicated. The suspect was a locally prominent attorney who appeared to be intoxicated when tracked down. Ted was reminding his staff every 'i' was to be dotted and every 't' crossed in that case.

He arrived at the barracks a little later than he wanted but he had no special appointments for the remainder of the morning. As he put his hat on the coat rack in the corner of his office a yellow sticky note placed in the middle of his desk caught his attention. He couldn't help but remember a similar experience from nine years before. It was a déjà vu moment as he looked at it and saw it said to find Captain Rondell and go to Colonel Sawyer's office as soon as he arrived. The setting generated some apprehension.

Ted Vallan was comfortable with his position in the force and he was quite comfortable with the men he worked with, especially Rondell. At Ted's level in the force there was a notable lack of bullshit in his work. Colonel Sawyer had been appointed to run the force only about four months before but Ted had known him for years. They got along fine although they never really socialized since Dan lived in the St. Albans area, pretty far from Ted's home in Richmond.

Captain John Rondell was still Ted's immediate superior. They had worked well together for years and had a satisfactory friendship and respect for each other. All these men were right up at the top of running the force.

There wasn't anything else of immediate concern on Ted's desk so he walked down the corridor to Rondell's office as the message advised. Rondell was doing paperwork at his desk.

"You're here. Okay, let's go to Sawyer's office. He wants to talk with us. I don't know, but I'd guess it's about the ME case."

"Yes," Ted said, "I guess so."

They walked back up the corridor to the large open area of cubicles and desks for most staff and turned into the only other corridor, where the director's suite was located. Mitzi Davis, Sawyer's secretary, waved them by and they walked to the open door to Colonel Sawyer's office. Ted let Rondell enter first then followed him in. The director's office was very different from every other in the building. It was at least twice as large as any other and it was carpeted and furnished with a huge desk for the director with two comfortable padded armchairs in front. Off to a corner, by a large window with a pleasant southern exposure, there was a round table with four lightly padded chairs circling it.

Colonel Sawyer was a large man but not particularly imposing. Notably, he had more of a gut drooped slightly over his belt than most troopers. He also was older than most previous new directors, a reflection of his long struggle to climb to the top of the force. Becoming the leader of the small Vermont State Police was a coveted position to cap a career in the force. Appointment was based on a number of factors and longevity was one of them. Dan Sawyer's age and many years on the force already probably was a signal to the other officers that his time at the top would not last too long. So the newly promoted Colonel was considered more a nice guy and placeholder than a man likely to have a distinct impact or lasting imprint on the function and policies of the force. To many his most memorable feature was the way his trooper's hat looked so small on his large head.

Two men, the Colonel and Lieutenant James Dixon, were seated in two of the chairs at the table. Ted knew Lieutenant Dixon well. Dixon was the head of Internal Affairs, in charge of investigating the force's own. Walking into the room and seeing Dixon rapidly re-enforced Ted's growing unease with the whole setting. It was another clear reminder of the time nine years before when an asshole treasury agent accused him of committing a felony with evidence from a homicide Ted was investigating. He had to remind himself now how stalwartly the force stood behind him during that attack.

Lieutenant Dixon and Ted continued to cross paths many times since as leaders of the force. For some reason maybe this setting reminded Dixon of that prior fateful morning also. Dixon decided to make a comment referencing that day.

"Hey, Ted. So how's your father, Thom, these days? Remember that crazy mess that treasury agent slob hit you, me, and John with that time?"

Ted decided to take Dixon's words as a friendly recollection that did seem to come to mind this morning. "Oh I guess I learned to keep my dad on a pretty short leash since then. Last summer we built a nice porch for my house and we keep him busy enough with projects these days so he isn't poking into anyone else's business anymore."

As he was saying this Ted recalled his father had tried to talk with him about something related to Ellie Stanton during a recent little league game. Did Ted dare ask his father what he wanted to say? Nine years ago his father really complicated Ted's life and career. He never wanted to go through that again. But...he did wonder what it was his dad wanted to tell him. Maybe he should ask him. But, if he did, he'd have to explain all the ground rules to his dad to ensure his dad never got in the middle of police work ever again.

Ted felt a little anxious, almost off balance, as some of that past flashed by him as he sat there after speaking. He reminded himself his position was greatly different now. For one thing, nine years later, his career was well established. Sitting there looking at Colonel Sawyer he realized why his confidence was still a little shaken. Sawyer's face looked as grim as when he sat in the back of the duty room a few weeks before listening to Ted insist one of the troopers in the room was guilty of murder. What was about to happen?

"Ted, guys, thanks for coming. You know guys I'm not sure I've had a good night's rest since Ted said a trooper murdered Dr. Stanton."

Ted could relate to that. Even his evening beer wasn't guaranteeing his sleep. But he never actually said a trooper murdered Ellie. He had said a trooper was involved in her death. This didn't look like the moment to correct the director.

The Colonel continued. "This whole damn thing just sits in my gut. It's affecting my appetite."

Again, not one of them was going to play with that statement either and suggest losing some weight might be good for Sawyer.

"So Ted, we have to tell the media we now believe Dr. Stanton's death was a homicide. There will be lots of questions. And just when I've been talking all week with Public Safety and, frankly, the Governor's office also, about how to handle all this with the press, now you've told John some assistant in the morgue is missing and he could be involved in this case."

Colonel Sawyer started out in a pleasant voice. Now he leaned forward and directed his comments to Ted but looked at all three of them. With his face turning red he was unable to hide his anger. He spoke more forcefully and louder.

"Ted, how the hell do you know that assistant didn't kill the Doc and not one of our troopers? I mean, from what you've told us there's not a lot to go on, so far, to implicate any one of those troopers. I know you're working hard to figure this all out but is this really the time to say we know this homicide was by a member of the force? Because do we really know that? From what you have how can you be so sure? I can't let the public be told there is an errant trooper out there unless we are positive that's the case. You know what I mean?"

The others sat quietly, mostly looking at Ted. No one else spoke. 'Errant trooper,' Ted thought? What the hell did Sawyer mean by that? He wanted to sanitize the force in this sordid business? Part of Ted understood where the director might be going with all this. Ted had sparse hard evidence so far. He and his investigator were learning there were some surprising connections between Ellie Stanton and the troopers he was following. He was formulating some theories but it all remained highly circumstantial so far.

Ted patiently reviewed findings and information that could, potentially, be tied to a member of the force. As he listed what he had he realized it was far from enough to convince the group he was sitting with. He was angry at the challenge though. He was sure he was right. He wasn't sure why but, as he was talking, he decided to say nothing about the second button or Liza's astute observation about one of the female troopers.

Dixon spoke up. "Ted, couldn't someone, anyone who killed the Doctor, stuff a brass button like we use on our uniforms into her mouth? Someone could have done that to throw us off or for a bunch of other reasons. Don't you think?"

"Exactly," Sawyer said, his mood noticeably buoyed. "You know, Vallan, especially since that assistant disappeared, this whole thing sounds far from clear to me. You seem to be insisting we have a bad apple on the force. I don't see how you can be saying that…and I'm not happy saying anything about your theories to the press now."

Ted didn't agree with the director. He really didn't care what was said to the press but he still felt a trooper was involved with Ellie's murder. He responded forcefully also.

"Dan, you can tell the press whatever you want, and just tell me not to say much and, of course, that's what I and my investigators will do. But you have to be aware that I'm not looking for a bad apple, Dan. Dan, I'm tracking down a rotten apple who participated, in some way, in the brutal murder of the State Medical Examiner; a young woman."

Everyone around the table stiffened.

"Ted, it's still your investigation." Sawyer showed no intention of backing away from his own judgment. "I'm not telling you what you can and can't do. But I'm concerned you have narrowed your focus to the force, and only the force, while there's at least one guy out there who's missing who could be the killer and I want to be informed more about him and what's happened to him. Understand?" He turned a little red again showing his anger.

"I think that session here a few weeks ago when you accused that group of troopers was a mistake. Maybe a big mistake. If any one of those troopers decides to say something to the press that stunt could mean big trouble for us. I'm worried you shouldn't have done that. Now you're searching for a bad apple who may not even exist. The way you're going, Ted, I'm worried this case may become a needless blemish on the force. And you know what that could mean for me.

"If my career is going to get tied up in this then yours may also, Ted. I don't know why I let you and John talk me into that meeting. I don't think it ever should have happened. Those eight troopers are among the pride of the force. What on earth were they all doing there?"

He turned and spoke to the two others and then back to face Ted.

"John and Jim, I want you two to begin to think about what we might say to those troopers to get them to put that meeting out of their minds. For good!

"Ted, find that missing man. You better move along with your investigation, quickly, and keep us closely informed about what you find. Understand?"

Ted knew the Director would have no interest in hearing the Vallan family was supposed to leave in a week to drive to the Washington, DC area for a week vacation. How was he going to tell Liza what today's meeting meant for that?

* * *

THE JIG IS UP?

"No."

"No? What do you mean, no?" Annoyed.

"I mean it took us forever to coordinate your time off, my time off, and a time when the kids could be taken out of their activities to do this trip. And your badge is going to make it a lot easier to get into some of the places we're planning to go. Ted, we have to go next week. If you won't go I think I'll go without you. It's not fair to the kids.

"What about that assistant you've spoken so much about, Trooper Barry? You used to be so high on him maybe it's time for you to let him do the leg work on this for a while? Call him twice a day. I don't care."

Ted stood up quickly and stiffly from the comfortable padded chair he was sitting in on Liza's porch. He hoped his face didn't show any sign of his anger or exhaustion. He walked to the kitchen.

"Where are Kathy and Henry? Isn't it getting late for them not to be home?"

"It's Friday. Kathy is spending the night at Sandy's and Henry is staying at Henry Thayer's tonight." In a sweet and welcoming but maybe by now in their lives, slightly sarcastic voice that still always excited Ted anyway: "Ted, it's you, me, and George for the night…"

His hand grabbed the handle of the fridge. "…So if you have any interest in a threesome you might want to skip the beers tonight."

Damn doctors! For just an instant when Liza spoke to him and he felt an immediate twinge in his crotch he recognized a thought; a fear he wasn't sure he ever had before: his frustration and exhaustion might make him unable to rise to the occasion. He was transparent to Liza and there was nothing he could do about it. How could she know? He assumed she knew what she was talking about and dropped his hand from the fridge door handle.

"Whatever you think" was his signal he was up for the night.

Clearing his mind and relaxing that night was much harder than he would have ever imagined. He wasn't happy with Liza's trip ultimatum and he supposed she had some anger also. Long ago he had constructed an image of her positive enough, he thought, to never, ever be chipped away much in a lifetime. He saw her as fearless.

That night he marveled at the affection she offered him. He relaxed. They made love at an early bedtime. It had been awhile. It was good but Ted knew he was changing. Slowly, it was becoming clear to Ted he did better and making love was more satisfying in the early morning the last few years. He had some ideas why.

* * *

These days instead of sex in the morning one or the other often ran. This morning they took a run together. They kept it short since it was already getting hot. Then Ted sat, on the porch, with a yellow pad and wrote down some pluses and minuses of publicly implicating the missing diener in the murder. It seemed like he had been instructed to consider it. Around noon he heard a car door slam in the front of the house and he could hear the cadence of

Kathy running on the walk and up the front steps. She practically bounded through the house to the porch where he was sitting.

"Hey Pops. How are you?"

"Good Kat. How are you doing today?"

She gave him a quick peck on the cheek and stood by his chair. She hesitated but just a moment.

"And how was your night at home without kids, dad?" Eyeballs looking to the ceiling.

Ted was dumbfounded. Did she mean what he thought she did? Why would she even think about such a thing? To this day he never thought about his parents having sex. Despite the reality of his sister and himself he assumed his parents never made love.

He stammered, "Well, we finally were able to have a quiet dinner, if that's what you mean?"

Kathy bounded out of the room and he heard her quizzing Liza as they met on the stairs.

"Well Kathy, you know George stayed home so we all played cards."

The risers shuddered as Kathy bounded the rest of the way to the top of the stairs, laughing.

Liza came down quietly.

"How come you always know what to say?"

"Ted, how come your face is all red?"

* * *

A SIGNIFICANT ATTRACTION

Several Years Earlier

The first two times they spoke in person she felt a sudden, cool chill in the back of her neck. It confused her. Then she recognized he frightened her a little. Why was that? He was a little older than many of the other troopers, policemen, and residents and young doctors who attracted her. But she had been with a number of older ones and none ever had that effect on her. No, even as they parried back and forth with light personal banter, the beginning of flirting replacing the professional interaction in the morgue, Ellie had a curious reaction to him. There was something different about him.

He was more self-assured than most in this setting and he took to the game much more quickly than the others. Despite the adventure she played over and over with lots of men this one felt different. He was more exciting to her. She was so used to feeling she was controlling everything, even with men who were aggressive with her. But this trooper made her wonder if he was actually staying ahead of her and seemed to remain absolutely relaxed and confident in the chase.

Now and then the more aggressive ones turned her off because they rapidly tired of Ellie's battle for everything to proceed at her pace; in the way she wanted. This guy very quickly understood her insistence on timing and was attentive in playing along, although often feigning an almost detached interest. Ellie felt the truth of his intentions were telegraphed in his eyes. He would have been shocked to be told that, believing he kept his face a mask to the outside world; a visage he developed in the war. Superficially he reminded her (and others) of a good old boy, relaxed but up for most anything and, pleasantly sharp. Or was it clever? His eyes told Ellie he was taking it all in but keeping a piece of himself removed from total immersion in their new relationship. Was that what made her feel a little frightened?

He moved slowly and with grace, just as she did anywhere but on a mountain trail. His control with Ellie was that he sensed her terms about how the game was to go and had no problem with that. He was comfortable with his ability to out maneuver her if the need arose.

As with so many of her other brief sexual liaisons, her involvement with the Trooper began with his testimony in person to the ME about an investigation of a death that required the ME to do an autopsy. The Trooper had come to the morgue with physical material from the scene and his trained knowledge of the circumstances and setting of the death. She sensed he was different but they seemed to hit it off right away so Ellie spent longer than usual going over the Trooper's details. As usual, when she liked a man, she encouraged him to stay for the post.

Later she was still unsure if this was a man she wanted to take home…yet. She worried it might be awkward if she delayed making a decision. Before her uncertainty and yet her obvious flirting made either of them angry the Trooper indicated he remembered something else at the scene that might be helpful and could bring it to her at the morgue the next day…if she wished. She asked when he would be able to do that. He suggested he could return at the end of his shift; around five-thirty. Ellie would have a day to make up her mind. Signaling both his interest and patience gratified her. He was able to keep it in his pants better than most.

Anticipating his return over the following twenty-four hours, almost girlish excitement removed any doubts about her interest and plans for him. If he didn't return she would have some regret but a good feeling because of her initial unease about him. When he did arrive in the evening they each acted like everything was all planned out. He drove behind her to her home on the lake in Colchester.

Ellie Stanton had no reason to think their time together would be any different than with many sexual partners from before. Arriving behind Ellie at her lakeside home the Trooper already was beginning to sense the kernel of an idea about the possibility of a big and promising solution to his worries about money.

* * *

The sex started quickly and was satisfying for each of them. Ellie's unusual post-coital pattern was well formed from early on and surprised and upset many partners. But this man was a talker. Either her demons didn't concern him or he figured a way to re-kindle or maintain the post-coital relationship that few others could manage. When Ellie looked tense, distant, and even unhappy he just chatted on. He was able to almost remove her from the recent act and she gradually returned to being at least a sociable person. He wasn't interested in being rapidly pushed out but neither did he make any effort to go after her again, which he rightly suspected would further turn her off.

So when she felt better, relaxed again, she tried to make sense out of this pleasant, chatty man who was able to charm her. She was not entirely comfortable. Maybe the battle would be joined again. Maybe later that night; or some other time. Like many others, he seemed to trust her more than she trusted him, but she really wasn't sure how she felt about her. She no longer felt frightened. She began to key on her perception he seemed supremely self-confident and suspected the word 'experienced', indeed, 'very experienced' applied to many parts of him. He exuded a been there, seen it all manner that could not be missed. A most different and entertaining man for Ellie Stanton.

At Ellie's request he did not stay the night. As he drove home, well after midnight, he was excited. What a great turn of luck. He hadn't felt as good, such a sense of well-being, since the early, successful, years of building his old business overseas. He almost could not believe his good fortune. He certainly never considered telling Ellie Stanton he was already in a relationship; quite a serious one. Now he assumed he was beginning another sexual relationship and that was fine with him. Just like before; the more sex the better.

* * *

THE THINGS WE DO FOR MONEY

His other relationship would stay hidden from everyone as long as he managed not to marry her. Force regulations would take care of that. She understood there was no alternative. His relationship with that Medical Examiner also had all the earmarks of a secret affair given what he thought he could assume about the Doctor. Over time he would work to ensure that. First he had to make their sex critical to her. Then, at some point, he would probably need to make the secrecy of their relationship a necessity for her also.

He needed money, very soon. Months before he decided he refused to try to exist on a trooper's salary. He figured ways to get money before and he would do it again. He had all but admitted to himself that, even though so much had changed and he was happy with his life and Nancy Devers, even illegal methods of getting money would be acceptable. He could think of no other way. Involving Dr. Stanton in the scheme that had popped back into his head after meeting her was a remarkable thought. If he could figure it out it would bind her to him and perhaps go some distance towards getting him the money he needed. Yes, he thought, with some more luck he might be able to work it all out.

Getting money, anyway he could, and contemplating continuing to have sex with two women exhilarated him. He recognized his challenge was to be patient, think things through, and plan well. Sloppiness had almost done him in years before. He told himself he was more disciplined now and would be able to stay fixed on his goals better this time. As he drove in the dark up the long dirt road to his home in the forest he was increasingly excited. Shortly after, laying in his bed, thoughts and ideas were bombarding his brain. He could not sleep.

As he tried to organize and prioritize in his mind what he needed to do, there was absolutely no reason for him to even consider what his continuing relationship with that Doctor would require from him.

* * *

At first there were only the minor challenges to maintaining secret relationships with each of the two women. Ellie Stanton's rules required that sex, and only at her home, be the only recurring component. She would not allow herself to be seen with any of the men beyond the morgue or at her home. (And that activity was only in a darkened house, at night.) Even repeat partners had to adhere to the simple rules. No one stayed the entire night. The small house by the lakeshore in Colchester was hidden from other dwellings and her long, thirty-yard, dirt driveway emptied into another well treed dirt road making any exposure of the traffic to and from her place reasonably infrequent. Of course, her distant neighbors might draw their own conclusions about even occasional vehicle activity.

* * *

Vermont State Police regulations about professional and personal conduct were very simple and clear. Buried lower on the list of bulleted warnings it stated there was to be no fraternizing between troopers. With fewer than two dozen female troopers the issue had never been high on anyone's list of concerns or worries. What had initially appeared to be an impediment to a serious relationship between him and Trooper Devers now struck him as a good opportunity for him to be with both women, with little to worry from Trooper Devers.

Their private romance flourished and they developed deep feelings for each other but they both strongly desired to maintain their professional careers as troopers. Trooper Devers had struggled through a lot to get to where she was. After two years of community college studying criminology she hoped to train for a police position. She applied to many law enforcement agencies around the country and kept at it for almost a year until she met some success. She thought long and hard about her choice when she finally was accepted to train as a National Park Ranger, in her home state, Arizona, and as a Vermont State Trooper. Despite the disagreement of her family and the friction it caused she realized she longed to be a police officer and moved to Vermont.

Trooper Devers thought she was in love with him. He thought he felt about her in a way he had never before felt about a woman and presumed that meant he probably loved her. As a matter of fact, he was the one who first brought up the idea of them getting married and Trooper Devers leaving the force. He knew she wasn't ready to give up her career so his words were no real risk to his plans. She declined to consider even discussing it. But after bringing the idea up he realized any possibility of that happening sometime in the future was a reminder he would have to figure a way to replenish his slowly dwindling money at some point.

Both troopers grew to enjoy the limited time they were able to spend with each other, almost exclusively in his home nestled deep in the woods bordering the Kingdom. They felt safe there. Safe enough to go on hikes and picnics. But they never allowed themselves to be seen together in public settings unless other troopers were present.

* * *

Ellie Stanton led him on a fateful sexual exploration. He was required to manage to tread a fine line where he offered the threat of violence and pain without ever actually hurting her. And so, while making love he would cover her face with his massive hand or put fingers in her mouth. Or he would put a large hand around her neck and close it just enough to make her feel it but never choke her or put much pressure on her carotid arteries. It excited both of them. He felt control and pleasure from knowing he knew when to stop.

Ellie had been with a woman two times. From those experiences she learned pleasure from using a vibrator to explore every opening that could be found. At first, only with him did she feel relaxed enough to have him penetrate her rectum. He had done that several times before with others. Initially there was excitement about what he was doing but, in general, the act did not lead him to feel much pleasure. He wondered if his reaction to doing that was because he felt it was a dirty or filthy thing to do. But Ellie was very much into it.

In the pattern of their lovemaking there often came a point at which she would gently, but with some pressure, direct his head to that region. Before encouraging him to penetrate her she wanted him to lick her vagina and then her rectum. She reacted with great pleasure to his wet tongue. But he did not enjoy doing it. Once he penetrated her she encouraged him to oscillate rapidly and intensely inside her.

He did what he had to do. Ellie was excited by the intrigue and mysterious nature of his scheme to make money. Once she agreed to participate she was helpful in making it work. But it was very clear to him the patterns of their sexual relationship were essential to her and therefore very necessary for him to maintain.

To his surprise, over time, he gradually came to almost dread their time together making love. Slowly the realization became obvious to him. He was no longer allowing her the illusion of control during sex; she was in control. The rules were hers and there was nothing he could do about it. The whole scheme depended on her and this was what she wanted in return. It was a dramatic change from his entire adult life where he prided himself on the way he managed to dominate women; certainly his sexual partners.

He grew to despise her, especially as he became unable to deny a primary method of her domination: Her knowing their sex was unpleasant for him. She was using him also. If he wanted the money to continue to flow he knew he had no option with Ellie.

* * *

INTO THE WOODS

The second crime lab report on Ellie's big Ford Bronco didn't have the impact her second autopsy did. Basically nothing new or different was found. Despite being told, in utmost secrecy, that Ellie had likely been physically placed at the spot she was found, the techs still insisted there was nothing in her vehicle to suggest a brutalized dead body ever traveled in her truck. Was she killed on the mountain or, as Shawn had speculated early on, could there have been two vehicles? One actually carrying her body and someone else driving her truck to leave it there so it would appear Ellie left it and went hiking?

From what he had been told about where her body was found and how challenging it was to move her out Ted still had some difficulty accepting the idea she was placed there. He could understand it was a clever way to make it appear she fell or jumped but how could someone, even with help, accomplish that? The crime scene remained poorly explained and her clean vehicle was a reminder of that.

Ted hadn't done any bushwhacking since he worked to become an eagle scout. Hiking now meant well marked trails with his family in tow. Liza and Kathy had done Camel's Hump and Ted had actually talked about doing it as a family, now with Henry also, in the fall. Ted thought he really should try to get to the site where Ellie was found. A police marker was placed there but who knew how long it would remain? He knew it wasn't likely much would be found but it continued to vex him how she could have been placed there when it was so hard to get her out. How difficult would it be to get to the site?

In the evening he told Liza he was thinking of going there but wanted to go on a weekday so the area wasn't as crowded.

"Any chance you'd think about taking some time off and coming with me?"

"Ted." Using his name presaged it wasn't going to go well. "I know with us going away next week I can't take any time on short notice to do something like that. Especially in the summer when other people are already away. And I'm not a bushwhacker. I'm not sure you should be either anymore. You said you haven't done anything like that in years. It's July, Ted. The woods are hot, wet, and sticky; and probably very buggy right now. I do my hiking in the fall, on trails."

"Yeah, I know that…"

"So should you really be doing something like that right now? You know, you've agreed to go to Washington so getting messed up in the woods will exhaust you and might affect our trip."

Then she plunged the dagger in. "And you know there isn't likely anything much to find out there anymore. What kind of crime scene stays unchanged in the middle of an impenetrable thicket of woods anyway?"

"Naw, I really have to do it, babe. Something's missing. I can't spend more time on theories about Ellie's murder and then find out later we missed things that help explain what really happened… again; like the first autopsy. I'm gonna clear my schedule and do it day after tomorrow. That'll give me a few days to get over any soreness and clean things up for us to leave on Saturday. Okay?"

Liza surprised him.

"No, I don't know if it's okay. Ted If you think you've got to check that area out I definitely don't think you should do it alone. That's wild forest you're talking about and you shouldn't be out there for a day trying to remember your bushwhacking skills from twenty years ago. And don't suggest your father, Ted. Don't bring him into it. Get someone from the technical team to guide you. Don't you think that makes sense?"

He didn't like Liza's tone which lately, more and more, reflected the way she spoke to him. Recently, he thought Liza's comments and attitude toward him were often more critical and less patient than were necessary.

But, in this instance, no matter why she had that tone, she was right. He was beat. He knew it. His impulsiveness was a bad sign and now he recognized it. He agreed. But he decided he wasn't going to make a fuss and enlist someone from Search And Rescue. He called Shawn Barry and told him to arrange to go and to plan to meet him where Ellie's truck had been found on an east entrance to some trails. Ted said they'd probably go rain or shine, but even he wasn't sure he'd go in rain.

* * *

The temperature the night before the planned hike cooled down considerably by two or three in the morning; typical even after a hot summer day in Vermont. But it was muggy and Ted thought still far from feeling cool when he got up just after first light. The sky was cloudless now but afternoon thunderstorms popped up commonly in July. About six-thirty he met Shawn at the east trailhead where Ellie's truck was found. Ted wanted to start early to lessen the chance of being caught in rain. He hoped if they were lucky and able to find and examine the spot they were after he might be able to return to Waterbury to do some other things later in the day. He had a lot to do before vacation.

Shawn lived in Burlington so his trip out to the mountain took a little longer but he was already parked and lounging on the side of his cruiser when Ted pulled up. Ted was struck by what he saw.

Ted got out of his cruiser wearing hiking boots, a long-sleeved chambray shirt, jeans, and a State Police ball cap. He clipped a water jug to his belt. Shawn also was wearing hiking boots and a State Police cap. But that's where the similarities ended. To Ted's surprise, absent his tie, Shawn was in full uniform. His duty belt and revolver were in place and a sizable backpack, with an attached water jug, was sitting on the ground next to him.

"Shawn, why the uniform and all that gear? All the times I've seen you, lately, you've been in a suit. The brush is going to wreck your uniform."

"Dunno, Chief, jus thought it's best to look official. No telling how busy these woods will be today. Since it's work I thought I'm supposed to have a firearm with me. And I got a bunch of stuff in the pack; mostly for safety. I brought one of the new beacons that can stay active for at least a week if we find something we need to mark. Stuff like that."

Except for the uniform it made sense to Ted. Ted didn't miss his uniform, but he did realize he felt more secure with Shawn and his gear with him. Liza was right. Travelling through brush was a mess but Shawn would do okay even if his uniform wouldn't. Both Ted and Shawn assumed Ted had the better orienteering skills, but that was probably incorrect.

Ted stuffed some energy bars in his shirt pockets and they headed into the forest. Compass settings and a visual plot from the well-known 'chin' rock outcropping of the southeast summit of the hump was all they had for trying to locate the area of concern. As they left the marked trail behind and penetrated the forest Ted quickly realized their task was tantamount to looking for a needle in a hay stack.

"Figuring where to go from here is just a guess." His right cheek pulled towards his ear; an occasional expression of uncertainty his family knew well.

Shawn's response jarred him.

"Yeah, just like so many Bob Dylan songs about relationships continuing, ending, whatever. You just can never figure what direction the next one might take."

Ted paused his next step for an instant, clearly confused. He thought this might turn out to be an exceedingly long day if Shawn Barry continued saying things like that. What was he talking about?

* * *

Ted had a feeling he would enjoy going into the woods. At the beginning of the trek he was especially struck by the peace and quiet. The only sounds came from their feet traversing the underbrush. The forest was damp but cool and smelled nicely of wet evergreens and moist wood. Brush could be pushed away and stepping over downed trees and occasional rocks and streams were only a problem because they slowed their hiking progress. Each had a knife and Shawn's pack included a small hatchet, but none of that was needed yet as they plowed through the brush. Most of the time they walked parallel to each other so they were not slowed by one of them constantly pausing to hold back branches from slapping the other walking behind. It was obvious that bringing a body in or out would be completely different.

Figuring out where they were was the major challenge in the beginning. Ted thought his readings indicated they were heading in the right direction. But then they reached a slight valley with thicker brush underfoot and more dense shoots and trees. It became muddy. Ted decided to try to backtrack a little to see if they could go around that area. In short order that meant going more steeply uphill. There was less under foot but they had to hold onto branches and sometimes use the ground to pull themselves up the steep incline. The hike was no longer just a walk.

They were sweating profusely and took a break. It made sense to keep going higher since Ellie's body wasn't found much more than a hundred feet from a summit. Going more directly straight up the steep mountain, however, was the most difficult way to try to do it. They were making some progress and they knew they were doing so on the most challenging part of the mountain. The team that removed Ellie's body said it took them about two hours to get to her. Ted and Shawn would probably take a little longer to get there but not necessarily too much.

Over two hours in Ted decided they were close and it would be best if they split up and walked directly south for a while. They would never be more than about fifty yards apart and stay within earshot of each other. It was hotter and buggy now. Ted couldn't imagine Shawn's uniform wasn't ruined. Whoever he thought they might run into deep in the forest in the middle of nowhere to justify wearing his uniform seemed a remote possibility.

Ted remained worried about how they would find the spot they were looking for. Whether there was any use finding it in these dense woods was becoming less important to him now. Fighting to get to where they were proved the immense challenge it must have been to get Ellie's body into this area. A tremendous diversion, in theory, but maybe too difficult to ever actually execute. She must have been thrown from somewhere at the summit.

Ted's path flattened a little and he moved a bit faster, calling out to Shawn every minute or so to maintain contact. Shawn was walking east of him but he couldn't see him. It was hard to tell in the forest but he thought the sky was clouding up. Forging on and lost in his thoughts he began to feel the challenge of the hike itself had become the main reason for the day and had to remind himself of his goals. He stopped to take a drink. There was movement in the brush about thirty yards ahead of him. He yelled out for Shawn. Shawn's response suggested Shawn was still located below and behind him.

As he moved forward his path opened up and flattened even more. He passed a clearing and he thought he could see up to a rocky summit. The rustling in the brush was closer. Cautiously, he walked towards the sound. It was an animal. Ted stood still and the animal appeared ten to fifteen yards in front of him. 'Holy shit, it's a fucking bear cub'.

"Chief, Chief, I think I'm at the spot! There's something on the ground!"

"Shawn, there's a cub just ahead of me! I think I'm in big trouble!"

It was unclear who shouted louder. Ted knew the birthing season wasn't that far past. More importantly he knew wherever there was a cub there was an insanely protective mother somewhere nearby.

When he turned around he saw her. She still was far off but he was in-between the mother and her cub. A disaster. The sweat from hiking paled compared to the drenching sweat he felt now. He knew he was supposed to stand tall and make some noise but, no matter, he wasn't supposed to be where he was. It was a terrifying moment.

"Shawn I'm right between the mother and the cub!"

"Lieutenant, don't stay there! Go up the mountain as straight and steep as you can! I'm coming up! Once you're at least twenty feet above them shout and I'll put one round in the air! Go!"

Give Trooper Shawn Barry credit. He ran, or at least climbed, toward danger. Ted had no idea how the momma bear would react to the sound of the shot but he agreed that clearing her path to her cub sounded like a good idea. He used his hands and feet to grab onto rocks hugging the mountain and found enough energy to scamper more than ten feet almost straight up. He didn't look back until he almost reached another flat area.

"I'm clear, but she's running now; closer!"

Boom! The shot echoed through the woods. Ted kept climbing. He could see that momma slowed and was more cautious, moving towards her cub, not after him. Once closer he could tell she was a medium size black bear and now he could see she looked a little ragged and scruffy. She made soft noises, appearing anxious, then started making small circles but didn't seem to be looking at all at Ted.

"Shawn, please don't try to shoot her unless I see her come at me! I think I can make you out now! Don't go south! Come directly up the mountain!"

The momma bear probably knew there was more than one possible enemy around now. With her cub at her side, she paused. Then, almost like lightening, they each charged down the mountain, away from the intruders. Ted stopped climbing and sat to catch his breath.

"Shawn, I think they're gone! Come up to where it flattens out but keep your revolver out! I'm coming back down!…Shawn, I think I found a trail!"

* * *

Shawn tumbled forward up to the level just above where Ted had met the bears. Ted was sitting about ten feet farther above him. Everything was quiet. Shawn pushed himself to climb almost straight up the next distance to get closer to Ted. Carved into the side of the mountain was a flat trail; almost three feet wide. Ted was perched against a rock hugging the mountain. The clothes of both of them were torn and soaked with sweat. Shawn stood up after climbing to the apparent path and holstered his revolver. He could see Ted was okay. He turned and walked north about ten yards, back to the clearing, and looked down.

"Chief, when you're ready you want to come look at this."

Ted hoisted himself up and walked the narrow but flat trail to where his deputy was. The area above and below was open and directly below, maybe less than twenty feet, was the marker for where Ellie Stanton had been found. They each sat down on the trail. They drank some water but decided not to eat anything out of worry about attracting that bear, or any critter, to their location. The clouds were darkening.

"Well, this trail is walkable. It's not wide enough but it almost seems like an old logging trail. There is remarkably little underbrush; maybe because of all the rock." Ted took out his map. The path was nowhere to be found.

"Shawn, let's follow it back, if we can. No sense going down to the marker. Question is, if this path stays as passable as it is here, if that's a way Doc Stanton's body could have been brought here and then slid down the small drop from here." Ted didn't seem to want to talk about the bear so Shawn said nothing and grabbed his backpack as he stood up.

They re-settled their gear and headed off to the north. In ten yards the path ended.

"It's probably gonna rain Shawn and if we go south instead we have no idea whether this path ends also or even where it goes. If we follow it it could lead to nowhere. And even if it leads to a trailhead or a road we might wind up miles from where our cruisers are; and likely soaked from rain. What do you think?"

Trooper Barry gave him an exasperated look.

"Of course we should follow this trail. We've come this far. I figured a really long day, Chief. I brought a poncho. Don't know why you didn't."

Well Ted hadn't. And he felt a blister forming on one foot. He really had barely prepared. But he agreed this wasn't the time to turn back. They might be on the cusp of answering a very difficult question in this case.

"Fine, let's try it. In about an hour or if there's a sustained rain we can mark where we get to and cut east and hope to intersect a road. If this trail disappears we'll have to cross it off and go east, like I said."

* * *

But the trail going south didn't end at all. It wound around in long arcs, descending down the mountain in a slow, lazy pattern. The forest appeared all but impenetrable on each side. The gentle grade down strongly suggested at one time it was more than a hiking trail. It, too, was slowly being absorbed again by the forest but it was obviously the easiest way to get to the spot where Ellie was found. It was passable. Even being able to traverse it with more speed since there was less underbrush, and they were going down, it took a long time because it looped so gradually.

After an hour it started to rain. Ted and Shawn battled over the solitary poncho. Shawn tried to get Ted to wear it, which infuriated Ted. He told Shawn to put it on but he refused since Ted was going to get soaked. There was no earthly reason they should both get soaked, but that's what happened. For a while they tried walking with each holding an end over their heads but the footing was too uncertain and doing that slowed their progress down the mountain almost to a crawl.

It was daylight but dark under the forest canopy. The rain, warmth, and bugs were annoying but they were increasingly excited by the persistence of the trail. Since it continued for a long time they both hoped, and gradually came to assume, it would come out somewhere. Long before Ted had given up trying to use the little he had with him to figure where they were. Streams and maybe one or two trails intersected their walk. Their path was easy hiking but, even if it's existence was well known, it's doubtful taking it to where they began it, actually where it ended in the middle of nowhere, would have made it of much use to many hikers. And because it wound around forever, its grade was so gentle it seemed an unsatisfactory way to go up anyway.

Of course the path did, finally, end. Interestingly, just yards away, through thick brush, there was a trailhead with a parking area. Several trails were options from that spot but the path just descended by the troopers wasn't named or listed. They embarked on their hike north-east of the summit and came out almost due south of the mountain. The rain stopped. It was after two and the two cars in the small lot might not see their owners again for several more hours. They were bit to pieces and felt and looked like shit.

Ted was limping.

They walked a half mile to paved road and followed it east. Without hesitation Trooper Barry flagged down the first vehicle they saw, fortunately also going east, and requested assistance with an official State Police investigation. It took twenty minutes to reach the trailhead where the two cruisers were parked.

Despite Shawn's uniform the older man in the truck who pulled over at Shawn's direction was uncomfortable about stopping for the two ragged-appearing men. His nervousness increased when Trooper Barry crammed himself into the small jump seat behind the driver and Ted, in no uniform, and looking more the mess, climbed into the passenger seat. No one had much to say and Ted fell asleep on the ride. The man did as he was asked but didn't relax until he saw the two cruisers parked at the original trailhead. At the trailhead Ted thanked Shawn Barry for doing good work, shook his hand, and they each headed for their homes to dry out, clean up, and rest. It was getting close to four o'clock.

* * *

An hour later, luxuriating in a shower, Ted had nothing but good thoughts about Trooper Barry. But he wasn't sure if, technically, Shawn had saved his life. The events of the day re-enforced his assumption that Shawn, in no way, should be considered a suspect in Ellie's death. That had never been something he considered likely anyway, but now he would remove him from his grand list of direct ME contacts, just as he had done with his own name on that list.

Despite all his soreness, blisters, and itching Ted knew the day had been a great success. The stiffness to come was a small price to pay for confirming the possibility, maybe probability now, that Ellie's body was brought to a spot and dumped just a few feet to appear the consequence of a fall from far above. Getting her to that spot still must have been a difficult effort but certainly was doable. If more than one person was involved, rolling her body up in something would have facilitated slowly carrying her along. It was a dead-end trail and it's possible moving her body could have been accomplished without crossing paths with any other soul. Whoever got her to that spot knew the mountain quite well.

* * *

While Ted and Shawn were bushwhacking through thickets and discovering bears and a path suitable for dragging a body to where Ellie Stanton was found the crime lab team spent the day at Ellie's home in Colchester by Lake Champlain. A detailed examination had taken place the day after her body was found. Nothing significant turned up. No signs of a struggle certainly, and nothing was found to give the slightest indication Ellie might have planned to leave her home and take her own life.

Her lab, Locie, was found inside. She was anxious and had peed and pooped in the house and looked very hungry. There was some question about Ellie going without her but troopers found out the dog didn't always hike with the Doctor. The dog's status and everything in the house suggested Ellie was planning to return home at some point the day of her disappearance.

The second go through by the techs didn't turn up anything especially new. But this time, on the phone that evening as Ted listened to the team's senior investigator, the possibilities and things they looked for reflected a different perspective on her death. They had looked more closely for signs of disturbance; signs or indications of people Ellie knew. Everything was fair game now; potentially of significance.

Given the violence of her death the crime team looked carefully for anything they might consider a sign of disruption, struggle, or even that she left her home suddenly. There still didn't seem to be any suggestive findings. Ted insisted the tech review the entire report with him. Listening to the report, two things attracted Ted's interest but only a little.

The first was a more complete description, indicating the small amount, just four mid-sized boxes, of medical supplies neatly placed in a corner in a guest bedroom. Ted had learned Ellie was collecting and every few months sending medical supplies to a hospital in Thailand. Tonight he wondered how helpful sending a small amount of supplies around the world could be? While he was away Shawn would have to learn more about that charity Ellie was involved in.

And he wondered, and asked the technician, if there was any reason to think Dr. Stanton's home was actually too unremarkable in appearance and neatness?

* * *

VIETNAM AND AFTER THE WAR

There are men who thrive on the battlefield in time of war. Unfettered acceptance and permission to kill suits some personalities. A man might not have known of his killing potential until placed in such a setting and encouraged to kill other humans. Success and pleasure from killing can act as a powerful stimulant to the right personality. The question, and often the problem, that arises after living the experience of being encouraged to kill others, is what happens to that person after the war is over?

Vietnam, like every war, served as an incubator for a portion of those men to accept the pleasure they recognized from killing and sometimes the need to murder others. A prominent image of the large white (or black) warrior in the teeming Asian nations became problematic as the war wound down and after. Of course, some of those men went home and never did kill again. But some men didn't want to stop or thought they couldn't. Some of those inclined to enjoy being killers channeled their murderous passion into a menagerie of criminal behavior and acts.

He was so successful as a killing Marine they made him a corporal. The second time he was pulled off the battle line for R&R (rest and relaxation) he wound up in coastal Thailand. The location was filled with sex and drugs. He learned those things kindled intrigue and violence and he, rather quickly, managed to get involved. While he was there the war ended; badly. He began to conjure a future for himself and considered he was an almost perfect fit for both the literal 'soldier' and 'fortune' parts of a soldier of fortune.

No one was going back to Vietnam. He managed to get posted with the Marine guard at the U.S. Embassy and Consular Service, initially in Bangkok. Over time he was able to serve at more outlying locations. There he had the ability to be more independent which suited him well. A culture of gangs and gang control of the various services being merchandised bred a type of harsh violence which he was comfortable with and immediately successful. For a time, as his reputation grew, he was an enforcer and he enjoyed it all; the murders and mutilations, the sex, and the people and the country. He was satisfied to live in the present and had no other real desires for his future. For re-enlisting they made him a sergeant.

Several years passed. He pretty much controlled not only his own group of enforcers but also pimps and drug distributors. A level of unwelcome stress developed but he felt he knew nothing else. Trust was an oxymoron in his strata of society. Although he had a natural aversion to most drugs, sex, and lots of it, was always satisfying and became his best go to method for relaxation. A new industry was developing in Thailand, sex tourism, and he was right in the middle of it.

Years later, when he mused about missing those parts of that life that became idealized in his memory, he also had to admit he had become sloppy and his risk-taking foretold trouble. Finally he made the kind of error he knew could, eventually, topple the structure he had carefully built.

He had been posted again to Bangkok and he hated it. He manipulated his schedule and hours so he could flee down the coast to his own small empire at least two nights a week. One day, in the middle of a warm and muggy afternoon, when he set out for his territory he had no idea he was followed.

Dinner was ending and he was wrapped up in trying to decide if he would go to a room with one or two of his women when the fully uniformed Marine walked in. He wasn't just following him. The

Marine was an investigator with the military police who seemed to know what was going on and quickly implied as much.

The women flanking the Sergeant were suddenly pushed aside and the Sergeant turned beet red, his neck veins puffed out, visibly pulsating. It was an instantaneous rage. Like a reflex, he reached down under his pants leg and unsnapped the holster on his left calf. He pulled out the small Walther P5 compact 9mm pistol he tried never to be without and shot the Marine, once in the face and once in his chest. Then, in a fury, he picked up a knife from the table and plunged it into the man's gut and twisted it and twisted it until it looked like bowel was coming out. He was already dead. The room became still, with blood splattered about and the Marine's perforated bowels filling the small area with a fetid odor. There were four other people in the room who were still alive.

Then he sat down; still flushed, angry, and breathing heavily. He knew a great part of his anger reflected his knowledge the life he was living was over. The rapidity and level of his rage didn't surprise him. He tried to tell himself he had done well; that his skills and ability at self-preservation were still superior. But he sensed a line had been crossed and trouble was ahead.

The two men in the room helped him gather the body. Since the man was an American and a Marine he couldn't be just dumped somewhere which was the usual plan. The dead Marine was taken to a field behind a small hill and completely incinerated. After his ashes were buried and shovels and gear were being gathered he shot the two men who had helped him. They had been wary but not wary enough. Their bodies were dumped in a usual spot for those who had been executed. He then returned to his whore house and killed the two women at dinner with him. The rambling shack was put on fire. He had no idea who was and who wasn't able to get out. But he had no illusions that someone among the many locals he operated with wouldn't figure most of this out.

He was nervous and vigilant when he returned to Bangkok. There he gradually recognized he had little to worry about from the Marines. By a great stroke of luck his dead Marine apparently was working on his own initiative probably with the intention of either blackmailing him or trying to get involved in his activities. The man was missed but no one appeared to be concerned about the Sergeant. However, the Sergeant was now without his fiefdom and assumed it was likely relatives of the natives he killed would eventually find him. Recently, before all this happened, a new idea had been percolating in his brain. Maybe, he thought now, even considering that idea had been his warning that things were about to, or had to, change.

A month before the killings he was seeing a local doctor for treatment of a venereal disease he contracted. Unfortunately he knew the man fairly well. As they chatted the Doctor asked the Sergeant if he had ever used any substances to enhance his sex. The Doctor spoke about a new rage, using pineal extract, to prolong and heighten intercourse. The Sergeant knew nothing about it and had only rarely tried one or two of the commonly available enhancements men easily procured for sex.

The reason the Doctor brought the topic up related to his belief that human pineal extract far surpassed the potency, and therefore effect, of the much more commonly used animal forms of the extract. Something about curing human pineal glands in sunlight supposedly made night-time sex more exciting and longer lasting. Or so he said.

The Sergeant understood the implications of the Doctor's comments immediately. He was a little disturbed to find out he apparently had the kind of reputation that someone would suggest he go into a business that involved harvesting human body parts. He took it as a warning and said he had no interest. The Doctor insisted he take a tiny vial of human pineal extract and instructed him how to use it.

First he gave half the contents of the vial to a Japanese businessman who was becoming a regular customer. The following morning the man asked for more and was ecstatic in praising its effects. So the Sergeant tried the remainder. The extract had to be snorted, apparently an effort to presumably get the material as close to the location of the human pineal gland as possible. He had no practiced facility with snorting and assumed user error, or something like that, accounted for the minimal impact of the extract on his own love-making. Though It didn't affect him adversely either.

Several years of work allowed him to accumulate a sizable amount of money, all safely converted to dollars carefully placed in a few accounts that would be easy to transfer to the states. In fact, he already had a significant amount in a local bank back home. After the killings his outlook changed. He told himself to forget about any very lucrative, but obviously dangerous, trade in human pineal glands. He actually shuddered at the thought of what a business plan for that would entail.

This adventure was over. The killing in Vietnam had ended and his overtly criminal enterprises in Thailand were supposed to end now. He was not unhappy. Whether he could find his way in the states was unclear. But he did have plenty of money to ease his transition.

He was able to manage a transfer to Pearl and stayed there just over six months. He was struck at the difference of life in the states. Everything was spread out, more relaxed, and even the cities were bright and clean. The more regimented lifestyle suited him now. The Sergeant was surprised at how easily he re-integrated into Marine routine. Over time he decided it would also be plausible for him to return to the mainland and try to resume a life without killing and intrigue. For a time in Thailand he had given up on any such possibility.

Before his stint in Hawaii he prided himself at the way he used what he recognized about his personality and his impulsiveness to initially stay alive and then to achieve so much. For a long time he considered himself a very successful person. Eventually it wasn't difficult for him to sense the challenges of attempting to continue that life. His experience in Hawaii helped him believe he really could become someone else. That hope lifted his spirits and generated optimism about the future. It was a kind of excitement he thought he had given up on for himself. But he also recognized a nagging worry about what he might do when his money ran out… someday.

When his enlistment was up, still with some sense of uncertainty, he left the active force and returned to the mainland. Unattached, he returned to the only state he really knew; where he grew up happily enjoying all it had to offer in the outdoors. With his long military background he hoped he could find a place in policing. Vermont had a special program for returning vets and the Sergeant's application was accepted by the Vermont State Police.

* * *

THE SLEUTH WORKING IN A BUREAUCRACY I

Colonel Sawyer was bound to continue to be displeased with the pace of Ted's investigation as long as it remained active and any state policemen were still considered suspects. However, at the meeting this morning he wasn't able to be vocal about Ted's pending time off since both Captain Rondell and Lieutenant Dixon were away on vacation. The Colonel had made it very clear he wanted to meet and be briefed by Ted before he left the state for a week. Ted brought Deputy Investigative Trooper Barry with him for moral support and to assure the colonel the investigation would stay very active. Ted was stiff and sore from the recent hike the day before. A break sounded nice but if he could have stayed in Vermont and continued to work on the case that would have been his preference.

He was pleased Shawn Barry knew enough to wear his uniform. Showing up in a suit probably would have dismayed the Colonel. Ted hoped he wouldn't call the Colonel 'Chief'. Shawn was suitably impressed to be meeting with the Director of the force and behaved accordingly. He annoyed Ted, only a little, by looking perfectly fit and comfortable despite the prior day's exhausting effort.

"We're making significant progress Colonel. Just yesterday Trooper Barry and I re-visited the area where the body was found and we were able to find a path close to the marker for her body that would have made transporting a body to that site much easier than anyone might have imagined."

The Colonel sat with his hand on his chin and showed no obvious reaction to that important information. Ted continued.

"We also are learning quite a bit more about Dr. Stanton's personal lifestyle. That apparently included a quite active sex life, with an unknown but, again, apparently large number of males; including some members of the force."

Ted began to get it as the Colonel furrowed his forehead and questioned him, more like a defense lawyer…for the troopers!

"So there were other partners, not just members of the force?"

"Yes. We have no idea how many partners she had. We may never know. But we do know of at least five from the force in the last year."

The Colonel didn't react. Ted decided to move on.

"We also know Dr. Stanton was working, through the Burlington hospital, with a hospital in Thailand to send them medical supplies every few months. Some of our troopers were helping to bring supplies from hospitals around the state and would drop them at Dr. Stanton's office. We need to find out more about what that was all about."

The Colonel sat back in his chair and looked at Shawn and then Ted. The sequence gave Ted a feeling he was actually looking to see if Shawn agreed with what was being said. That was odd and Ted took it as a sign of lack of confidence in him.

"Ted, what about the missing pathology assistant? I've asked you to explain his absence and find out why you say that isn't related or has no role in the Doc's homicide?"

After all Ted had reported the Colonel was still really only interested in focusing on the diener who was missing. Sawyer remained convinced he was responsible no matter where Ted's investigation was going. Ted realized Shawn was going to have to key on this while he was away despite Ted's continuing belief the missing diener was, at most, a consequence, not a cause of what had happened.

*　*　*

ADVANCING MEDICAL SCIENCE

A Little Over Two Years Earlier

If you were a fly on the wall watching Dr. Ellie Stanton complete an autopsy you would never have had a clue about her true personality. In that setting you would have observed a slow, organized, and methodical process. All business. Morty Stern was overjoyed she chose him, whenever possible, to assist her. He worked very hard to learn how she wanted to do things and what she wanted him to do. He felt they were a team and he prided himself on his ability to anticipate her next move. Morty tried to have whatever instrument she needed ready when she reached her hand out and anticipate when she needed him to remove or re-position a body part.

When she explained to him she was embarking with another, out of state, doctor on a study of pineal glands he was only too happy to help, feeling like he was a part of a grand study for the advancement of medical science. So whenever there was an opportunity to harvest a pineal during almost any autopsy Morty quickly learned the special technique Dr. Stanton told him she devised to extract it from the base of the brain and preserve the gland for further study. The method was entirely different than the way the rest of the brain was fixed for later gross and microscopic analysis. Actually it was only a quick spray of the extracted gland with liquid nitrogen, but she told him it was special.

Because she was working with a physician who was not part of their medical center she told Morty it was best none of their work be shared with anyone at the hospital. She said something about cut-throat competition in research. He was told she and the other Doc had a generous grant to do their research and Morty was very pleased when she said he, too, would receive a stipend for his role in securing usable pineal glands. Together Doctor Stanton and Morty worked out a plan to harvest, fix, and lock-up in her office the material she needed without anyone else in pathology having the slightest inkling of what they were doing. It was actually easy.

Each of the two dieners, or pathology assistants, carried a beeper because many post-mortem exams needed to be completed off hours, especially ME cases. For years there had been a call schedule so one diener was always available by page. But for the last two years Morty always left his beeper on and he was the one Doc Stanton paged. Steve Dunham, the other diener, was getting increasingly angry at losing the overtime off hours posts generated. Morty Stern was beginning to become reliant on the overtime plus the generous stipend for harvesting pineal glands. Doc's secret seemed safe with him.

* * *

THE SLEUTH AND THE BUREAUCRACY II

The Vallan family vacation and being away from the case for a week loomed over Ted. He dreaded the pause and the Colonel's thinly veiled threats at him for the delay. Ted then did something he had never done before. In truth, he had never before dreamed he would ever do anything like it. He planned a news conference to announce Dr. Eleanor Stanton's death was a homicide and one Morton Stern, a pathology assistant, was missing and considered the prime suspect in her death.

It was not unreasonable to include Morty Stern on his list of suspects. He certainly had stayed missing and it was well documented he worked especially closely with the ME. But Ted didn't believe he murdered Ellie.

Morty Stern had a daughter living in upstate New York and Ted sent Trooper Barry to speak with her, for a second time, to prepare her for the publicity to come after Morton Stern was publicly named the prime suspect in a homicide investigation. Trooper Barry was managing the investigation of Morty Stern: his disappearance and relationship with Dr. Stanton. Not much had turned up. Morty's daughter was all but estranged from him and her mother divorced him many years before and she died a few years ago.

His daughter and the few friends Morty had, basically drinking buddies, had little to say about his life over the last few months.

Everyone agreed he liked his work. Dr. Fowler and Ms. Perdy agreed he was never a problem on the job. Despite his penchant for drinking there were no absenteeism or behavioral issues. No one believed he would intentionally disappear and, more than that, no one was comfortable with any idea that Morty would harm Dr. Stanton. His daughter and friends believed something terrible had happened to the diener.

On his second trip to the outskirts of Peru, New York Trooper Barry didn't alert Morty's daughter he was coming. This trip he noticed some things that raised a degree of suspicion about Morton Stern's life. Shawn expected Stern's daughter might express anger that her father, who remained no more than missing as far as she knew, was in the process of being accused of murdering a prominent doctor. But his daughter seemed generally more uncomfortable with Shawn's un-announced visit than anything else.

A newer vehicle was parked out front and in her house a newer TV and stereo system were prominently displayed in the living room. None of those things were there last time. The car had New York plates and was claimed by the daughter when Shawn asked about it. Shawn felt he had no basis to press her about any of those things. Morton Stern's bank savings account had a nice bump over the prior year or two but apparently not enough to raise any major red flags before. His daughter seemed to have difficulty responding innocently to the few questions the Trooper asked. As Shawn drove away he thought sure he could see part of the beat up old AMC Eagle he had noted on his first visit, now parked behind a shed in the back of the house. He wondered if the two vehicles had switched positions for his first, announced, visit.

* * *

"Folks, Lieutenant Ted Vallan, a senior investigator in the Major Crimes Unit, is going to make an announcement about an active criminal case. Lieutenant Vallan is not planning to take any questions at this time. Further details and information will be released to the public at a time and at intervals that the State Police believes appropriate."

As he spoke Sergeant Kern carefully went from face to face of the four most important media representatives who were assembled before him in the small duty room. The media had previously been told the room wasn't large enough for any video and the four he looked at understood, from prior phone contact, this was not going to be a typical press conference.

Public Information Trooper Sergeant Thomas Kern was a veteran of his job. He had taken enough time speaking with Ted before setting up the brief meeting with the press to understand Ted's concerns about this case. Ted insisted his own presentation would be brief, direct, and devoid of significant information. They all realized the announcement and topic would set off great interest and a myriad of questions. Ted told Tom Kern he just wasn't going to say anymore; maybe not for a while. He didn't explicitly tell Tom the information was not completely truthful or reliable but he hinted at that. Tom Kern got it and assumed his job was to protect Ted's case and decision. He handled it masterfully; at least for the moment. Next, Ted stood to speak.

"Ladies and gentlemen the Vermont State Police have developed major new findings related to the sudden death of the State Medical Examiner, Dr. Eleanor Stanton, in May of this year. Dr. Stanton's untimely death was initially thought to be related to a tragic hiking accident. More recent information and investigation has confirmed Dr. Stanton's death was a homicide."

There were gasps in the small room but Ted continued on, trying to minimize the drama and remain as matter of fact in his presentation as possible.

"While there are aspects of this investigation that remain unclear the State Police have developed a major suspect for this heinous crime. Morton Stern, a pathology assistant in the Burlington hospital and Medical Examiner's Office, has gone missing. Mr. Stern worked very closely with Dr. Stanton. At this time we have no evidence of a personal relationship between them. We believe Mr. Stern planned to leave for Canada on July fourth for a scheduled vacation but his whereabouts have remained unknown since the evening of July third. As best we have been able to determine Mr. Stern never crossed the border. We consider Mr. Stern our prime suspect in this case at this time.

"Sergeant Kern will give you copies of the last known pictures of Morton Stern. The Vermont State Police strongly encourage Mr. Stern, wherever he is, to turn himself in to the nearest legal authorities. We also are asking the public to contact the State Police at the number Sergeant Kern will give you if anyone has any information about Mr. Stern that will aid us in his immediate apprehension. Thank you for your cooperation."

With that Ted immediately walked away from the lectern and out of the room like he was in a hurry to get somewhere.

There, he did it. He hoped that would satisfy the Colonel and take some pressure off the investigation (and himself) for a while. He refused to worry about any impact on Morty because he felt sure he was dead. Standing in the front of that room at the brief press conference he had felt awkward and somewhat ashamed.

Naturally, Ted wondered what the eight troopers were going to think about his statement when it showed up in the media. After the press conference was over and he had some time to chew on it he began to feel a little differently about what he had done. Although he still thought it was unethical Ted found himself considering if his action might somehow shake up the investigation. And, after all this time, maybe that would be good.

He decided he wanted to believe there was a chance this unexpected public pivot could actually help him with whoever was guilty. Who knew what reaction the guilty trooper might have to this? The publicity surrounding implicating Morty Stern in the homicide had to be a confusing jolt to the troopers who had been targeted by Ted. Would they think they were now off the hook; no longer under suspicion? Surely they would wonder what was going on? None of them received any communication about this apparent turn of events from Ted or anyone else in the force.

Of course, if Morty Stern happened to show up, alive, Ted would be forced to do some quick explaining about other theories the State Police were considering. That would likely blow the whole sordid case wide open, challenging, by implication, the fundamental integrity of the force. Given Ted's history with missing pathology assistants, he had a feeling this guy was dead. He remembered the terrible end of the last diener he was involved with years before.

Morty Stern was missing. Dead or alive, he was now a very wanted man…probably by everyone except Ted Vallan.

* * *

A DANCE WITH DEATH?

For some time Ted planned to return to Ellie's house to look at it again now that murder was in the equation. From the very beginning he was suspicious about the circumstances of her death but the new developments encouraged him to want to re-assess almost everything and look at every part of her life; now from the perspective of a homicide investigation. The findings of the hike up Camel's Hump re-affirmed to him the need to continue to check out everything again.

After her death Ted relied on Trooper Barry's report of his and the crime lab's first investigation of Ellie's house. There was very little in it. The features of her home they noted all suggested Ellie was probably planning to return home sometime the same day she left. Even though the homes in the neighborhood were spaced considerably apart it was the persistent, mournful howling of her dog that ultimately alerted her neighbors something might be wrong at her place. A day after her absence was noted her body was discovered on the mountain.

He wanted to drive there late in the afternoon the next day, before he had to be at a retirement dinner for a senior trooper at the St. John's Club in Burlington. But he was late getting out of the Waterbury Barracks and realized he didn't have time to go to her home first. He thought he'd still try to go after the dinner if it wasn't too late. Many of those attending had to drive some distance to get home so he thought the affair would break-up by around eight-thirty.

As he was working on his second beer Ted reminded himself of his plan so he put the beer down and stuck with soda for the rest of the evening.

* * *

The thinking of at least one of the eight troopers was affected by the sudden news about Morty Stern. The Trooper reasoned the recent announcement suggested he had done well in his interview with the force and had successfully deflected suspicion. He thought it was very significant Lieutenant Vallan was the investigator who publicly said they were following a different path. Evidence challenging the Lieutenant's original assumptions must have turned up.

So one thing the public naming of a suspect did do, for sure, was embolden that Trooper to go ahead and go to Ellie Stanton's house in hopes of retrieving the final shipment, if it was still there. He had argued with himself for weeks about going. After all, he reasoned, he had a key. He drove there the following night. To encourage anyone who might see him to conclude he was on police business he figured it was smart to go in his cruiser and in uniform.

It just happened the night he picked was also the same evening Lieutenant Vallan made his long-planned visit to Ellie Stanton's home.

* * *

Getting to Ellie's, even at night, was not a problem for Ted. He had been there several times over the years. By the time he left paved road for the narrower dirt lane that served Ellie's neighborhood it was mostly dark. The dirt road was shrouded by a canopy of trees so whatever hint of light still persisted around nine was immediately extinguished as he headed down the narrow road. Beyond his headlights everything was black.

Ted was startled when he turned into the path to Ellie's and saw a light on in her house and a State Police cruiser parked close to her back door. For a few minutes he sat in his cruiser and thought about what might be going on. He was about to call dispatch with the number painted on the rear of the parked cruiser when the back door opened and State Trooper Corporal John Davies stood in the doorway silhouetted by the light behind him in the kitchen. What was this all about?

Ted exited his cruiser slowly, reflexedly brushing his right hand over his service revolver, ensuring its presence. He was uncertain what was going on and he was not pleased. As he walked past Davies' cruiser on his way to the house he placed his hand on the hood. It was quite warm. Only as Ted was practically at the door did the corporal step back to leave a narrow path for him to enter.

It was an awkward moment for each of them.

Ted was immediately suspicious and the corporal was tense. Ted appeared unaware of the extent of the corporal's reaction to his arrival. Davies flushed with anger...and worry. Instantly he was battling hard internally, desperately fighting to control his emotions about Ted showing up. He began to sweat. He felt the call to action; the instinctual behavior that began a cascade to violence. He was totally focused on the Lieutenant. Suddenly, for him, It was as though everything turned silent and time was standing still.

At first he assumed Ted must have been following him. That, and all that implied, infuriated him. Was he caught? They stood just inches from each other talking almost directly into the other's face. It was not lost on either of the troopers that there were revolvers holstered on their hips.

There were very few times in Davies' life he felt confusion and uncertainty in a setting like this. Davies believed he knew why he had survived so much danger. He assumed his continuing survival was dependent on suddenly initiating lethal damage to any adversary who threatened his ability to live as he wished. The tension continued to build.

Davies glanced at the dish drainer by the sink. Several long knives were interspersed with forks and spoons. He knew the light switch for the kitchen was at the doorway directly behind him.

But the force had trained him well.

With an almost herculean effort he was able to recognize this was a moment to control his anger and avoid violence. Killing Lieutenant Vallan, at least right then, might be very difficult to cover up. Would there have been any reason for Ted to know or think he was in grave danger with this Trooper? That Davies' longstanding modus was to act first and then destroy any evidence of his violence?

"What the hell are you doing here, Davies? Why would you come here? How'd you get in?" Ted's anger was obvious. The more he spoke the more angry and intense he got.

Davies stared for a few seconds. He knew he was sweating. He struggled to find a way to calm his fury. If he could de-fuse the moment maybe he could control himself.

He decided to tell Ted the truth.

"I told you before, Lieutenant, I have a key so I could drop off some of the charity supplies we collect from time to time. There's a batch still in the house and I thought I should try to figure out how to get at least this one last shipment to the hospital." He was satisfied with his answer and was pleased to sense his body begin to relax perceptibly. He knew it would be a battle to continue to control his emotions with the Lieutenant.

Ted, very formally, told him everything in her house was potentially evidence and he could not take anything. "I assume that's why you've got gloves on. So you don't contaminate the scene."

Davies tensed again. His facial expression actually frightened Ted. For a brief moment he looked homicidal. But he was able to catch himself again and resumed his difficult struggle to back off.

He smiled. "Then I guess you'll be wanting this key I have to the Doc's house?" As he spoke he reached in his pocket and pulled out a solitary key on a small chain and dangled it for Ted to grasp.

Ted was furious with this Trooper. He also had a sense something was wrong with Davies. Standing, late at night, in an isolated setting with this strange man, he pushed himself to back off...for now.

"Yes, that's right... Corporal, I think it's best for you to leave now."

Then Davies started to talk like a good old boy and Ted had a thought the Corporal was trying to take over the discussion, which made him even more suspicious of the Trooper. The way the guy was talking to a superior annoyed Ted.

"I can see you're mad at me Lieutenant and I'm sorry I came here. Just was hopin' to finish the job, if you know what I mean, since I knew there is some stuff here ready to go. Guess I didn't think of the place as a crime scene until I got here; especially after all this time. So then I figured best put gloves on." He moved back a foot or two and looked around.

"Say, Lieutenant, my guess is you're so ticked at me you're not gonna want to leave those supplies in the Doc's house anymore. So while you look around why don't you let me help you bring it all out to your cruiser, sir? I understand. We'll get it to where it's s'posed to go eventually. Help ya?"

Ted thought he was beginning to get a feel for this guy. And he didn't like much about him. He was angry with himself he wasn't able to completely shake some nerves about being alone with him in Ellie's house, at night. The Trooper looked dangerous. Ted wasn't sure if he had a game he was playing or what exactly was going on but Ted decided he didn't want Davies doing anything for him or even to be with him outside in the dark.

"No. Thanks anyway. You better go now. I want to check some things and then I'm going to leave soon too." Davies gestured one last time that he'd carry out some boxes but Ted waved him off.

He watched Davies walk, slowly, towards his cruiser. Davies stopped a few moments then continued to his cruiser and slowly drove away. Ted put his gloves on and walked around the place, first turning on every light he could find. He realized he was too tired to do more than look around in a cursory way. When he saw the cluster of small boxes in the corner of a spare bedroom it occurred to him it was such a small collection he might have missed them if he hadn't run into Davies. Ted wasn't sure what he should do with them. Davies' seeming to tell him what to do made it confusing for him. And he was a little worried about even walking outside just then, with or without the packages.

'Best take the fucking stuff with me and park it in Waterbury or Williston tomorrow,' he thought.

It was a warm summer night. There was a cadence of crickets and a slight rustle of leaves in the trees. It took two trips to bring the boxes out to the trunk of the cruiser. After the first he stood for almost a minute, listening. He decided to close his trunk all the way so it locked before he went back in the house again. He didn't think he was being watched but he wasn't sure.

Other than running into a trooper Ted thought the trip was a bust. He was too tired to take the time to look for the little things that might have been overlooked. He went through the house a last time turning off lights. The front of the house was now dark and he sat in a comfortable chair that faced a bank of windows overlooking the lake. He got up and drew open the curtains revealing a moonlit night reflecting on the lake. What would happen to this lovely house, he wondered?

A car door slammed in the back. He raced to the kitchen in the rear, turned out the light, and looked out to the driveway path. Nothing. He found a light switch that turned on floodlights lighting up the whole area. Nothing. Cautiously, he ventured outside and looked around. No other vehicle was in sight and he heard no engine sound. All four doors to his cruiser were closed. His holster was already unsnapped and he kept his hand by it as he opened the driver's door and all the courtesy lights went on. Nothing in the front or back seats. He doubted any of the few things he had left in there were gone. He closed the doors, confirmed the trunk was locked, and walked back to the house.

Unless someone was looking for something inside his cruiser, or the door slam he heard came from somewhere else, Ted had no explanation for what he heard. It sounded close but he didn't know for sure. The whole trip to Ellie's house seemed unhelpful and had become unsettling. There was still so much to do before his vacation. He and Shawn had to plan Shawn's week. And Ted had to pack; something he hadn't even thought about until then.

As he drove from Ellie's house he wondered if Trooper Davies just seemed to have moved to the top of his suspect list?

* * *

THE SLEUTH ON VACATION

It was far from a working vacation for Ted but the case was never far from his thoughts. The days were filled with activity and the Vallans travelled and enjoyed themselves as a family. It took Ted two full days to truly relax and gradually feel a notable lessening of the relentless pressure of his work and, in particular, this investigation. The next two to three days were almost magical. He felt different. Relaxed. Despite the enforced closeness of all four of them in one room, especially with one a teenager demanding her privacy, he was enjoying the trip; and the rest.

Prior to the trip Ted had no idea he would get so intensely interested in where they were and what they were doing. The places they went brought out his not so latent sense of patriotism. For a fleeting moment he even wished he had worn his uniform. Ted, and also the kids, he noted, were surprised Liza did not direct each day's activities as completely as usual. She was more quiet and laid back than they expected. But he and the kids were into it so Ted took the lead at the monuments and especially the FBI tour and various Smithsonian Museums. 'What the hell's with her?', Ted thought. Liza seemed to perk up at Mount Vernon and Monticello.

With two days left in the trip it all began to return to him. Later, by the time they did get home he started to wonder if a one week vacation wasn't more cruel than pleasant. Just as he was finally consistently relaxed the pressures of the job seeped back with the anticipation of returning to work. Someday, he vowed, he and Liza would take two weeks or more to really feel on vacation.

Two days to go, starting to feel the return of the tensions of his job, especially Ellie Stanton's unsolved homicide, Ted recognized he had been irritable most of the afternoon. He was going to call Shawn at five. Flashes of the threads and problems of the case kept popping up in his thoughts as the family did some sight-seeing but with the knowledge they were driving back to Vermont in the morning. Ted and Liza were each a bit detached from the activities as thoughts about their work began to infiltrate their lives again.

He hadn't spoken to Shawn for two days. Ted was getting anxious about returning and the forty-eight hours without contact also increased his sense of worry. Moreover, Ted was angry with himself for realizing, only the day before, he had forgotten all about those medical supplies he had taken to the Williston Barracks just before he left town. The day before, as the Vallan family toured the Gettysburg battle field, he remembered them. It hit him then it was possible there could be a more sinister explanation for that Corporal going to Ellie's house for those supplies. Maybe there was something about those boxes.

* * *

Shawn was active on the case all week. He worked mostly out of Waterbury and Williston barracks organizing information about topics they would review together on Ted's return. Morton Stern and Trooper Nancy Devers were each still missing. Both were presumed dead by Ted; Morty definitely and Trooper Devers possibly.

Initially Ted was not pleased to hear Barry spent most of the week behind a desk. Before he left town he told Shawn about his evening run in with Corporal Davies and asked Shawn to try to look in more detail into the charity and, in particular, Corporal Davies' involvement. Shawn still didn't have much to offer.

Information about the charity responsible for sending medical supplies to the small hospital in Thailand remained sparse; an obvious concern. Shawn was contacting U.S government customs and treasury agents and international aid agencies to find out about the hospital in Thailand. He also was talking with the Burlington hospital about any role it had in the apparent effort to actually send the medical supplies overseas. He was struck, now that Ellie was gone, there wasn't much known by anybody there. Trooper Corporal Davies was unknown to the staff.

The Burlington hospital donated regularly and troopers from around the state picked up occasional donations from three or four of the few small hospitals that dotted the state. The police already knew that was, possibly, the sole reason for some of the trooper's visits to the ME's office and Ted and Shawn assumed coordinating that was the extent of Corporal Davies' involvement. Ted had asked Shawn to try to find out if any other groups were involved also. There appeared to be none.

"Ready to wind up your trip, Chief? Time to come back to the cool mountain air? Actually hotter'n blazes up here this summer."

"Gotta be hotter here. Yes, Shawn, I think we're all ready to come back. Sleeping four in a room isn't my idea of restful. But it's been a good trip. Glad we did it. We've seen a lot. Leave it to Liza to make me get my head out of Vermont to learn about our history and see how big this country is.

"So tell me what else, if anything's come up the last day or so?"

"Chief, you were right to tell me to try to learn more about the program the ME seemed to be running to get medical supplies to that hospital in Thailand."

Ted was not surprised. Whatever donation program was set up had been concerning him. When he talked about it with Liza they both agreed it was the kind of thing they could see Ellie getting involved in. But Ted was getting stuck, not on the idea of Ellie helping out but the idea of Ellie possibly starting or even coordinating something like this. And what possible connection could Ellie really have had to a small hospital on the coast of Thailand? Wouldn't

Liza have had some awareness of Ellie doing something like that? Liza didn't recall Ellie ever mentioning even being in Thailand.

"I checked with BPD and some other departments. I called every frickin' hospital in the state. You know, Chief, I'm getting an idea whoever was running this charity was mostly getting donations from our hospital here in Burlington. Stuff she often just walked around the hospital and picked up from what I hear. And only a small amount of stuff from about three other hospitals. And, get this…those three hospitals all got their donations to the ME by state trooper. No other agency or place a part of this. Nadda. The Doc, the hospitals, and the force. And no one in Community Relations on the force or at the hospital seems to know much more about this than we do. There's one short paragraph in a force Community Relations newsletter about Corporal Davies' involvement and support for a 'charity donation program for medical supplies overseas' done through the Burlington hospital. That citation is in his file.

"We're still waiting to hear from the agencies I contacted to get info about the place this stuff has been going to. Despite the charitable nature of all this, Chief, I can't find almost any publicity about this in Vermont.

"So I began to think about all this, Lieutenant, so I went to Williston to look at the supplies you put there that never got shipped because she was killed. It hit me that someone set up this whole program, with the paperwork and records we have, and yet the pile of stuff I was looking at was really not a lot supplies to send for all the work it must have taken to coordinate, ship, and all. So I wondered if the supplies themselves might mean something. Yesterday I figured I should look more closely at what had been sitting in that corner of her spare bedroom for weeks."

"Good thought, Shawn. Just yesterday I realized I had forgotten all about that stuff and had the same idea. Today I planned to suggest you do just that. Find anything interesting?"

"Well I think so, Chief. I think I may have found something that's kind of a worry. That whole thing as a charity may not fly, Chief."

The last two days Ted was just beginning to consider any charity as something else too, but Shawn's words still startled him. He also was thinking 'enough with the Chief business' but he didn't bring it up.

"Tell me."

"Well, first I laid out all the packages on the floor. Then I picked up each one and opened it. Pretty unimpressive stuff, Chief. Mostly different types of sterile bandages; different types of what they call surgical tapes; some plastic urinals, IV tubing, small curved basins. Things like that. I guess you could call them dry goods. No medications, needles, IV bottles, or anything you would consider as valuable. Know what I mean?

"So I kept at it and made sure I looked at everything. One of the bigger boxes had four identical boxes of gauze pads inside. But when I lifted each box out it was obvious one box was much heavier than the other three. I opened them all, but the heavier one may be something, Lieutenant. In that box there's another box, wrapped in heavy brown paper. Something is written on it in red ink, maybe in thailandese? And there is also an address on it, maybe. To me it looks like there's a name in the middle of the writing. It starts with 'Dr.', I think. Box is heavy; feels like it's metal."

"Really, Shawn. You think it was safe to open it?"

"I didn't. Didn't even take the wrapping off, Chief. Figured we should look at this thing together; and maybe with the crime lab. I mean, I didn't have gloves on. Never figured something was really going to turn up. Know what I mean? So I got an evidence bag and sealed it up. Put the rest of the stuff back on the shelves. No, Chief, I figured I should wait for you to get back and we'll sit down with the crime lab folks and check it out. Good idea?"

"Good decision, Shawn. Sounds like an important find."

"Yeah, Chief. Maybe real big. Anything in that box and one of us may be on our way to Thailand to investigate. Think?"

Ted answered in a light tone. It was obvious he was smiling. "Right, Shawn. I was just telling Liza we need a longer vacation. Wonder what language they actually do speak over there?"

* * *

DAYS OF RECKONING

MAY, 1985

Ellie Stanton did not feel well. At all. Just as many times before when something came up related to health or how she was feeling Ellie's mind ticked through a list of possibilities of the many diseases she always worried about. After so many years of her lifestyle she was more than a little fatalistic about possible health consequences. Long ago any guilt about the life she chose to lead had faded and she considered its risks the price she paid for its enjoyment.

She liked sex. The problem was that one of the things that excited her about it was going from partner to partner, usually strangers; frequently. By now she realized her patterns and relationships were unlikely to ever become anything different. There were so many opportunities for her. What a great job she had. Contact with zillions of doctors; of all ages. And bunches of cops. And most of these guys were really under her control. She could do anything she wanted. Although only recently, more and more, she found herself thinking about the two times she played around with a woman a year or so before. She found it awkward then, but now she had some new ideas and had been wondering if she should try again. Not right now when she was feeling so crappy. No, sex with anyone wasn't appealing right now.

In all the years she had been sexually active only twice did she need treatment for a venereal disease. She was quite comfortable functioning as her own doctor, monitoring her health. Once she fantasized she was like a doc for a brothel doing checks on the girls and monitoring them for VD. Ellie figured out an ingenious way to submit smears and cultures she performed on herself to the lab with fake names and IDs that fit the hospital requirements and skirted the billing system. Rarely, she would use a name from the ME office files. She didn't do that frequently and putting her name down as the attending physician had never seemed to raise an eyebrow. Coming increases in computerization might make her scheme more difficult but, especially now, feeling so sick, she wasn't going to worry about that.

It was difficult and clumsy but using lights and a speculum with a mirror to collect vaginal smears was doable. Drawing her own blood was easier and not nearly as challenging as she thought it might be. Two hundred years before Dr. Hunter injected himself with syphilis as an experiment. All Ellie wanted to do was get some blood out. She was worried about the usual way to wind up with syphilis; among others.

She couldn't recall feeling this rotten in a long time. A month or so before she had a bad flu-like episode but it passed and now she was sick and coughing again. She was having sweats every night. Her last period came right on time, like always. She knew her IUD was intact.

Ellie delayed a few days hoping each new morning she would start to feel better. Wasn't happening. To start she decided to keep it as simple as possible and only do a complete blood count and what was called a comprehensive chemistry profile. So far, over the years, nothing more had ever been needed. Except for those two times her venereal studies always stayed negative and the occasional bloods were always perfect. This time she recognized she was more worried than usual. Even when she submitted the samples she found herself thinking about other possible labs that might become necessary.

The next morning she was apprehensive as she arrived at her office and quickly moved to the hospital mail in-box in a side area behind the secretaries' desks. She was purposely early so she could go through the pile before anyone else arrived. As she started picking through the mail she could feel her heart rate pick up and was plainly worried. She snatched a large white lab envelope addressed to her, folded it, and put it in her coat pocket. To make sure there were no others being sent to her she quickly went through the rest but found nothing else. Once back in her office she closed the door and sat at her desk.

With a sense of resignation and a lightly pounding heart she pulled out the envelope and opened it, placing the enclosed sheets flat on her desk. Her heart sank. Something, probably something significant, was wrong with her. She was anemic with slightly elevated white blood cells that broke down to indicate, she assumed, an acute infection. Her blood chemistries were notable for a depression of her proteins. Minor abnormalities related to liver and kidney were also noted but of very uncertain clinical significance.

These were the lab results of a sick person. After her initial upset at the findings she realized the labs indicated illness but these findings were a non-specific sign of illness; no specific disease diagnosis could be made from what she had in front of her. What was wrong with her? Was it serious? What should she do next? At least, she thought, in her profession if she was infectious to others she wasn't a risk to dead bodies.

Later, after she thought about the results some more, she realized the breakdown of the white blood cells might actually show a deficiency of lymph related cells rather than an increase of typical acute infection cells. More labs would be needed. Only for a brief moment did she think about seeing another physician.

Who would she ask? Liza came to mind. How judgmental would Liza be? Not yet she decided. Liza was living the American family dream life. Could Liza or most any of her colleagues begin to understand the way she chose to live? Ellie opened her office door to begin her work day and planned to do some reading that night.

She would bring home everything she'd need for more blood samples.

In the evening she read about venereal, connective tissue, and several specific autoimmune disorders. Early the next morning, still feeling weak and sick, she made sure she hydrated well and drew some more labs. In the back of her mind she recognized the beginning of a fear of another disease so terrible her brain worked hard to suppress even the thought. Her Lab rescue, Locie (after Dr. Edmond Locard, one of the fathers of modern forensics), was her only comfort.

Ellie arrived extra early at the hospital and submitted the bagged and authorized labs in her usual anonymous fashion. Even so she was anxious because she had never previously ordered so many tests, some quite specific and sophisticated. Then she began working. Only when Morty Stern, her favored pathology assistant, said she didn't look well and asked if she was okay did she begin to accept she might be losing control of her situation.

Some of the labs took several days to be completed. Ellie soldiered on at work but her worry intensified, as did her reading. Results came in drips and drabs over four days. She came into the morgue on Saturday and sat at her desk staring at the final reports. Still no clear diagnosis. Then she placed every result around her desk and looked them all over one more time. Her gaze drifted to a framed picture on the wall, a copy of Picasso's Don Quixote. Tears moistened her eyes. She felt so discouraged. There was no one for her to talk to. No Sancho Panza for her to unburden her upset and fears. At the sink in her office she washed her face and used paper towels to dry it. All the lab slips were put back in her briefcase and she went to the lab to pick up more blood drawing equipment. Then she went home, to Locie, who always offered unquestioning affection and love.

Ellie felt limited pleasure about how well she had been able to disguise the source of her occasional lab studies. If the study she anticipated doing on Monday came back positive it would not only be a reportable disease to the state but would cause quite a ruckus in the lab and the hospital. The test had only been available a short while and everything about this disease was a big deal. Could she manage to do it and keep the source a secret?

She wasn't sure why it mattered to her but she didn't want anyone to know the test was hers. In the midst of all her upset she still was clear headed enough to accept that a positive result was tantamount to a death sentence. So why would it matter at that point? Ellie didn't know. A part of her always felt she was fooling so many people about her life she seemed to think she should be able to do that forever.

She would draw her blood again early on Monday morning. Before then, over the weekend, it was only logical that she spent some time ruminating about how she might have wound up with such a disastrous problem. Some might say her exposure was almost unlimited but Ellie quickly narrowed her focus to only a few possibilities. In fact, in her mind, from what she knew about many of her partners she decided there was only really one person who was the most likely to have done this to her. She vacillated a little since she really had no way of knowing who it might be but she kept returning to him. There were lots of reasons, she thought.

* * *

Ellie was surprised but, of course, pleased she was feeling better on Sunday and again on Monday morning. She decided to only re-check the blood count and chemistries instead of submitting the worrisome test. She knew the lab only ran that test on Wednesdays anyway so she would still have time to submit it if there was no improvement in the basic studies. She had already decided she would label that lab test with the name of a forty-six-year-old male who died in an auto crash the week before who was known to be an alcoholic. It was the best she could come up with and hoped she might be able to get away with it. At least for a while.

Even though her symptoms were better the test results were unchanged. Ellie, reluctantly, admitted to herself she was continuing to have drenching sweats each night. She drew and submitted more blood on Wednesday morning. At three-thirty the chief microbiology tech came to her office, personally, to tell her that man's sample was ELISA positive for HIV.

Ellie stumbled through the rest of her day completely distracted, nauseous, and numb. A weakness and sense of despair she had never known overcame her. Her face felt hot and her heart raced. she had difficulty following any discussions. Everything around her seemed distant. She was devastated and it all felt unreal. She left early. Ellie drove home and walked into her silent house. Greeted by her dog she got on the floor and pulled Locie to her lap, bent over her, and cried.

* * *

Denial is a phase of grieving that doesn't make too much sense to a physician. As she sensed all the parts of her carefully constructed life tumbling down and falling apart, Ellie Stanton recognized she was going to be stuck on the anger phase of grieving...for a long time.

She could accept her diagnosis and its likely very poor prognosis. But any sense of guilt about the way she pursued her sexual pleasure was just not a part of how she had chosen to live her life; for many, many years. She understood this was a disease she could have acquired from any one of her many partners, although probably in the last few years rather than very distant past. Why she trusted her instincts about the source of her own infection, rather than consulting an expert to learn so much more about all aspects of this disease, seemed to satisfy her desire to feel sure she knew the answer and, therefore, could focus her anger and hate on one person.

Ellie had been aware for months he was unhappy to be performing sex in the way she often encouraged him. She knew he was stuck. He wanted all that money much more than she did. She felt a kind of perverse control during sex with virtually all her partners. But this man was actually controlling her at the start and now, almost each time they had sex, she was truly in charge, for sure. Ellie had been reluctant to have this kind of sex with almost anyone else. Saving it for him kept the excitement and pleasure of their relationship more alive. It had not been lost on her during the time they were having anal sex that she occasionally saw blood when she cleaned her bottom after they finished. Now she thought the implications of that periodic bleeding were obvious.

Ellie never had any illusions about his lifestyle when he was in Thailand. After all, how else was he likely to have met the quack doctor they were working with? If he whored there, he probably did here also. She chose to not think about why he didn't seem ill; or how many of the men she slept with had multiple partners of their own.

She wanted him hurt too.

While focusing her anger at him and on hurting him she did less ruminating on all the many other parts of her life that were about to fall apart. When she did feel flashes of what was about to happen to her she willed herself to return to thoughts of ruining his life and in that way managed to actually get up each morning and return to work for a few days. People at work knew there was a problem. She was distracted and did not look well. But she ignored their looks and quickly brushed away any comments of concern about her.

* * *

END OF A LONG ROAD

Human beings are animals. How high an order you can decide for yourself. Animals have urges, needs, desires; whatever you wish to call them. Even in terrible and disastrous times and settings men and women copulate…because that's just something animals do. Dying, and planning to hurt the man she held responsible for her fate, Ellie could not help fantasizing one last pleasurable sexual episode with the only man she knew who would perform it reliably. Following the added pleasure of knowing he disliked what she made him do she would then tell him she would no longer be a part of his scheme to harvest pineal glands for profit.

In her mind Ellie focused on how she could upset him the most when she told him she was finished helping. She knew that was what he cared about. Confronting him about her sickness would only make her feel weak with him. No, she wanted him to think refusing to continue to collect the glands was what she wanted to do…to hurt him.

First, one last time in bed.

* * *

She left a note in her truck signaling him the next time he dropped off supplies she wanted him for an evening. There was no indication of a rush; it was a routine they had followed for well over a year. He wasn't pleased but he was determined to keep the money coming. So when he drove in her driveway a few days later they were each cordial. She kissed him when he walked in and he determined to perform his role to her satisfaction.

But their love-making wasn't what it usually was. Ellie tried, very hard, to slip into her accepted role and act out the recurring fantasy that excited and haunted her. He tried to accommodate. But it wasn't the same. She was distracted. She wished for the fleeting fulfilment that came with this sex but, not surprisingly, she was too upset to completely relax even for this: a pleasurable experience she had re-created so many times. He sensed her mood was off. He sighed and tried to play his part more diligently. 'What more does she want from me?' He consciously reminded himself he was doing this for the money; for him and Nancy; to maintain his ingenious and fabulously successful money-making scheme.

When it was over, even though they lay side by side, he accepted the distance and darkness of her mood which was her way.

"I'm not going to do it anymore." Her tone was flat, maybe with just a tinge of anger. But even that wasn't so unusual.

In this setting and with his increasing despair over his own role in her bed he assumed her words were about the sex. She had never ever even hinted at such a thing before so his guard was raised, just a little.

"It's whatever you want Doc, but you know I'm always ready when you are." He wished he had said it with more conviction. He realized just how much he had grown to dislike her. He thought he had to do better. "I think…"

Ellie sat up in bed. After sex she always covered up when she pulled away from her partner. This time she hadn't. Davies caught the movement of her beautiful large breasts lagging slightly behind as she re-positioned her body. Nancy had small breasts. Nobody's body was like the Doc's, he thought.

She had tears in her eyes. She wasn't listening to him. All the hurt of a lifetime was in her anger. She didn't tell him she hated him and what they did. She didn't tell him he meant nothing to her. She didn't tell him she held him responsible she was going to die. She only told him what she knew would upset and hurt him the most.

"No more goddamn pineal glands to Thailand. I'm out of that business. No more."

They stared directly at each other. At first his face drained. He tried to think as fast as he could. Why was she doing this? What should he say to her? He saw her tears; her anger. Her expression was grim. He reached over to gently push away tears from her cheek. She didn't stop him but she spoke; firmly.

"No. Never again. No more. I'm finished. You'll have to figure something else for yourself. I'm done." Her words didn't satisfy her. She turned away from his hand. Her anger was only building. It wasn't enough.

"I'm going to tell the hospital what we have been doing."

Initially, as he sat there he was angry with himself he had never considered such a possibility. He had gotten sloppy again. His anger quickly grew into a fury. She couldn't do this to the scheme; to him. His reflex for self-preservation, brewed even greater with the anger and hate he had developed for her, exploded.

Ellie began to move her legs to get out of bed. His left hand and arm that had seconds before tried to offer tenderness suddenly recoiled and returned in a crashing blow to her face, smashing her nose and right eye socket. His huge Marine Corps gold ring caused terrible damage to her face. She was out before she fell. Instantly he shoved her body to the wood floor before her blood could destroy the sheets and her mattress.

Immediately he started to figure out the situation he was in and what he had to do. He was pleased he was now thinking quickly again. It wasn't until a day later that he would allow himself to reflect, in any way, on what he considered the larger problem of the end of his business.

The barking of Ellie's dog on the other side of the closed bedroom door alerted him to managing his immediate environment. He pulled all the bedding onto the floor next to her. With a towel he opened the bedroom door, went downstairs and found a large bowl which he filled with kibble for the dog. Then he went out to his cruiser and brought latex gloves and a regulation canvas tarpaulin from the trunk back to the house.

When he moved Ellie to the tarp covered with her sheets she didn't move and he assumed she was dead. It didn't matter just then as long as she was out. He cleaned up the floor with wet and then dry towels. There was plenty of other bedding to make the bed. Then he carefully and awkwardly dressed her limp body. He didn't care if the panties, bra, plaid shirt and jeans got bloody while he did this. That was okay. He found heavy socks and hiking boots and put them on her and placed her keys in a pocket of her jeans. He rolled her up in the tarp; bedding, towels, and all.

Before he grappled with moving the tarp stuffed with Ellie and bedding he took a moment to find her wallet and made sure her driver's license was in it. He ran outside and put the wallet in her truck's glove box.

The dog watched him carry her to the trunk of his cruiser. There was no barking now. He returned to the house and placed a bowl with some cereal and milk in the sink and an empty coffee mug. He walked through her house one last time carrying a barely moistened towel and wiped down everything he could think of. He thought he had finished and turned off all the lights. Just before going out and locking her door he turned the hall light on again and opened the closet door. He took a beat up rain poncho off a hanger and brought that with him as he walked to his cruiser. It was about eight-thirty.

* * *

He drove, cautiously, to Trooper Devers' apartment in Johnson and was pleased she hadn't gone to bed yet. It wasn't much but a trained eye could tell there were several small blood stains on his uniform. He needed her help and had prepared the story he would tell her.

"Something terrible happened tonight, sweets. The Doc made me do bad things with her again and I just couldn't take it anymore. I said 'no more' and she went crazy. She started threatening me with all kinds of things; about the money...and us. She said she would accuse me of rape and forcing her to be part of the deal with the Doc in Thailand. She would stop getting those glands." His voice had emotion and concern and conveyed a sense he felt trapped.

"She started to beat me on the chest with her arms so I grabbed her. She spit right in my face. I just lost it, sweets. It was like everything was falling apart all at once; so quickly, you know. I...I wasn't able to think. I wanted her to stop screaming at me. I just hauled off and hit her; hard." He stopped for dramatic pause and looked down at the ground. "Sweets, I think I killed her. She hasn't moved since."

Nancy Devers put her head in her hands. She felt her eyes moisten. How suddenly disaster can strike and your life can change forever, she thought.

He wasn't going to let her think about tomorrow.

"Sweets, I need your help; tonight. I got a plan to make Doc's death look like an accident. It will take all night to do this right and we have to get to work in the morning so we got to move; now. Will you help me, sweets? Our future together depends on it."

What could she say? Recently, more than ever, their lives had become forever united. She knew this only too well. He was the force in her life for most of the last two years. What he did, he did for them. She fervently believed that. It was too late to think in any other way. She felt confused and overwhelmed by his words and emotion. At that moment the only thing that made sense to her was to follow him. Distracted and struggling to hold back tears, her voice was barely audible when she said they should get going. First he had her put on a uniform so she could go right to work in the morning.

As rapidly as his behavior could land him in murderous trouble he also maintained an amazing ability to quickly plot an effective attempt to disguise his disastrous actions. He spent little time re-living his impulsive act. Effective flight now meant removing himself from the crime and suspicion. The challenges excited and energized him. He tried to get Nancy to feel that way also but that was not in her make-up.

They drove back to Ellie's and he got in her truck and followed Nancy, driving his cruiser, back to his home in the woods, which was about fifteen minutes north of Johnson. As they pulled behind his house it was still before midnight. His dogs were in their kennel and were barking furiously. He told Nancy he would put the dogs in the house to quiet them and then they would move the body to his truck.

It became quiet. He was still in the house and Nancy stood in the dark, bewildered by all that was happening. She thought she heard sounds from the trunk of his cruiser. With his key she slowly opened the trunk. The stuffed tarp took up the entire space. Soft squealing. She slowly bent over the tarp and unrolled some of it. Ellie's lower legs became visible. As she bent farther into the trunk to unwrap some more bedding and tarp a leg with a large hiking boot kicked out, hard, and jolted Nancy in the stomach. She was pushed back, in pain and in fear.

The tarp further unfurled as Ellie's arms pushed at it. Nancy was furious at being kicked in her enlarging belly. She leaned back into the trunk to grab Ellie's arms. She started shouting:

"She's not dead! She's moving all over! She's not dead!"

Nancy pushed hard on Ellie's left arm and Ellie's shoulder fell back. That put Nancy off balance and her forearm fell against Ellie's face and Ellie bit down, hard. Nancy struggled to try to pull her arm back.

He came running over and dropped the flashlight he was carrying. He leaned in also and helped Nancy reclaim her arm. As Nancy pulled away he fell into the trunk. His shoulder then was on Ellie's face and she, in turn, tried to bite down on him. He felt his uniform tearing. He was infuriated.

He picked up a rusty three-foot metal rod that was in the trunk. He had stopped his cruiser on the interstate a week before to get it off the road. In a rage he brought it down on Ellie's face, destroying it in a line from her forehead to her mouth and jaw. Blood spurted everywhere but not on them.

"Are you all right sweets? Why did you open the trunk? I thought she was dead, but I guess not. Listen, I have to smash her up anyway so it's gonna look like she had a big fall. Just help me lay her out on the ground and then you should sit in my truck until I load her up and we can head out."

Later Nancy remembered the sound of that pipe thudding into the Doc's arms and legs. She heard no sounds of life from her anymore.

He had managed to slip the poncho on her and rolled Ellie's beaten and bloody body back up in the tarp and they placed her in the back of his capped pickup. He put the bedding in a big plastic bag and locked it in a shed in the back. He had a backpack he brought from the house that had two head lamps, some apples, water, and two ponchos. He told Nancy they were going to place the Doc at a spot below the summit of the hump so it would look like she fell to her death while hiking.

"I don't have boots! Climb that mountain now? In the dark?"

"You'll see, sweets. I thought you could get rid of a body there this way years ago when I used to hike all over that place. No boots needed."

So she drove Ellie's old Bronco, following him in his. They stayed on Route 100 until they were south of the interstate and cut onto dirt roads to reach the best known east approach to the mountain. Ellie's truck was left in the empty lot. It was just after one-thirty on a cool, partially moon-lit night. Next they headed for another approach parking area due south of the mountain. There was a car parked in that lot, a reminder there were people in the woods.

He was intense and it was obvious he was pre-occupied and unhappy but he remained very focused on his plan and goal. They spoke very little. She loved him but that moment wasn't the first time she recognized his impulsiveness sometimes frightened her. The entire situation numbed her mind. She always hated that Doc. She knew they had relations; strange relations. Any sex with the man she loved was bad enough. She wondered for the millionth time why he was willing to do anything for money; even if it was a lot. Then she felt pain in her belly and she was fearful and hated that Doc even more.

Head lamps adjusted, he strapped on the backpack and they slid their cargo from the back of the truck. He remembered exactly where he wanted to go and in only minutes Nancy was amazed to find they were walking on a fairly wide flat path with much less incline than she would ever have anticipated. It was still dark despite head lamps and footing was far from perfect. All Nancy had to do was support Doc's wrapped legs while he managed the greater bulk of her body. His adrenalin was pumping. He knew what he wanted; had to accomplish. He was greatly buoyed by the good time they were making. He wanted to be off the mountain well before six.

Nancy held up well and they trudged up the mountain at a decent pace with their gruesome cargo. Neither spoke. If he was worried about running into any travelers he didn't let on to Nancy. His revolver was on his belt. The cool air was damp but maintaining their footing was not really a problem. She had no idea how far they had to go but found her job was not exhausting. Almost two hours after entering the trail they reached a clearing where they could see stars and maybe, just maybe, a rock formation way above them.

They walked about ten feet farther on the trail and put the tarp with Ellie on the ground and then he unrolled it. Nancy stayed back, not wanting to look at her. But he decided he needed her help. He motioned her over and wordlessly signaled her to pick up Ellie's legs. They stood near the edge of the path, swung her back and forth, silently counting to three. On three Ellie Stanton's broken body was heaved over the edge of the trail and cascaded down the mountain almost twenty feet or so. Nancy quickly walked back down the path about ten feet. She felt sick.

He stood at the edge and stared down. He could barely make out the position of her body below. He was in a hurry to get back down but decided he wasn't satisfied with how she lay on the ground.

His uniform was a mess and would have to be changed anyway so he jumped over the edge like a skier heading straight downhill and slid and skipped down to the clearing where her body was. There was a strong image in his mind of how he thought her body should lay there so he quickly positioned the Doc accordingly. He struggled to get back up the steep drop to reach the path again. He folded up the tarp and didn't look back. He didn't really look at Nancy. When he reached where she was standing she joined his pace and they walked down the mountain.

It was first light when they were in his truck and drove away from the parking area. They hadn't seen another soul. Parked in front of her apartment he reached over and squeezed her shoulder. Few words had been spoken through the night. He thanked her for her help. He said he hoped she understood they had no other choices for handling this.

"I couldn't be more pleased and proud of you tonight. You really are something else, sweets. Don't know if I ever could have thought I'd be able to find someone like you. We're gonna be fine, sweets. This stuff is all over now. You'll see. In a few weeks I bet you we won't hear any more about that lady."

Nancy gave him a weak smile and got out of his truck. His idea of wearing their uniforms did not work out and they each planned to clean up and change. They both made it to work on time.

Around noon it rained hard on Camel's Hump.

* * *

SURPRISE IN A BOX

Ted was startled when the first thing Ed Clark, Director of the Crime Lab, did was pull out a stethoscope and start to put the ear pieces in his ears. He was even more amazed when he thought he recognized the stethoscope.

"Sure, maybe you should. Your wife gave it to me. Guess I should say she donated it to the force"

Liza had a bunch of them and this one reminded Ted of one of her first, from medical school.

"You know she saw me put my ear to a cabinet at an investigation once. These days we listen, more and more, for ticking or mechanical sounds, or even for signs of life before we open something up. Next thing I knew Mrs. Vallan dropped by and gave me this a week or so later. It's great. Gonna save someone's life someday."

With that Clark began a process of carefully opening the package. He listened, first, through the heavy wrapping paper and heard nothing, then indicated he would listen again when the metal box was exposed.

Chief Crime Lab Technician Edward Clark was a tall, slim, middle-aged man with a full head of gray hair and a matching thin silver moustache. Ed Clark was easy going and friendly but also conscientious enough to have a reputation for running an excellent detection lab. Nowadays his strength was more in the lab than at crime scenes. That probably was a reflection of the challenges of working odd hours and conditions in the field as an older man rather than a skill or interest issue. The lab was a brightly lit room with built-in cabinets and counters where everything but the walls were finished in white plastic laminate and stainless steel.

With a variety of tools and techniques he managed to remove the thick brown manila wrapping around the box. He did it in a way so it could probably be re-applied to the box and appear never to have been manipulated if that was desired. Shawn took photos of the wrapping and the writing on it and the steel box that was now exposed. No evidence of any internal sounds on repeat auscultation. The steel box was just larger than about four inches by four inches and a little less than two inches deep, with a top and bottom piece. There was no reason to assume it had been custom made. A metal clasp secured each opposing end of the small box. There was no lock. No prints were found when the box was dusted.

"Well, let's open 'er up and she what we've got." Ed was using a chair with wheels. The other two sat in folding chairs, each on a side of a small stainless steel table anchored to the wall on the fourth side. With some kind of special gloves that Shawn remarked reminded him of space gloves Ed Clark slowly and carefully removed the top half of the metal box. The contents immediately visible were gauze pads, probably four inches by four inches, tightly packed. Clark wheeled his chair to a close workbench and rolled back with a sizable tweezers and a plastic bowl that was larger and deeper than the box they were examining.

He used the tweezers to pick up individual gauze pads, placing each one in the bowl.

"If you find only a few more of these pads then this may be a box filled with nothing but white gauze pads," Shawn said.

Ted was thinking along the same lines. "Maybe there's something special about these pads," Ted wondered. "If…"

"Whoa!," Ed interrupted, since he was the first to see something as he lifted up another pad.

Peeling that pad away exposed a flat, clear plastic bag containing about twelve large gray peas placed in three rows. A few more gauze pads were under the bag.

"What are those things?"

"No idea Shawn. What about you Ed? Any thoughts?"

None of them had the slightest idea what they were looking at so they assumed it was something to do with drugs.

"I thought things like drugs were being smuggled into the US instead of being smuggled out." Shawn glanced at Ted and then Ed, but neither had a response.

After a short while Ed spoke up. "I guess we'll have to get chemistry to do some tests. Just not sure what could look like this. I mean they're each almost shaped like a ball but it's obvious they are actually each a little different in size and shape. You know, I have no idea."

So chemistry became, briefly, involved but made it clear, right away, the material was unlikely to be a form of a drug. When the tech carefully removed one of the large peas from the bag he remarked that the material felt rubbery. He doubted it was artificial or from a plant. With that Ed Clark took a clear glass slide and barely brushed a sterile blade along an edge of the material trying to scrape a tiny piece onto the slide. He placed a cover slip over it and clipped the slide to the stage of a microscope.

"Lieutenant, I'm not sure what this stuff is. But it could be some parts from an animal of some kind. I think you guys are going to have to take this to Jim Phelps, who we use in Zoology at UVM. He'll know how to check this out correctly. Okay?"

Ted kept staring at the package and its contents while he listened. He was thinking about what any of this stuff could be and how that could relate to his case.

"No Ed, everything in this case, so far, has involved the Medical Examiner. I'm not sure what's going on here but I'm going to take this box to Dr. Fowler, the Chief Pathologist, in Burlington. What he thinks might make this a very big deal." Ted looked away from the contents of the box and then up; first at Ed, then Shawn. The implication of his words were clear.

Shawn re-settled in his chair. "Got to be some kind of drug, Chief. Can't imagine what else." Ed said nothing.

"We'll see; we'll see" With that Ted asked Shawn to help Ed put everything back while he called pathology to ask Dr. Fowler to stay at his office until he and Shawn could get there.

* * *

It was later in the day but Ted refused to consider any delay in finding out what these small things that looked like big peas were all about. The almost assured involvement of Ellie, the Medical Examiner, in this business raised a few incredibly serious and troubling concerns. He wasn't going to wait another day. He and Shawn walked out to their cruisers.

"Shit! This stuff has been sitting under our noses for two months. No matter what this crap turns out to be you know it's gonna turn the whole charity business into an obvious diversion for some kind of smuggling. And international! Shit!"

"Yeah, this sounds like the kind of bad stuff that gets people killed, doesn't it Chief?"

"I guess so Shawn; I guess so." Shawn caught how Ted repeated himself just as he had done only minutes before in the crime lab. He wasn't sure what was going on with the Lieutenant. Ted's words reflected how he looked: diverted and almost enervated by the new direction being opened by the finding of the last hour.

Actually Ted was thinking a few moves ahead. He wasn't sure what he had at that moment but he thought he was beginning to know where to put the players responsible for all that had been going on.

Shawn picked up on Ted's interest in getting to Burlington and, hopefully, a final explanation of the contents in the box.

"Guess I'll see you at the hospital, Chief…Say in about twenty-five minutes?"

Ted cracked a slight smile, winked at Shawn, and they each climbed into their cruisers and immediately reached under the dash to activate flashing lights. No sirens, just lights as they headed for the interstate.

It was still a sunny August afternoon. The sky was deep blue with clusters of big, lazy, billowy, brilliant white clouds, especially to the west over Lake Champlain, where they were headed. They were two distinctive, flashing, large green and off-yellow sedans racing, in tandem, at a notably high rate of speed down the asphalt. The ribbon of black and brown colored highway was dwarfed on each side by endless large expanses of very green fields and forested foothills and mountains, attesting to the notably wet summer.

* * *

Dr. Fowler had another doctor in his office when they arrived. Ted motioned with his eyes and an ever so slight twist of his head and Dr. Fowler asked the man to leave. Ted got right to business. As he filled the pathologist in on the history of that box, so far, he also directed Shawn to put some gloves on and get the box out and open it.

"Dr. Fowler, you will probably want to get a sample of this material to look at with a microscope. Our lab technicians don't know what these things are but they are thinking they may be some type of animal-related material. They're not sure."

Fowler leaned forward into his desk to look at what Shawn was displaying. He stared at the box and its contents only a short time. He looked up at the two troopers with a kind of puzzled look on his face; almost a squint of one eye. From his expression, for a second, Ted wondered if Dr. Fowler might be thinking they were joking with him. Then he spoke to them but it looked like his mind was somewhere else. Fowler's words were just shy of sounding angry.

"Well, you know, it's not that easy. You can't just scrape something like this and tell you what it is a few minutes later. You need to fix the material. Although it looks like someone's already done something to it to try to kind of preserve it. Then we use a special cutting machine to make micro thin slices. And we usually also do some stains to enhance features. We'll do a frozen section now. After that it can be looked at.

"We'll get on that right now but it may take thirty or forty minutes to get to that point."

Ted couldn't conceal his disappointment about the time needed to find out what he was looking at in the box in front of him. Dr. Fowler picked up the box and got up to assemble the help he would need to do the job. As he rounded his desk he stopped and looked at Ted. He appeared a bit flustered but it was the anger that flashed across his face that startled Ted.

"Lieutenant, we'll have a microscopic diagnosis of what this is in a few minutes. But I can tell you right now these little specimens look to me like they are going to turn out to be pineal glands… and they could be from humans. Now how the hell could that happen?…You know what the hell that means?" He no longer hid his worry and upset.

He turned towards the door but after just a step turned back again and pointed as he continued to speak.

"And, Lieutenant, this box these specimens are in; this is the type of container we use when the department needs to mail slides for a consultation with the AFIP, the Armed Forces Institute of Pathology. Pathologists from all over the country send uncertain, ambiguous, and unknown specimen slides to the institute in these boxes for an opinion."

The Doctor walked out the door. Ted and Shawn looked at each other.

"What the fuck is a pineal gland?"

"I don't know, Shawn, but some really strange stuff may be going on. If Doc is correct something terrible has been going on around here. And I mean maybe right here."

Pineal gland meant nothing to either of them. If it was a human body part it sure was small. Where would something like that be in a body, they wondered?

* * *

FAMILY SUPPORT?

Ted knew he was getting closer. Corporal Davies was the most likely of his group of troopers to have killed Ellie Stanton. And Trooper Devers probably was involved in some way. At least she was involved with Davies in some way. He knew that. Nevertheless, all his suspicions didn't leave him anywhere close to proving Davies was the killer.

Although most in the force seemed to find Davies a pleasant and reliable trooper every contact Ted had with the guy left him with nothing but distrust. He accepted the Corporal was probably a clever guy and smart enough. But his history probably meant something so he might not be so smart it was unlikely he hadn't made any errors. They always do, Ted knew. Ted would look back and find things that didn't add up about this man.

Davies' and Ellie's Thailand connections, still ill-defined, seemed to remain their only unique bond. Shawn was too patient with federal and international authorities. The true connection of that hospital with John Davies' and Ellie's past in Thailand had stayed missing for too long.

Ted ruminated over all this as he drove home, earlier than usual, on a Thursday afternoon. A summer cook-out was planned at the Vallan house. His parents and his sister's family were coming. Liza said she felt pushed to have it by Ted's family because they all wanted to hear about the recent trip. Leaving Vermont to tour the country was not a usual summer vacation activity for many Vermonters. Ted was fine with doing the BBQ mid-week and managed to get home on the early side to help out.

Naturally, his parents were already there when he arrived. Both his mom and dad had finally settled into true retirement. His father, Thom, initially had some rough years after being laid off as a machinist at the end of 1975 when he was sixty-two. A good part-time job in the Essex Town Department of Public Works shop and some volunteer work with a local charity turned out to be a nice fit for being active and busy. That still left ample time for his hobbies and to do projects around his and his kid's homes. So far his masterpiece was the porch he and Ted built. It was much harder and more work than either had anticipated, taking an entire summer to complete. Liza's frequent expressions of eternal gratitude never let Thom or Ted ever think it wasn't worth the effort.

Ted wasn't sure which of his parents were more of a surprise to him over the last few years. Thom had some brushes with health issues years before but as the years passed he was the one who seemed to have the most energy, remained truly sharp, and maintained the more positive outlook about life. For virtually Ted's whole life his mother, Sheila, had been the more dynamic parent in his life. She was the take charge, get the job done person for the family. The rock who watched over them all; reliable as day following night. Everyone looked to her for the tough decisions and guidance. That seemed to be changing now.

His mom was fine; active and always pleasant and interested. But not as sharp. Sometimes she seemed just a half-step behind in conversations. She was fine, he thought, but he realized the word 'dynamic' might not fit his mom any longer. She looked notably older the last year or two. It was almost as though she had decided to stop fighting the battle of life as actively anymore.

Before he went out back with the others Ted locked up his weapon and ran upstairs to change. Coming back down the stairs his father was waiting for him.

"Okay dad, before we go outside why don't you tell me what you've wanted to say about you and Ellie Stanton?"

"Well it's about time that I tell you about it, don't you think, Ted? I mean I'm sure it's something you should know; something you need to know. And you keep brushing me off about it."

"Come on. You know you and I haven't talked much about any of my cases for years. At least ever since that major mess up with your use of the *ABC* during that big case in the seventies. I almost lost my job because of that, you remember?"

Thom had a look of resignation on his face and started to walk away. "Fine. I'll let it go; forget about it. You can get important information from everyone except your own family, right?"

"Dad, I said I'm ready to hear what you have to tell me, didn't I? Sorry if even though that last mess was long ago it still sits in my craw when I think about it. You know it won't work out if you decide to do any investigating for me. Shit, you wouldn't expect to go into a medical office and start examining patients for Liza, would you?"

"Okay, Ted, that's enough. Forget it."

"No, I would like you to tell me so we're done with it. Okay?"

Thom knew from Ted's tone he was still more angry than interested. But Thom had carried his story with him for weeks. In his mind he just knew it had to mean something to Ted. Despite his difficult audience he looked right at Ted and spoke in earnest now.

"Okay…So here's the thing. I did know Dr. Stanton, you know. I met her about one or two times when we all were at your apartment when you were still in Burlington or maybe at this house. About two years ago she called me up, out of the blue. We chatted about nothing for a bit then she asked if she could ask me a question; in fact, about the *ABC*. Isn't that a coincidence, huh Ted?

"I said 'sure' and she said she wanted to know if the *ABC* gets sold or, at least, sent around the world at all? You know, to other countries. I told her I happened to know it's read all over the globe by collectors everywhere. Did you know there's a promo on one of its pages every week says 'read on all seven continents...even Antarctica'? And you know I've shipped some records to South America.

"Then she asked if I ever heard about anyone ever using the *ABC* as a way to send messages to someone?" Ted flinched a little. "Well, I told her her guess was as good as mine, but I assumed that using the *ABC* and some kind of pre-determined code could make that doable. I mean, every issue has hundreds of small ads. Anything's possible.

"After I heard she died I remembered that call. That's all."

With that Thom started to walk towards the kitchen which would lead him out back where everyone was. Ted called after him.

"Wait dad. That's it? Did she say anything else to you then? About that or anything else? Did she ever bring anything up about that when you saw her after, or did she ever call you again after that? Did you and she talk about what sections someone might use?" Ted wanted every detail Thom could recall.

Almost as if on cue Thom stopped and turned to Ted. "No Ted, that was it. Don't think we ever spoke again... I'm sure it was nothing." Then he resumed his path through the kitchen and porch to the back yard.

Ted was amazed. That damn ABC. Back to haunt him.

Among Thom Vallan's interests was a decades long hobby collecting, by buying and selling, novelty records, mostly 45's from the late fifties and sixties. There were lots of them. Titles like "The Purple People Eater," "The Chipmunk Song," and "Please Mr. Custer (I Don't Wanna Go)." Each time one came out he bought ten or twenty copies. Over time, as some became valuable he was able to get into the business of buying and selling to other collectors; making some money doing it. The main vehicle for transactions for Thom and innumerable other collectors of myriads of things was *Applegate's Better Collectables Weekly*, commonly known as the *ABC*.

Creating a long distance message for someone unsafe to contact in any other way could be done easily through the *ABC* as long as quick contact wasn't of the essence, since it is a weekly. Ted knew this from simple common sense but also because of an incident in his past.

At just this point in the case his father's report to him was as startling as it was striking. It seemed to answer some questions just as it raised new ones. Whatever was happening with these crazy pineal glands probably had been going on for two or more years. How could that be, Ted thought? Ongoing trafficking in human body parts; smuggling continuing un-noticed for all that time in the hospital morgue? How easy could that be to accomplish?

Before going out to the backyard to join the others Ted stood in the kitchen, thinking, staring at nothing. Then he sat down. The information stunned him. Here he was, after all this time, still getting more completely new pieces of the puzzle. But this piece was tied to a new, huge, crime in many ways equally as serious as Ellie's murder. A wave of weariness came over him. He felt physically drained.

Ted was tired of continuing to find new questions that needed to be answered. The idea of the Ellie Stanton he and Liza knew masterminding some kind of a diabolical scheme to use human body parts for…for what? He didn't even know what the stuff was for. If it was for profit Ellie's financial records showed she was quite well off but Ted assumed that was because she was a single doctor; a Chief Medical Examiner and pathologist, who, not surprisingly, made a lot of money. They'd have to go back and look again for any odd patterns, especially deposits.

Ted joined his family outside but he was completely distracted.

What was going on in Thailand and how deep was Ellie into it? That's where Ted's thoughts stayed for the rest of the evening. The more he went over it in his head the more he felt there was only one way to get the answers he needed. Someone was going to have to go to Thailand to piece all this together. By the time everyone was gone and everything was all cleaned up from the evening Ted had decided he should be the one to go.

It was time to go to bed but he was beginning to get excited. He thought he should at least start to introduce the idea to Liza so she'd have some time to adjust to all the implications.

She was not impressed.

"What? Do you or I even know where Thailand is on a map? Well, you anyway? …Sorry."

But she was correct. Because of Vietnam he probably could pick it off a map, although he wasn't sure. But he was still pissed at what she said.

Liza may have quickly apologized for her words but that didn't stop her from continuing to shoot him down.

"You remember what happened to you in New Yor…"

"Wait a minute. What are you saying?" While he was speaking he realized Liza was actually giving him the opportunity he needed to gain her acceptance; whether she agreed or not.

"Liza, you're not talking to Kathy or Henry when they go into one of their lame 'you're not the boss of me' routines. You really don't get to have the final word when it comes to me. You might earn a lot more than I do but we each have important careers and I intend to succeed in mine just like you do in yours."

He stopped her dead, probably just as she was revving up for the battle. His words put her off balance. She stared at him. He figured he had her but they each were still angry and that left that discussion officially unsettled.

"Your friend, Ellie Stanton, appears to have been deeply involved in shipping some human body parts across the world. It's a big crime. In fact, looks like a big criminal enterprise she was involved in for some years, and it's probably what got her killed. So she's gone now and I suspect most of the answers we need are somewhere in Thailand. Tomorrow I'm going to set up meetings with all the brass for Monday. And also early next week I'll probably need to meet with the people at the hospital. I will find out how many federal and, maybe, international agencies I have to brief and work with. Whether I'm here or in Thailand I don't think you're going to see much of me for a while."

Liza had no response. They went to bed not speaking and didn't talk again until later in the day on Saturday, both clearly finally tiring of efforts required to avoid conversing.

Liza's tone was bland, but it was obvious she had thought about his plans. "If you travel to a place like that you are going to need some special immunizations. The sooner you get them the better. On Monday I'll stop by the travel clinic at the hospital and find out what's recommended."

Ted responded with a sharp, guttural "Thanks."

That was enough to convince Liza it was okay for her to add, "If Shawn Barry went with you the two of you could probably get more done quicker, don't you think?" It came out sounding more a plea and Ted took it that way.

"No, Shawn has plenty to work on here. No matter what happens over the next week or so we're going to put a lot more pressure on one of the troopers who must be a part of all this. If I go it will take some time to get it all organized, but I will have to go alone." He walked away, signaling the end of that immediate discussion and that some of his anger persisted. Liza had many thoughts but decided she didn't know exactly what she wanted to say so she said nothing.

Ted was going to Thailand…at least in his mind.

* * *

On Friday he arranged the meetings he needed. Mid-morning on Monday was set with Colonel Sawyer and other top echelon officers. Then early Monday afternoon he, Colonel Sawyer, and some officers would meet with hospital staff. Dr. Fowler, the hospital CEO, and lead legal counsel would come to Waterbury to be briefed on this major development. The CEO was difficult and insisted Ted call personally if this was so important. Over the phone Ted could only hint at the gravity of the problem. He found the man pompous and abrupt, more concerned about his busy schedule than being able to grasp a major problem had developed at his hospital. Ted tried to envision, with this man's attitude, how the hospital was going to handle the coming fallout.

Ted and Shawn spoke on Friday and through the weekend. He wanted Shawn at the meetings but he also wanted him to find out, for sure, names of Feds, US Customs and Border Protection agents, Treasury, and maybe even Interpol agency people they needed to contact. On Friday Shawn reminded Ted he had been working on some of that for a few weeks but hadn't gotten much. Ted gave him a look that served as a quick reminder of the problems he all but held Shawn responsible for at the beginning of the case.

Ted contacted Internal Affairs and a State's Attorney to arrange to meet on Tuesday to talk about initiating the process for internally making Corporal Davies a formal suspect in Ellie's murder or at least in the trafficking in human body parts. That way they could gain access to his banking and phone records and possibly a few other things. Ted envisioned a lengthy interrogation later in the week. He would try to go as far as they could without Davies having a lawyer present but that would have to be discussed. He might need a lawyer soon. Especially if there was a decision to place him on suspension and keep an eye on him.

Ted continued to consider the need for someone to go to Thailand. Why not him? He was getting more and more excited about the possibility. He said no more about that when he and Shawn spoke periodically over the weekend. They each were working on reviewing their research and making sure of their facts and suspicions so Ted had solid notes for all the pending meetings.

Later, Saturday night in the den when no one else was up, he pulled out a volume from their multi-volume 1980 edition of *The World Book Encyclopedia* and read all about that country. On Sunday he cut the grass and did as many chores as he could think of. Who knew? Soon he might be going away for a while.

* * *

THE BEST LAID PLAN

The Vallan family backed off over the weekend and on Monday morning. It was clear Ted was fully absorbed in his work. The kids thought his efforts at doing chores were only a way to take some breaks to divert his mind from all the work he was doing for his job. He was up early on Monday. Everyone was cordial but they left him alone. Even the kids wished him well when he left home for work.

As he drove Ted was actually more relaxed than anyone would have thought given the looming presumed intensity of his work for the next few days. He was thinking which meeting and at what point he should bring up the idea that someone from the force, in particular he, should go to Thailand to finally figure that part out? Ever so softly, but out loud, he hummed and then sang, "Goin' to Bangkok city, Bangkok City here I come."

* * *

The first meeting was set for ten. Shawn was supposed to meet Ted in his office around nine-fifteen for one final review of what they had and how Ted was going to present it. Shawn didn't show. Immediately displeased, Ted tried to go over his notes again for about five minutes but he was distracted and increasingly annoyed. He got up from his desk and walked the corridor to the large open room where Shawn, along with many others, had his desk. Ted was incredulous seeing Shawn sitting there on the phone. Shawn saw him. Ted shrugged and pantomimed a what gives? Shawn stayed on the phone but raised his other hand in a please wait signal. It was obvious he knew Ted was waiting for him. Ted returned to his office; angry.

This was a day for everything to go well. Certainly at least at the start. He was increasingly pissed as a few more minutes ticked by. Just as he began to get up again Shawn walked briskly around the corner into his office. His face warned Ted something was not right.

"Chief, I was just on the phone with an agent from Customs and Border Protection. I first talked to him about two weeks ago and he seemed to get it then about what we've been working on but he never got back to me. I called him again on Friday and told him this looked to be much bigger now and he just called this morning. Chief, if this guy is right in what he's telling me the whole case is changed."

Ted was instantly wound up tight. What was going on? While driving in he wondered how he could feel relaxed despite so many problems and challenges. Even just now as he was preparing for a slew of meetings he didn't know who killed Ellie Stanton and maybe others. And he still had no idea why anyone wanted to ship human pineal glands to Thailand. He felt a cold sweat. How could he have organized all this when he had such sparse evidence? It didn't take much for his confidence to fade.

As he waited for Shawn's apparent bombshell his mind reviewed the facts that motivated the last few days. Clearly it was all the evidence pointing to Ellie Stanton as the prime suspect and motivator in human parts trafficking. With her death the Thailand and trafficking part of the case could soon be lost without someone physically investigating that location before whoever else was involved could fade away from the scene.

With a sudden sense of resignation, Ted asked him: "Well, what do you have, Shawn?"

"This Agent Smith, from Customs and Border Protection, told me they checked with the Thailand Border Customs and Immigration Service and asked for records on both Doc Stanton and Corporal Davies. Well, we knew Davies was there with the Marines and Customs wouldn't keep track of that. But the years when Doc had to have passed through everyone had to get some form of visa; even a short-term tourist visa for a quick visit.

"But Chief, they have no record of an Eleanor Stanton with our doc's DOB, social, etc. ever being in Thailand."

Ted slumped down in his chair. His right cheek pulled to the right with a slight twitch; a not surprising reaction for Ted in a situation like this. What astonishing news!

"Now, Customs tells me Thailand has had leaky borders and sometimes not the most reliable records but only really dedicated or more masterful criminals would try to sneak in and out. Pretty unlikely for our Doc."

Shawn sat and looked down. Although this news wasn't terrible for the case, he knew it put a big dent in the scenarios they had worked on the past few days. The imminent meetings and plans were all based on Ellie Stanton being the prime mover and organizer of the whole business.

Ted's initial response was something of a surprise to Shawn. He spoke quietly, in a flat tone.

"No Shit." To his credit Ted showed he was willing to follow where his case led and try to move beyond mistakes or errors. Well, not entirely.

"So this probably changes just about everything we were planning for, at least in the meeting with the brass in a few minutes… And I need to think through if I… I mean anyone still needs to go to Thailand… That fucker Davies! He's really our man, isn't he? What a fucking bullshitter. That lyin' bastard. What a storyteller."

"Yeah. But you still think Doc must have been in on it, don't you?"

Ted wasn't sure what to think. "Of course. Somebody was responsible for the criminal activity in the morgue and that couldn't have been Davies. Davies and Morty Stern? Nah, I don't think that fits. No, Davies and Ellie Stanton both had to have a hand in that and that had to be what got her killed.

"Shawn, you need to work with all the agencies that connect with smuggling in Thailand. Tell them someone at that hospital is receiving those supplies and then taking those glands. I don't think they're for research. Make sure the stuff written on that brown wrapper gets to them. I aim to find out what that fuckin' stuff is for."

Ted started to put his papers in a folder and stand up to go to meet with his superiors. His story now was sure going to be different. Good thing he didn't make a fool of himself trying to sell his trip to Thailand.

* * *

The person who was disappointed the most was Ted but he got over it fairly quickly. The meeting with Colonel Sawyer and other high ranking officers went reasonably well except for one thing: Everyone, except maybe the Colonel, agreed with Ted Trooper Corporal Davies was now more highly implicated in the smuggling than ever before. His lying was catching up to him. But his involvement in Ellie Stanton's death remained no more than circumstantial. Just because he lied about Ellie and Thailand didn't have to mean he killed her. But his association with Ellie and probably some involvement with the still missing Trooper Devers definitely made him the one to go after hard now.

Everyone who was going to be at the Tuesday meeting to talk about Davies was still needed. That meeting took on greater urgency and importance now. Ted suggested bringing in Davies right away or at the latest after the Tuesday morning meeting. Colonel Sawyer, clearly thinking about the publicity that would be generated by his arrest, asked Ted to hold off until later in the week when he hoped there would be more evidence to make the arrest easier to explain.

By now Ted and the other officers sensed the Colonel was only trying to delay the inevitable.

The Monday afternoon meeting with the hospital people was probably not appreciably affected by the day's revelation. Human parts were being removed from bodies and smuggled out of the country. No matter who was the mastermind, someone or people in the morgue were involved and that was bad enough.

The hospital counsel got it quickly. The CEO and Dr. Fowler had a tougher time coming to grips with what the investigation of this crime was going to subject the hospital and local community to. It just kept getting worse and worse for them as Ted, Colonel Sawyer, and Captain Rondell quietly and patiently explained this case would continue to be investigated by the State Police but also a variety of federal agencies from the FBI to Customs and Border Protection would claim jurisdiction and become very involved. This would be a major criminal case. Finally the CEO began to get it. None of the police or the lawyer had a definite response to his nervous question about any possible impact of all this on the hospital's accreditation. That's when the CEO's and Dr. Fowler's mouths fell open and stayed that way. A bug could fly right in.

* * *

"Well why else would that Trooper have risked everything to get into Ellie's house to get those supplies." Liza was not asking a question.

"Exactly, babe. Without those glands we found the true story of the medical supplies shipments probably would have died with Ellie. But I didn't think he acted like he was too worried about going to her house. That worries me. And I allowed myself to assume Ellie was responsible for organizing most of that mess. I mean this guy couldn't have been getting those glands cut out of bodies. It had to be Ellie."

Ted started to get carried away. "Then we went away to D.C. and somehow I managed to forget about the supplies and why on earth that bastard was at her house."

"Drop that, Ted." Liza's face conveyed her displeasure. "Don't tell me one of the best times this family has ever had wasn't worth interrupting your investigation. In a few more years Kathy won't want to go anywhere with us. Baloney. Not buying that, Ted. So catch up if you think you fell behind. Maybe you spend your time in too many meetings…and dreaming about visiting exotic locales…by yourself."

It no longer took much for them to get on each other.

It was Monday evening. He did do a lot of meetings, didn't he? The burden of senior leadership. After her comments he decided not to tell Liza about the Tuesday meeting to plan the strategy for going after Corporal Davies. The Colonel was trying to get Ed Bradley, the state Attorney General, to come. If he wasn't going to be there Ted assumed a top aide would be sent.

Temporarily hampered by the Colonel's caution, he wanted Davies suspended, and maybe in custody, at least by the end of the week. Monday afternoon he told Shawn they had to go hard on Davies by Thursday afternoon or Friday at the latest. No more time to delay. But they also had to meet, personally, with a bunch of different federal and state agencies about the crime in the morgue and international smuggling. After dragging their heels for a few weeks now the feds wanted to talk about all of this…yesterday.

Ted still had ongoing responsibilities for other investigations his division was running. He smiled when he thought about the police detectives on television who always only seemed to have just one case at a time to solve.

* * *

ANY GOOD WAY OUT?

At first, finding out she was pregnant confused him. He thought he really did love her; as much as he might be able to love anyone. But after all that happened her pregnancy now seemed like it was a warning signaling his time in Vermont was near an end. Managing a family while forced to figure out how to stay free and alive was more than he could remotely imagine. Maybe if things hadn't turned out this way but that wasn't the case anymore. Increasingly, as he thought more about it he was repelled by her situation and, even many weeks later, her rejection of sex the last time they were together.

He was angry at himself for the direction all this was taking but he also had more than enough anger for her and the state policemen after him. He ruminated for days on what moves he could make to save himself. The most practical sounding solutions involved leaving the country again. But his ideas ranged wildly, even considering if he could plan the deaths of Troopers Vallan, Barry, and even Devers; preferably all three of them in one large incident that would free him from suspicion; suspicion for their deaths and even Ellie Stanton's. Nancy Devers' role and situation were very unclear to the force. They didn't know where she was; but he thought he did.

In a confrontation where everyone had a firearm, he reasoned, any number of violent and bloody endings were possible. He knew

Trooper Devers was good with weapons but suspected troopers like Vallan and Barry, who didn't know her, would assume otherwise. If he could wait until she returned and have her help him set them up he could make it appear as though all three of them died in a firefight. Would their deaths and his apparent absence from the scene with a well-planned alibi be enough to end the investigation into the ME's death? Was it a sign of his desperation that he tried to convince himself he could find a way to implicate Nancy in Doc Stanton's murder?

It was a scenario he wanted to believe could work but knew would be very difficult to accomplish. Disappearing, with as much of his money as he could quickly get from his accounts, was the more reasonable path. But it was also more discouraging, he thought, after all he had achieved since being back in Vermont. And any likelihood he would ever again be able to stop running or return to the US was minimal. A third world country made more sense. He sighed audibly. It had been such a long time; the thought of doing anything like that was almost overwhelming.

Now he regretted not killing the Lieutenant when he thought he had an easy opportunity at the Doc's house. Maybe there was still a way to get at those supplies locked up in Williston or Waterbury? That was where the evidence was that would, eventually, tie him, personally, to the case. If there was a way to have Doc Hananratin in Thailand disappear who else could implicate him besides Nancy? Fat chance; but maybe. Then he thought there still might be a way to work with the Doc if he re-located him…somewhere. So then he wasn't sure his death was necessary. He had so many different ideas he could barely focus his attention. But none were any good. He knew it.

He spent the better part of a weekend he was not on duty trying to think his way through all of this. If he didn't do something first, and soon, he was sure something was going to happen to him. Probably very soon. Would they think to look at the contents of the shipment? His efforts, at that moment, to find where Nancy was were failing. What happened to her and when would she be back? And the baby? Thinking about the baby reminded him she probably would never be of any use to him anyway.

The fewer good ideas he could imagine the angrier he became. He battled with conflicting feelings of satisfaction about killing Doc Stanton and despair it had come to that. He couldn't let Nancy refuse to help him. He became furious with Nancy for what she had done to him and now disappearing so he could not rely on using her in planning for his own salvation. She was a necessary sacrifice that had to be made. He would put more pressure on his contacts to find her and get her back to Vermont. He would use whatever money was required to have her returned. There was no possible scenario for him out of this without her.

Going down in a hail of bullets held no attraction for him. He had always been a survivor; someone who not only survived but excelled in disastrous situations when his life was on the line. Despite the time and intensity of his effort though, after days and days, he remained confused and uncertain. Somehow he was unable to see or sense a clear path for himself. That realization frightened him. And he knew without a plan he could believe in there was no telling how he would react when he came in contact with anyone who was a part of this. Especially now, could he control his magnetic attraction to sudden violence?

He returned to work on Monday but each night he lay on his bed in the dark and stared at the ceiling most of the night.

* * *

WEDNESDAY EVENING I

It was doubtful Ted Vallan could feel any more pressure to solve a case than he did for Ellie Stanton's homicide. But, somehow, the way Liza reacted to his investigation seemed to make it even more stressful for him. Liza almost always had an interest in Ted's bigger cases. But nothing like with Ellie. Practically every evening she queried him about the status of the case, often just as they were going to bed. It was like she expected a daily briefing. Whether she said or suggested something after Ted responded, or said nothing, it left Ted feeling he was constantly being pressed to succeed; to solve her murder as quickly as he could. It often didn't make for a restful journey to falling asleep.

And yet Liza had insisted and pushed him to take the vacation week. Life clearly went on for the Vallan household. It was what they both wanted for their family. But it didn't help their marital relationship, which showed some signs of fraying.

Ted had difficulty with subtle changes in Liza's personality. Changes he might have treasured in her, such as her relatively new found directness and concern about her appearance. Though likely reflecting continued maturation of her self-confidence some of the small differences actually worried him a little. Maybe it was just worry. Or maybe he was becoming envious. Now was a moment for him to perform and solve Ellie's homicide. He wasn't doing as well as he thought he should. At the same time Liza seemed to be succeeding just fine, morphing into someone more beautiful and impressive.

Ted had difficulty putting his feelings and reactions in a context he could understand. He sensed something was wrong with their relationship. Serious? Damaging? Hopefully not, but he just wasn't sure. They didn't really argue much or much more than they ever did. They did seem to openly challenge each other more recently. Or at least he thought she was challenging him a lot.

On Wednesday night two weeks after their vacation, despite how incredibly busy he was, Ted assumed the role of putative baby-sitter for Henry; something that really hadn't happened in years. Not since Liza was in training and had to be in the hospital all night and their nanny wasn't around. Liza was going to an awards dinner at the med school. Kathy was staying at a friend's so it was Henry and Ted for the evening.

The boys were assembling a dinner for themselves when Liza could be heard coming down the stairs. The moment and image of her arrival in the kitchen caught Ted and was fated to stay with him and affect him for a long time. She looked beautiful. She was all dressed up; even in heels. Make-up, perfume, really nice dress, and signs of obvious extra attention to her hair. She moved quickly around the kitchen, advising them on their effort, retaining her sense of being in charge. Ted felt uncomfortable.

He was uncertain if he could ever recall such a sudden, unexpected emotional reaction. He felt extraneous to her life. What was causing him to have a sinking feeling in his gut? Why such a sudden sense of loss? It didn't take long to figure his reaction out: He was jealous. Not an emotion he could recall in almost fifteen years since they first met and he wanted her all for himself.

Was Liza in some sort of relationship with another man? Was this a sign of the end of them as a couple? As a family? It fit and, of course, it didn't fit. But he couldn't shake his immediate sense of sadness. Was something happening? Had he missed something developing right under his eyes?

Still in a whirlwind, Liza grabbed her purse and started to leave. Ted wanted to say something, but he didn't know what to say. Not a moment to register his concern; certainly not any upset. No reason to express any suspicion.

"You look great!" Then he paused for an instant. "Don't be home too late, babe." He turned to the stove. 'What the fuck!'

* * *

WEDNESDAY EVENING II

The last time she had driven to this house in the woods she was a different person. Even after the tumult of the Doctor's death she hoped good things could still happen for them. This time, like in the past, although she was sure he was watching her come up his road he stayed inside the house. By the time she parked he must have been able to see it was her. He opened the door as she reached his deck.

"Sweets! Where the hell you been?" He was un-mistakably angry now even though she knew he was trying to act worried. She had no doubt he was very, very concerned about her by now. She wasn't sure how much he knew, or if he could understand what was happening even if he did get some of it. From what had been explained to her, and what she had figured out, if he knew he was probably the last to know, despite being the one who started it all.

Repeatedly trying to remind herself he never knew what he had done, since nobody really understood anything about all this until very recently, didn't assuage her hurt and anger. It was all too late now anyway. How much worse could things get?

"I'm glad to know you're okay but you never should have come here. Better to have called. The investigators and Internal Affairs still don't know anything for sure but they are making life difficult for a bunch of us. And I think they will soon figure out Thailand

and know I was a big part of setting up that donations front with the Doc."

She was so anxious in the moment she made no effort to try to evaluate the truth of his reaction to her showing up.

"They can't see you, at all or know you're back. They figured out you were pregnant and they're looking for you…"

She spoke for the first time.

"And so is my family. I haven't been able to do more than secretly let them know I'm alive. It's been terrible for them and me."

"I know, I know, sweets. What can I say? I thought I set you up in a good spot, near Pearl. Then nothing. I got nothing from you for weeks. Why did you do that Nancy? I mean you know you wanted that baby and I've been doing everything I could to make sure you're safe and comfortable. Then, suddenly, you disappeared. Hell, I've been a wreck."

"My money is gonna be going way down soon. The Thailand connection is too hot right now to even try to send over the fake extract I've made. Man, I thought that was going to be a great way to keep the money coming. The whole business was always a fake anyway. That gland shit was useless."

She could tell he was distracted while he spoke.

"Listen, let me move your car out there out of sight, okay? That a rental? We don't want anyone snooping on us. Gimme the keys, okay?"

"I'm not pregnant anymore. You never asked about the baby."

"Oh, right. I'm so sorry. I can see how upset you are. Okay, let me move your car and then we can get you something to drink and I want to hear everything."

The dogs barked away in their kennel. She flipped him her keys and he went out to her car. She was so despondent. Could he be planning to kill her? Would that really matter? She remembered his ability to become violent in a flash. He brutalized that Doc in a fury in such a short time. Then he was so apologetic to her, immediately making his case for why that had to happen. Of course she helped him get rid of her. She loved him. She was so surprised how he made his plans to dispose of Doc so quickly and cleverly, she thought. At the time she figured he knew more about that forest than anyone else. It was like long before he knew that spot would be a good place to put a body. Did he have other spots picked out in the woods?

All along during her long pilgrimage back to him she kept asking herself why she wanted to go back. But right now, sitting in his home, she realized it was her resolve that was being tested. How much anger and hate did she have? What he had done to them, intentionally or not, could never be fixed. Who cared how close the force was to catching him; or her. Why on earth should she care about them catching her? Could she ever go home again?

She stood up and walked to a closet in his bedroom where she knew he kept his service revolver. She had no idea he had again started to wear the small ankle holster around his left lower calf he used to wear in Thailand. The safety clicked off, she put his revolver in the pocket of the light jacket she was wearing. She certainly no longer looked at all pregnant. She looked thin and pale. And terribly sad.

He came back in the house. "Okay, that's done. Now let's talk in the kitchen. Tell me where the baby is and how that all went." He motioned to the coffee pot but she waved it away. He opened the fridge and brought small containers of milk and orange juice over with two glasses. Before he sat he looked at her. She felt like he was trying to look into her mind. They each had grim, unhappy expressions. He never kissed her. He did not return her keys to her.

"Or maybe you'd rather have something stronger? I mean if that's okay right after the baby, or whatever?"

She mouthed 'no'.

"So where is the baby? What is it, and how's he doing?"

Watching him closely, she sipped some juice. The past few weeks, in all her ruminations about coming here and confronting him, only in the last few minutes had she ever considered he might have plans for her also. For her to wind up on a forest floor and him to work some magic and move on was a terrifying thought for her. No matter what happened to her he must pay for what he did to them. But the words she had practiced came hard to her.

"You never told me the truth of why that Doc refused to continue to get you those glands, did you? You told me she said all kinds of things. Sure, you said she forced you to do things you hated. You said she wanted a bigger cut and she wanted you to stop seeing me. But she threatened you for a completely different reason, didn't she? She told you how you made her sick. And with all your anger and then killing her you never even thought that what happened to her could happen to me too, did you?"

She could see how quickly he stiffened when she spoke about this. He looked puzzled and tense. If this was to be the end, so be it. She decided he had never wondered if what happened to the Doc could probably also affect her.

He spoke earnestly. Was he unaware?

"Listen sweets, Doc treated me like shit. You know that. She had me do things to her I'd never dream of doing with you. You know that. She made me feel like a prostitute but we had to have that money so I had no choice. She never said anything about anybody being sick. I don't know what you're talking about. I figured she had an idea of pushing me out of the stuff we were doing. I wasn't sick and you weren't sick. What are you saying?

"Then she threatened me. She said I was going to pay. She was going to blow the whole thing wide open and we'd all be finished. Even her, she said. She said she didn't care anymore. Doc wasn't making any sense. Sweets we went over what happened a bunch of times. It was like in 'Nam; kill or be killed. Don't you get it?"

"No, don't you get it, you asshole?"

He pushed his chair back, astonished at the words she spoke.

"You killed all of us! The Doc, me, and our baby! You must carry that fucking disease and you infected us with that deadly bug. There's nothing they can do about it. It's gonna kill me slowly, but it killed the baby quickly."

His mouth dropped open. There was a good chance he still had no idea what she was talking about. But then his eyes quickly focused; on her. He understood whatever she was talking about didn't matter anymore. She watched his face and realized it was probably the first time he thought she might have come to harm him. She knew, from that moment, it would only be a short time until he exploded to try to ensure his survival.

Just before he upended the kitchen table to try to push it into her she pushed her chair back and reached for the revolver in her pocket. He grabbed the pistol on his leg and shot right through the upended table, which stayed standing on edge. Her left arm burned with a searing pain. It didn't hurt nearly as much as she always assumed it would hurt to be shot. Maybe by this point she was numb to pain. He didn't wait to see the effect of the shot. He bolted from his chair, turned his back to her, and reached for a knife in the dish drainer. She wondered why he would want to stab her instead of continuing to shoot?

She stood and fully extended her right arm. She, also, only squeezed off one round. It was aimed at the top of his neck. He was probably dead by the time he hit the floor. She thought it fortunate he fell backwards and was face up when she walked the few steps to where he lay, placed the barrel of his pistol in his mouth, and pulled off a second round.

She was a trooper. She knew all about weapons and had always handled them well. She took some pride in cleaning up the scene to make it appear a self-inflicted gunshot wound while he was standing at the kitchen window. His entire head was a mess. She took her time and thought through what they would look for in the room. Best not to move him. She had thought she didn't care if she was caught but now she felt a flush and a kind of perverse pleasure trying to construct the scene to suggest a suicide. Many little details passed through her mind and she tried to attend to them.

Her own wound was in her upper arm. Superficial. A dish towel served well as a bandage and tourniquet. It wasn't bleeding much and she made sure there was no dripping from the wound. Obviously no artery had been pierced, but she had no idea if a bullet from the small caliber weapon was in her arm.

One bullet was placed in his revolver and then it was wiped, briefly held against his fingers, and carefully placed on the floor near his right hand. She wiped his small 9mm pistol and placed it back in his leg holster. The table was put upright and covered, and most broken glass and juice was cleaned up. She decided to leave some glass and, of course, the spilled milk. She took her time, moving slowly and deliberately. She never looked at him again.

Proceeding from room to room she made sure there was no hint of her presence. Over two thousand dollars was in an old boot in the back of his closet where she knew he kept his cash and she took it. On her way out she paused, took one last look around the kitchen, and exited through the back door. The keys were in her car. The dogs, in their kennel, continued to bark from the time of the initial gun shots.

She drove to a motel in Burlington. The following morning, with the cash, she bought a plane ticket to Tucson, Arizona. It was time to go home.

* * *

DEATH BY BUREAUACRACY?

"Oh shit!" A pause for about five seconds. "Damn! Look, I want the whole team out there right away. Immediately. Make sure they do the entire outside quickly; before it rains. Listen Shawn, get that going and then call on the radio so we can go over this. I'm leaving now. Exactly where is his house?"

It was almost noon on Thursday when Shawn first called him. Ted was in Rutland. Shawn had just heard from Corporal John Davies' unit commander that Davies' body was found by a trooper after Davies didn't show for his shift that morning. When he saw the body through a window the trooper broke in to be sure he was dead. Barry was told it looked like suicide.

Ted excused himself from his meeting and put his lights on as soon as his cruiser was on a main road. He was really upset. Davies was his prime suspect. He was close to arresting him. Ted assumed Davies knew that so suicide would not be out of the question. Ever since Davies appeared to be tied to the growing Thailand connection in the case his likely involvement became much greater than just the fact he, like others, had a sexual relationship with Ellie.

Suicide. From what he was learning about Davies it didn't strike Ted as something a person like Davies would do. And Ted had convinced himself if Davies killed Ellie, and probably the pathology assistant also, he must have had some help getting Ellie's body to where they found it. Even the open path he and Shawn found was unlikely to be traversed by one man with a body; most likely in the dark.

The missing female trooper, Nancy Devers, like several others, was at least connected to the Thailand donations and going over her months before disappearing John Davies' name had come up several times. Liza was right, Devers must have been pregnant; possibly by Davies. Where was she? Was she dead or alive?

"So Shawn, tell me what you know, from the beginning."

"Right, Chief. Well, as you know, this Davies, other than being a little temperamental, has had a great record on the force. So his division commander told me he was always where he was supposed to be, whenever he was supposed to be there. Never late or anything. Always let dispatch know where he was when he was working. Well no word from him today so they sent the trooper to check out his house, which apparently is pretty isolated in the woods; almost off the grid.

"That's really it. I'm about five minutes away. No rain yet. His commander said his trooper told him back of the guy's head looks like it was almost blown off. Must've had the barrel in his mouth."

"Shawn, I'm really concerned about this guy's property. Out there in the woods, so isolated. I keep tying that missing lady trooper, Devers, to this guy. We need to check that property out; even follow any paths or trails into the woods for some distance."

"Yeah, I get it Chief. But man, that sounds creepy."

'Creepy?' Ted thought. Everything they were learning about this case was creepy. If Ted confirmed a few more details of his suspicions about John Davies' personality the guy might rival Norman, whatever his last name was, in *Psycho*. Corporal Davies was considered a model citizen for his hospital support program in Thailand while he intentionally made sure his own years in Thailand were a fog. His ability and aggressiveness as a killer in the war were well documented. What Ted was finding out made Davies sound like two different people; and that was scary.

Ted decided he had another reason to dislike John Davies. Davies got praise and some publicity for his Thailand charity work. Ted hadn't figured it all out yet but he knew there was plenty wrong with it. At the same time he had struggled through coaching Henry's little league team this summer and virtually nobody knew about it or offered anything like praise. Indeed, doing that coaching he felt his ability to do his job the way he needed was compromised. His coaching and his team were shitty. The idea it was community service was, to Ted, either a joke or that meant it was more like a punishment.

* * *

The dirt road leading to Corporal Trooper Davies' small house from the county road was dotted with cruisers pulled off to either side leaving only a narrow path for Ted's cruiser to slowly navigate its way to the house. The mobile crime lab was parked in front. Shortly after Ted arrived the new State Police morgue vehicle carefully made its way up the road. No rain yet.

Ted stayed outside even though all the talk was about the gruesome scene in the kitchen. He insisted the area around the property be carefully searched while it was still daylight and nothing was washed away by the impending rain. The Corporal's cruiser and his truck were in the back of the house. It was immediately obvious to the crime team there were tire tracks from another vehicle that appeared to end at a small open area between the door-less garage and the thick forest.

All that could be said about the tracks were they likely dated to within the last four days, since there had been a drenching rain in the area five days before. The tracks were also from smallish tires, probably a smaller sedan. Ted was very worried this was a significant finding and asked everyone at the scene to form a circle around the house and slowly walk away from the house, straight ahead, as close to about one hundred yards as possible. Everyone there knew what he was looking for: hard evidence like a weapon or even small pieces of clothing or signs of a struggle through the woods; or anything dragged.

They knew to look for any indication of disruption of the ground or a mound that could hold a body; or whatever. Any trail was to be marked for future further investigation. When Ted reached about a hundred yards he blew a whistle and everyone moved, laterally, about five yards to the right and turned around and walked back towards the house. That maneuver, stepping laterally again a few yards and walking away and then back to the house, was repeated one more time and the group re-assembled in the front of the house.

Nothing definite turned up. Davies' cruiser was next to the back door. His truck sat in the garage and ten yards away was a clearing with a steel drum used to burn solid refuse…and who knew what else. Ted spoke to the crime lab's superior and the team was divided into groups. The garage and shed and burn area were to be searched. First a tarp was constructed well over the boundaries of the burn pit to protect it from the threatening rain. Others would search the house. Most of the lab technicians were assigned to the kitchen, where the body was, and one senior tech to the burn pit. Examining that pit was critical to Ted and he made sure a really skilled tech had that responsibility. The two remaining crime team members were tasked with the rest of the house and the small crawl space under part of it.

Shawn followed Ted into the kitchen through the back door. Trooper Davies lay on the floor between the kitchen table and the sink and counter. Davies' contorted position was typical only for a lifeless body that had gone down in a heap to the ground. Blood and brain and bone were splattered over a notable area but mostly below counter level. Ted crouched down and looked at the dead Trooper. The crime lab team members moved back to let him survey the body and the scene.

"You know, Shawn, our job is to look at what we have here. We have plenty of time to consider what looks obvious; in this case suicide. But I want to consider as many other possibilities we can dream up that might explain this scene. That way we're less likely to miss something we need to find. So I'm telling everyone this Trooper was murdered. Tell me if you can find evidence of that."

The back of Corporal Davies' head was practically blown off from a bullet that presumably came from his service revolver. Most reliably if the barrel was in his mouth. But there were signs everywhere that complicated any simple assumption the Corporal was responsible for his own death.

Corporal Davies' revolver was on the floor, close to his right hand. There was a small accumulation of blood at the side of the tip of the barrel. Fingerprints were on the handle but they were not aligned and were smudged. A technician called to Ted to show him it was likely the handle had been wiped before the few prints that were present got there. Eventually, when the Trooper's body was re-positioned the small bulge in his pants from his ankle holster was noticed.

There was no obvious explanation for finding the ankle holster pistol handle had been completely wiped also. Like his service revolver, the pistol it contained had obviously been recently fired and one bullet was missing from the magazine. With that information, once again, there was an exhaustive search for any sign of a bullet or bullet hole in the kitchen, other than the area behind the position of the body. No bullet had been found there. A plastic tablecloth on the kitchen table was removed and a bullet hole in the table was readily apparent. Where the table was when the shot was fired and the trajectory the projectile traversed were not immediately clear.

Ted asked Shawn what was clear from finding Davies wore a leg holster. Other than in undercover situations it was unusual for a trooper to carry hidden armor.

"Well, I guess, like we suspect, Davies may have been involved in some unorthodox activities to feel the need to carry like that. And we can presume there may have been some kind of recent fight or altercation if both the revolver and the pistol were fired. That complicates drawing conclusions from this scene."

Ted continued to look at Shawn, implying he was waiting for more. But Shawn looked puzzled and barely shrugged his shoulders, indicating that was all he had.

"Shawn, look at the leg he wears his holster on. It's on his left ankle and the revolver is near his right hand. The location of the holster means he was left handed. The feel of Walther P5 compacts have also given them the reputation of being best suited for lefties."

Simple suicide was appearing less likely. After the death some housecleaning and alteration of the scene had taken place. Those efforts really disturbed Ted and Shawn. However incompletely the crime scene had been adjusted the idea whoever tried to do it had a professional criminology background had to be considered. Ted had been worried Trooper Devers' body might be in this neighborhood but now he began to wonder if she wasn't dead and instead she, or a third trooper or law officer of some type, might be involved in what took place in that kitchen.

Shawn Barry had a sick feeling as he found himself constructing any scenario where Trooper Davies was restricted, but alive, and had the barrel of a pistol placed in his mouth and then fired. In some ways no less brutal than the mangling of Dr. Stanton.

* * *

"What'd you got, Benoit?" Corporal Arnold Benoit had walked into the kitchen. He and another trooper had been tasked with examining the interior of the home other than the kitchen.

"Lieutenant, there wasn't too much on first go through except for what we found in a piece of furniture. In a spare bedroom he has a night table with a fake bottom in the drawer. Pretty easy to find. Two bank books and two bank statements from two other banks. Very substantial amounts, especially for cops like us, or really even anyone; especially the one in Honolulu. You should look at the statement. It's recent and there are a bunch of small withdrawals along with two transfers totaling almost $10,000 to local banks. Looks like there were no deposits into the Hawaii account for that month. The Hawaiian bank statement doesn't have his name on it; says 'Experienced Import/Export Company, LTD'. Wonder where the money for that account came from?"

Ted was hard at work on the Thailand connection, but he couldn't explain why small cash withdrawals were being made in Honolulu.

"Yeah, I'm not completely surprised by that from what we're working on, Benoit. Anything else, so far?"

"He didn't lock his revolver up. We found his belt in his closet, with most of the usual gear attached. On his dresser he had a pile of change, a pocket knife and a key ring with six keys on it. We'll have to check them out but one is obviously to his cruiser and two or three might be house keys. Don't know about the others. Harry says his wallet is still on his body. You decide when that and whatever's in his pockets should be pulled and checked."

"No cash anywhere?"

"Not yet."

Given the way the bank statements indicated some large amounts of money were going in and out of his local accounts Ted was surprised. Davies was getting wire transfers from a bank in Honolulu, but Ted had no idea how that was happening.

* * *

This was terribly difficult for Ted. He wanted to blame everything on Colonel Sawyer but it was more than just him. He kicked himself for being so close to getting Davies yet had to admit he had been taking his time. Too much time lining up all the parts he needed to be sure of success with his next interrogation. Now Davies was dead. And, of course, his focus on going to Thailand may have been a delaying distraction also.

Everything was important and there still was so much to figure out. He had just lost his main suspect, making the entire case more fragile again. Then again, really just how close over the last weeks was he or wasn't he to solidly implicating Davies in the dealings in Thailand and any real connection to Ellie's murder? He was getting there but it certainly hadn't all fallen together before his murder. And even now he had no hard evidence Davies killed the ME. But he had to be involved; just seemed certain. Who killed Davies? Ellie's killer? The probable killer of Morty Stern and Trooper Devers? Was Davies the missing link tying them together?

Ted stayed kneeling next to the body. Out loud, but to no one, "Shit!" He continued to try to make sense out of what he thought he knew.

Ellie and Davies were in some kind of business together. And they had sex, possibly more frequently or at least over a longer period than Ellie did with most of her partners. Morty Stern probably had something to do with helping get those glands, whatever they were being used for, and he probably paid a big price when whatever went wrong turned the whole thing sour. But where did Trooper Devers fit into all this?

Before he was killed Davies had steadfastly denied anything more than having occasional sex with Ellie, just like the others. He, of course, admitted knowing Trooper Devers since they were at the same station. But that basically was all he had admitted. He went to New Hampshire with her to help her buy a used car. If that was all that wasn't fraternizing.

Phone records were sparse for all of them. Nothing at all notable for Morty Stern or Trooper Devers. And exactly two calls from Ellie to Corporal Davies at his barracks in the prior six months. Although the most recent was probably only a day before she disappeared. The Corporal insisted both those calls were to ask him to make sure all supplies got to her very soon as she was getting ready to send a shipment.

Finally, the rain began. The driveway slowly turned into mud puddles as vehicles came and went. There was still a lot to do when the senior tech who was working on the burn area ran from the cover of the tarp to the kitchen. Ted looked up from where he was kneeling next to the body.

"So what do you think, Jenkins? Anything worth taking back to study?"

"Well, Lieutenant, it's been an active site; proly burned a good amount of his trash there on a regular basis. Might say the drum looks like it was really heated super-hot at some time; maybe pretty recently. I took some crust off the inside for testing in the lab. Bet a good chance there's been an extra accelerant used. So I sifted through the bottom but the residual is pretty fine stuff. Possibly burned and re-burned, you know."

"A body fed into that barrel?"

"Well, I doubt it, sir. But good chance we'll never know for sure. We'll take the ashes, do some tests, and put some under the scope and see if that tells us anything. No, Lieutenant, not much in there now. Maybe the only stuff we found are a bunch of badly burned and partially melted brass grommets."

"How many did you find, Jenkins?"

Jenkins gave Ted a puzzled look.

"Seven, sir."

"Well then there were probably eight originally."

Shawn Barry was following the conversation and now wrinkled his forehead trying to figure out why Ted said that. Ted glanced at him.

"Standard issue in the trunk of every cruiser is a six by nine canvas tarpaulin with eight brass grommets for anchoring. Has anyone cataloged the things in his cruiser? The trunk?"

* * *

POST TIME...AGAIN

After the debacle of Ellie Stanton's first autopsy Doc Fowler tried to refuse to do virtually any forensic posts for complex cases and absolutely declined to complete the one capital case that summer before John Davies' death. But he did work diligently to find a replacement for Ellie. He developed a good relationship with Dr. Agarwal from New York City and Dr. Agarwal made an effort to encourage someone from the pool of young forensic pathologists he was training and working with in the city to consider becoming the ME in Vermont.

With little warning or apparent choice Dr. Samir Balasubramanian was gently pushed by Dr. Agarwal to go to Burlington to complete a forensic autopsy toward the end of July. The case was an accidental death of a construction worker who was crushed by heavy machinery. The post was straightforward and 'Dr. Sam', as he instructed everyone to call him, managed it very well and appeared to be very efficient. Notably, he and Sarah Perdy worked extremely well together. She became an immediate booster and, more importantly, after that first post tried to encourage 'Dr. Sam' to seriously consider a permanent move to Burlington. They each were both super organized and very efficient, two traits that were never applied to Ellie Stanton.

Dr. Sam was in his early forties. Most all FMGs (foreign medical grads) were older even though still in or recently finished with U.S.

training because they had to complete residencies at home before becoming eligible to do often the same residency here in the US. So, depending on how you wanted to look at it, new docs like Dr. Sam often already had significant experience in their fields. He had a youthful appearance and was quite thin. He moved around a lot, appearing almost hyperactive. He talked as much about his love of soccer as he did about his young family in the city.

Doc Fowler did not intend to be very choosey about the next ME but he did, actually, take an immediate liking to Samir, as most everyone who met the man did. Judging his forensic skills, however, in the best of settings, would require monitoring his abilities over several cases. Fowler wasn't sure he had that luxury. He figured Samir actually as a potential star and he knew he was considering positions at several other places. Medical Examiners were increasingly difficult to find. Attracting a new one to such a small state as Vermont was appearing to Fowler an almost insurmountable task.

On his two previous visits to Burlington before the post of John Davies Dr. Fowler took Dr. Sam to the solitary Indian restaurant in the state which, fortunately, was in Burlington. For the second visit he wished he could have had a fake menu made up with a different name for the restaurant to try to have Dr. Sam think the city was filled with Indian restaurants. Dr. Sam made a point of praising his vegetarian meals at the restaurant.

It was very rushed and organized at the last minute but Dr. Fowler pressed Samir to bring his wife and two children with him for the post of John Davies. He arranged to have staff available so it could be done that weekend. The pathology department quickly arranged a dinner for the family at the vice-chair's home on Friday and Fowler pushed Liza Vallan to have the family for dinner the next day.

The Vallan family was not especially social but Liza thought they could do it. Samir's boy and girl were only slightly younger than Kathy and Henry and his wife was a pediatrician. Initially Ted thought it would be awkward but he recognized the absence of a true forensic pathologist in Vermont was a major disaster and anything he and his family could do to help resolve that was worth a shot. And who knew that Henry, a pretty poor baseball player, would show natural talent at soccer? Besides, solving every aspect of the death of Ellie Stanton remained foremost in his mind.

Liza correctly assumed quality of life in Vermont should be pushed as a major selling point for the young family. The major drawback of Vermont for a professional was the relatively small volume of ME cases. And Vermont's Indian population was laughably tiny.

* * *

Arriving at the morgue Saturday morning around nine Ted was surprised to see Dr. Sam already sitting at Ellie's desk engrossed in reports. He was making notes in ink on a pad next to him. A lefty, like Ted, Dr. Sam, had requested someone from the investigating team be at the post. Ted planned to be there anyway as soon as he heard when the Doc was coming to do it.

Liza had the more difficult task for the day. She was going to meet Dr. Sam's wife, Sujatha, just after midday to show her and their kids around Burlington and, since she was a doctor, the hospital also. Kathy, the budding matron-in-training went along but Henry went to a friend's. After showing them around Liza would bring all of them to the Vallan home for dinner, which she had put a lot of planning into.

So she had the more challenging schedule. Ted was to bring Dr. Sam home whenever he finished his work. If there was time Ted figured they could drive the area a little. Later there was some free time but Dr. Sam opted for going to the Vallan home and running around with the kids with a soccer ball. Henry's ball handling was an eye-opener to everyone.

"Really glad you could come Lieutenant. I…"

Please, Dr. Sam, Ted."

"Sure. Call me Sam, okay?" Ted nodded in agreement.

"You know Ted, during training in the city, there were times when the forensic residents had to go to the scene of an accident or crime. I almost always felt I did better work when I did that. It's really hard, for me anyway, to just look at a body and comfortably put all the pieces together. You know what I mean?"

One thing Ellie Stanton never did, for all her interest in physical activity, was leave the morgue to visit a crime scene. Ted often wished she had.

"I think that's a great idea. Often thought that made sense, but it just didn't happen since I've been around."

Dr. Sam and Ted were both wearing plaid shirts, jeans and each had a type of boat shoe on. The similarity was not lost on Ted.

"So Ted, please tell me anything and everything you think I need to know, or even might want to know, about the man we're about to post. You know, what I like to do is go into the prosection with as clear an idea as possible of what the most likely cause of death is and then I figure it's my job to consider as many other possibilities as I can think of and see what I find."

Ted was startled. If Shawn Barry had been there he would have done a double-take hearing Dr. Sam essentially repeat what Ted told him at the Davies crime scene.

"Sam, if you come here and ever want to check out any crime scene with me or any other member of the force, anywhere in Vermont, I will make sure you are picked up by a trooper and brought to the scene then back here or your home anytime you want. Just let the major crime staff know. Anytime. I mean it."

Sam looked up from his chair and smiled. "Thanks Ted."

"Before you really get going Sam can I ask you a question that's been nagging at me for some time that I think is more important now that we have John Davies' body here?"

Sam nodded for him to go ahead.

"Well the second post suggested that Dr. Stanton had some semen in her behind. We have some of that somewhere. Is there any chance that stuff can be checked to see if it could be linked to someone like this Davies?"

"Sure. Well we can do some things to determine his blood type factors and, hopefully, have enough of that seminal fluid to test that for the same things. If there's a match it narrows down the likelihood they're from the same person. Especially if the antigens happen to be less frequently seen types. So it can never be completely specific to one person but it can be a helpful addition impacting on suspicion. Of course, if the blood typing isn't a match then that means a lot also. I've read a few things recently about someday maybe being able to do some very specific genetic tests on biologic materials. But that's not something we can do here yet."

* * *

SAVING A LIFE IN THE MORGUE

Ted and Sam stood, preparing to walk across the hall to the autopsy suite to do the post. Standing at the open door was Sarah Perdy with some sort of file folder tucked between her elbow and her body. She looked apprehensive.

"Doctor, before you start I have to talk to you about something."

She looked directly at Sam. He motioned her into the office and glanced at Ted, implying to Ted he wanted him to stay. She closed the door behind her and all three sat. As she began to speak it was obvious she was fighting back tears. She had never impressed Ted as an emotional person.

"Doctor I can't let you do this examination until I talk with you." Ted and Sam were startled at her intonation and the gravity of her words. Where was this going to go?

"Please bear with me and let me tell you something very important." Some tears formed. She battled to maintain her composure. "I've done a terrible thing and I feel so bad. It's just awful. I can't really explain why I did it…I…"

She spoke slowly, with her head down. She was embarrassed.

"I guess, in a way, I loved Dr. Stanton. Sometimes she let me talk with her like a mother would.

"I knew; I guess a lot of people knew, she had this wild streak; maybe crazy. So she did things not a lot of women do, I don't think. Certainly not a doctor. I mean she was a wonderful person and cared so much about me and the others on the staff. But she was also devoted to living a life that I think was very different from most people. In many ways she kept so much to herself. Even if I couldn't understand why she was that way I guess I felt I wanted to try to help protect her any way I could."

Now her tears came more freely and she had to stop and use a tissue in her hand. Sam was dumbfounded and his face displayed a puzzled look. Ted had been present at many confessions and recognized something was about to come. From what he surmised about Ms. Perdy's personality he assumed it was less likely to be only a small fine point about some ME office procedure. Probably more likely a bombshell. Her presentation had all the earmarks of a major confession. She looked like she was about to fall apart. Ted knew he could have a role in reassuring her confessing was the right thing to do. His empathy and direction helped. Sam got her some water.

Dabbing under her eyes she regained some composure.

"Over the last few years I became aware that occasionally Dr. Stanton submitted laboratory tests to the lab with fictitious patient names. After a while It was pretty clear to me the tests were hers. I don't know how they were collected but I'm sure the samples were from her. Sometimes it was a fake name and medical record number and, infrequently, she used a name from an ME case.

"I'm so sorry… She didn't know it but sometimes I helped her if I received a call from the lab or a query from billing or whoever. I helped make it seem like it was all okay." She looked up and wanted to make a strong point. "I never opened any of the lab envelopes addressed to her. Even if she was away. I never said a word to her or anybody in this office about those envelopes. I never knew what lab tests or results were in them.

"Then, about a week before she died, I mean was killed, something happened that had never come up before." Ms. Perdy clasped her hands and looked down; tears began again. "I just didn't know what it really meant. I mean I'd heard about it but I didn't understand how dangerous it is. And I guess, then anyway, I thought mostly about Ellie; I mean Dr. Stanton. Although I didn't even really know what it meant for her. Since then I've tried to learn some more about it. I understand my terrible error now. I don't want anyone else to be harmed."

This was becoming a long confession. Sam was getting a little jumpy in his chair. It was probably about as long a period as a pathologist, especially a hyperactive one, ever sat and listened to a live person talk about what seemed to be a non-medical topic. He wanted to get started on his autopsy. Ted was used to hearing all kinds of confessions and, more than ever, at this point in Ms. Perdy's story he felt patience was required.

"Sarah, what was different this time?"

"Hillary Freeman is the chief tech in microbiology. We've been friends for years. She was in my office for something; I don't remember what. We were chatting. Then she said 'wasn't that something about that recent ME case who had HIV?' Before I could put it all together she said at least the man was dead and wouldn't have to worry about a slow terrible death from AIDS. Then she asked if our office had notified the state like Dr. Stanton said we would when Hillary had been to her office and told her the results the day before? I told Hillary we were taking care of it."

Ms. Perdy now had everyone's rapt attention again.

"Doctor I didn't say anything when Dr. Fowler or the other two pathologists did their posts. I never said anything to our assistants. It's terrible, just terrible; I know that now." She sniffled and dabbed and mustered strength to finish her statement.

"I know this dead Trooper was having relations with Dr. Stanton. I think he and some others have been on Lieutenant Vallan's lists for a while. I don't know if this Trooper could have caught that virus from relations with Dr. Stanton but from what I've read it could be possible. I don't know what that would mean for doing her post or his post but whoever comes in contact with her or this Trooper should have known about this.

"I'm awfully sorry. I should never have kept this a secret after she died. Dr. Sam, you seem like the best thing that has happened to this office in a very long time. And you have a family. You have a right to know this and take whatever precautions are necessary for this."

With that she placed the folder, obviously containing Ellie Stanton's HIV test, on the desk.

"Do you want me to stay to answer questions or may I leave? I've told my sister I've done something very wrong and she's waiting for me. We live together."

Ted quickly asked Ms. Perdy a series of questions about what she knew but mostly stressed to her he understood the dilemma she felt about Ellie's behavior. He told her he and Liza also cared, very much, for Ellie and he wanted Ms. Perdy to try to relax and let some time pass. He praised her confession, telling her it took great courage and was definitely the right thing to do. He saw no reason to think she was so upset she might harm herself. He gave her his card and re-assured her and sent her home. When she left the room Sam spoke up.

"Double gloves, a gown, eye protection, and masks, Ted. From what we know right now that's about it. Don't want to get any of this guy's blood or secretions mixed with ours." And he went off to do the post with a surprised and thoughtful Ted trailing him.

* * *

A BLOODY MESS AND NOT MUCH ELSE

Before beginning the actual procedure Dr. Sam palpated and marked an area over the Trooper's left chest with his double gloved hand and then took a large glass syringe with a huge needle from the diener. With some force he plunged the syringe between the ribs he had demarcated and pulled up on the plunger filling the syringe with dark blood from the Trooper's heart. The diener carefully took the syringe and filled appropriate lab tubes that would be tested for HIV and associated studies, plus blood typing and toxicology analysis.

What was left of the Trooper's head loomed over the post. Dr. Sam decided to start with his thorax. He worked rather quickly with the diener through the examination of Davies' chest, torso and then extremities. Ted sensed a nervous energy as Dr. Sam worked away, somehow moving about the table doing a million things seemingly at once. His mode of work was vastly different than the slow, deliberate process he had become used to with Ellie's posts. Dr. Sam was almost frenetic in his activity but he also was clearly intensely focused on what he was doing. There was little reason to expect significant findings anywhere but the head in a fortyish trooper who was presumed to be in otherwise good health.

There was a change in the way he worked when it became time to examine what was left of Trooper Davies' skull and brain. Dr. Sam darted back and forth to and from the body on the table. He picked up and exchanged various probes and tools, inserting or measuring within the blood-soaked matter. He stood or then sat on a stool with rollers so he could work at the back of his head and then slide away to stand again. Periodically he stepped back and observed the body a few moments then moved to it again. It reminded Ted of an artist moving around, trying to perfect the object of his sublime creation.

But this was a dead body. Instead of creating, the dance of the medical examiner was designed to determine the cause of its misshapen appearance. Ted felt he had pretty solid suggestive evidence the Trooper had not blown his own head apart. But it was difficult to think, even for a minute, there was any way anyone could prove the trauma to this man was caused by anything other than a bullet fired from in his mouth.

Finally, Dr. Sam stepped back and stopped moving. He asked Ted to come closer.

"With most of his posterior skull blown away it was no small challenge to figure out why the extent of disturbed brain also involved some of the frontal regions."

He asked his assistant to move the voice-activated dictating microphone to almost over the body's head. The pathologist then started describing various landmarks and findings and, using a thin probe, showed Ted what he found.

"The trajectory of a probable 45 caliber bullet, such as found in service revolvers used by the Vermont State Police, has a limited path that can be delineated with a probe, traversing from beginning about twenty degrees above the hard palate. The bullet exited with most of the posterior brain structures and skull. That suggested bullet path is an unlikely explanation for extensive but more focal damage to more anterior structures, especially including the left eye socket, which was destroyed.

"Probing posteriorly near the base of the neck there is small channel that ends after only a centimeter or so. But if the probe in that path is pushed further into the destroyed region and slowly manipulated ahead by very carefully moving it back and then forward when another small channel can be found there is a path that extends to the left posterior eye region. This is where a second bullet, probably the same caliber, is either lodged or exited. The two bullets will need to be found to find out if they came from the same revolver. One may be behind the eye. The posterior neck entrance wound has no powder marks so it was fired into the back of his neck from at least a few feet away. A 9mm cartridge is a less likely alternative.

"Either bullet would have killed the victim instantly. Therefore, this death cannot be a suicide unless the posterior neck wound occurred after he shot himself in the mouth. That really cannot be considered. Even entertaining that possibility, the more frontal brain and skull findings would not have been localized; an impossibility after all the initial posterior contents and skull destruction.

"Therefore, that sequence is all but impossible given these findings." He walked away from the microphone. "Ted, since no bullets were found at the scene there is a good chance at least a fragment of one will show up on x-ray in his eye-socket region."

Ted visualized the possibility of the event in the Trooper's kitchen involving two revolvers, beside the 9 mm. The origin of the one used to shoot Davies in the back of his head was the one he was most interested in. The weapon of another trooper or, at least another law officer, was his guess. Trooper Devers? Or…was it Davies' service weapon used in both locations?

Dr. Sam's conjecture was confirmed on a subsequent x-ray.

* * *

For Ted Vallan the pieces of this terrible case were coming together rapidly now. Corporal Davies' autopsy was critical but Ted had expected Sam was, in some way, going to confirm the Trooper was murdered. He also now expected this terrible disease, AIDS, probably was playing a role in this case. Sam said testing the Corporal was still possible.

He had mostly given up on ever finding Morty Stern, who he still suspected was long since dead. But now he felt finding Trooper Devers, dead or alive was very important. Where was she? What was her relationship to Trooper Davies or, less likely, to one of the other troopers?

Trooper Devers probably didn't know Ellie except through helping her and Davies' supposed hospital charity work. But how much more of a relationship did she have with Davies? The other female trooper impressed him and Shawn as purely helping with the charity. They needed to speak with Devers.

Ted called Shawn and told him he wanted to meet on Sunday and talk more about what they had and might get from Devers…if they could find her. He still had some suspicion she may have been dead for weeks; a very unpleasant thought. Beyond Davies and Devers he had no good ideas. Maybe even that connection was shaky now.

* * *

After the post was completed and Sam cleaned up Ted offered him a tour of the area. But Sam was tired and suggested they go to Ted's house. Kicking a soccer ball around apparently was his idea of relaxing. Ted was sure one of the neighbors would have a ball. Sam's wife had picked up their rental car and followed Liza to Richmond so Sam jumped in the cruiser with Ted. As they were leaving the hospital parking lot Ted remembered a question.

"Oh nuts! Damn! During the autopsy I meant to ask you to show me where the pineal gland is."

"Oh well, not today anyway."

Ted looked confused.

"Your Trooper didn't have one."

Ted thought he had been told everyone had one.

"Your Trooper's pineal was blown to bits with most of the rest of his brain from the two bullets that hit him from different directions."

* * *

CAN MISSING PIECES BE EXPLANATIONS?

Ted wondered how much Liza knew about HIV/AIDS. Ted liked Sam. He knew the evening ahead was planned to be strictly social but he really wanted to learn more about all that and get some ideas about how that might impact this case.

It was late in the afternoon when they arrived home. Henry knew exactly where to find a soccer ball to borrow and Sam and the two boys were out in the back yard shortly after having some lemonade and Liza and Ted made a quick sweep for any dog poop. The neighbor's kid who had the ball came over and after just kicking it around for a while it became two against two. Ted sat on the porch with the ladies and watched.

Sam was a skilled wizard with a soccer ball and continued with the high energy behavior Ted had observed in the morgue. The surprise for that scene was Henry's intuitive ball handling. Sam offered constructive advice which Henry seemed to understand quickly and his apparent natural ability blossomed with instruction. No one had ever seen him run so much, much less the ball control he exhibited. Sam's son, Ram, was very good also. And so was the next door neighbor. Sam and the folks watching from the porch were astonished at the surprisingly high level of their play.

Sam loved playing and would have continued. His wife was probably used to calling the game before everyone, especially Sam, got all sweaty, so she stood at the porch door and told them to come in. Henry didn't want to quit so the kids stayed with it. But Sam came in.

Ted, being a good host, socialized with Sujatha and the daughter, Gita. However, the case, and especially the post-mortem, stayed foremost in his mind. He had so many questions. For a minute he wondered if discussing any of this in front of everyone there, adults and kids, would qualify as talking about a medical topic or police work? Medicine and health topics passed muster for Liza's rules about what could be discussed in front of the kids. He wanted more information about pineal glands and about what HIV is and why it's so lethal. He wrestled with it only a short time and decided the context of the health issues he wanted to talk about wouldn't qualify for discussion with the kids around. He tried to think of a way to speak about some of this with the three doctors in his house at some point during the evening.

After dinner Samir and his family were tired and looked ready to leave. Ted was disappointed. How often would he have an opportunity to quiz three doctors, with different specialties, in his house? Liza probably knew a lot about HIV but he liked Sam and his wife. He guessed he could learn a lot from all three of them. Then fate, in the guise of Kathy and Henry, intervened.

Henry and Ram were getting along really well. Gita admiringly followed Kathy everywhere. Henry and Kathy suggested a short board game in the den. Later Liza chided Ted for for putting the kids up to it. He, unconvincingly, denied it although he really hadn't prompted them. Nothing wrong with leaving Liza a little uncertain.

Ted and the three doctors stayed on the porch. They each had something cool to drink. The sky was almost dark at eight o'clock now as the seasons were changing in Vermont. Liza planned to talk about the cachet of the state since that day they had already covered Burlington, Chittenden County, and the hospital. But Ted wasn't going to miss his opportunity.

"Sam, Liza and Doc Fowler have told me something about pineal glands. That the gland doesn't seem to do anything much. Certainly nothing that's very critical for life. Maybe something to do with being awake and asleep. I haven't told you, but this case with the ME's homicide may have something to do with pineal glands."

"Not likely I or Sujatha could tell you any more about it. Just like the appendix there's always been some mystery about what, if anything, those glands do. Maybe some use or importance in prior evolutionary development."

Ted leaned forward to make sure he had their attention, implying by the look on his face he was about to say something confidential.

"The thing about pineal glands, and Liza knows about this, is that the ME and the Davies murder cases are tied in with what looks to be the smuggling of many human pineal glands."

He stopped for a second as Sam gave out a soft "oh no" moan, probably contemplating the obvious source of the glands.

"Yes. We have reason to think shipments of human glands were sent from here to somewhere in Thailand, periodically over a few years. The only people we know of who were involved in this in the US are dead: Dr. Stanton and Davies, and maybe a pathology assistant. We have authorities trying to find the people on the other end… But why pineal glands? No one seems to know why they were being harvested from humans and smuggled to Thailand."

Sam's face developed a slight smile. He glanced over at his wife. She looked at him almost like she was blushing and then looked away with a more formal expression.

"Well Ted, I certainly don't know for sure why someone was doing this but I actually can think of a pretty good possibility."

Ted and Liza looked at each other with some surprise.

"Folks, there are some strange ideas and folklore out there in parts of the world. Different cultures than what you're used to that have very different views about what's medicinal, you know. Sujatha and I know that, especially in Asia, there are a great many animal and herb substances that get touted for their miraculous effects in people. What's big in Thailand?... What's always big are sexual enhancements and aphrodisiacs."

That raised eyebrows.

"It's usually really crazy stuff. But they make up bizarre stories about almost anything, or there's been a long tradition of believing in something so people believe it's true. There are places, I guess stores, you can go into all over Asia that are filled with all kinds of things touted to have sexual effects. Right on the shelves for anybody to buy. Who knows how safe some of that stuff is…and certainly whether it does anything at all. Imagine what goes on in black market settings.

"I bet that's what was going on. And think of it; advertising it as something like a human extract and maybe even saying it came from humans in the US. That might be a big deal there. Probably considered very exotic; so then expensive. If you've heard the phrase sex tourism, well that's what goes on in Thailand lately. Who knows, but I think it's a good bet for those glands. But don't ask me why it might be used or what it's supposed to do. I have no idea."

Liza spoke up. "I guess I'll have to go to the medical library next week and cross reference pineal glands and something like 'sexual enhancements' in the Index Medicus and see if anything comes up."

Sam responded, "Sure, but, you know, there may very well be nothing. Lots of that stuff is just crazy. Made up stories that sound good; hoping a placebo effect will kick in."

Sam and Liza looked like they could continue talking about those glands and a likely fantastic use for them. But Ted had heard enough and was anxious now to learn about HIV.

"Sam, you're probably right. Very bizarre and very sad, I think. I wonder if we will ever find out why Ellie agreed to be part of whatever that Trooper must have set up. When you talk about the sex trade in Thailand do you think that might be a link to Ellie having HIV? We'll know about the Trooper on Monday when the lab has agreed to run whatever test they do for that."

When Ted said that about Ellie Liza sat bolt upright with an expression of utter shock on her face. Liza looked shattered; like she was re-living the loss of her friend all over again.

"Yeah, babe. We just found out today Ellie somehow did some secret blood tests on her own blood shortly before she was killed that were positive for the HIV virus."

"That's unbelievable...Just like Reed? Oh, I can't believe it. It's such a quickly growing epidemic. I just keep hearing about it more and more; even in Vermont now."

To Ted, of the three doctors, Sam was likely to have the greater knowledge about this disease. He assumed pathologists should be experts on really bad diseases. In fact, Liza, the internist, a specialist in diseases of adults, knew quite a bit more about HIV/AIDS than Sam did. Sam knew it.

"Ted, the reason I know anything about HIV and the disastrous AIDS process it causes is because it's showing up in big cities right now. It is an epidemic, I'm sure. But I bet Liza knows much more about what it is and why it's so lethal."

Liza explained.

"Ted, HIV stands for 'Human Immunodeficiency Virus'. Someone can be tested for that specific virus but having it doesn't always mean you have to be feeling ill or be sick right away if the test is positive. You know viruses are not alive on their own like bacteria. Viruses have to get into a living cell and kind of take it over to replicate... I mean reproduce. Since this virus gets into cells in the body that are responsible for producing types of immunity, or protection, the body's immune systems are destroyed and the ability to fight infections becomes dramatically limited. We are seeing all kinds of strange infections and some tumors that can develop because of immunodeficiency. And that's, ultimately, why people die of HIV/AIDS. So AIDS, 'Acquired Immunodeficiency

Syndrome', is the term that's used to describe all the clinical, or symptom, features caused by that virus."

Sam spoke. "Ted, people are still calling HIV/AIDS a disease that only homosexuals can get. Indeed I had a prof who said it should be called the 'Gay Disaster Syndrome'. But that's wrong. It looks like it spreads through sexual transmission and it apparently happened to first show up in the west only in gay people. So we now know it's spread by an infected person's blood or body secretions or fluids getting in contact with another person's blood. That means it's not something that can be passed to another only by a gay person to a gay person. Anybody who's blood comes in contact with an HIV positive person's blood or secretions can become positive."

Sam paused and looked at Liza and his wife, who both nodded agreement with his words.

"This means that if someone were to get a blood transfusion from someone positive for HIV it's very likely they could become HIV positive and might develop AIDS. You can imagine the nightmare that is developing because of this. The entire blood transfusion system is at risk. A public health disaster for sure. So we need better and quicker tests to find out who is HIV positive and to test all blood before transfusing it."

Liza now spoke. "One of the many very big problems and worries about HIV is that after a person is infected it usually starts a process in the body that, for some, can take some years until that person develops the clinical symptoms and consequences of AIDS. Many people who are HIV positive have no idea they are carrying the virus even though it is likely gradually affecting their immune system and will cause them to explode with symptoms up to years after becoming infected; some sooner than others. So that's another part of the HIV public health nightmare: people feeling well can pass the virus to others without knowing they have it."

Sujatha was quiet during the discussion. Probably for many reasons. Different than Sam, she was still striving to find her comfort level in a foreign land. Her up-bringing and culture worked to stifle any tendency for a woman to be outgoing like her husband. And the topic they were talking about seemed a matter for adult disease; nothing a pediatrician would be involved in. But she did have something to say.

"I have seen nothing of this myself but there have been a few, only a few, articles in the journals recently talking about AIDS in children. Yes, this mostly seems to be related to HIV transmission from an infected mother to her baby. This may happen in utero…" She looked at Ted. "I mean while the baby is still in the womb or transmission at birth."

She didn't say why, but Liza was intrigued by what Sujatha said.

"Sujatha. Do you know if the progression for the baby from HIV infection to full blown AIDS follows the same several year timeline as with adults?"

"I have never been involved in a case so I don't really know much about this but I think babies can be born with immune problems and, probably, AIDS. I think some can be born with terrible consequences of immunodeficiency. So at birth, sometimes premature, they will not do well and may die then. I also believe there is concern that a mother infected with HIV may possibly develop AIDS at an accelerated pace with pregnancy, delivery and all."

* * *

The room became quiet. Outside it was completely dark. With the reading lights off the porch was only illuminated by a solitary low power overhead fixture causing the room to take on a dim glow. It was difficult to see the expression on anyone's face. But enough had been said.

Ted ruminated on the very big day and was glad it was ending. He and the others sitting there had quite a bit to absorb. Everything from that day was new to Ted. He sensed it was much the same for Liza and probably for their new friends, Samir and Sujatha, also.

As they sat in silence, every few minutes one or two of the kids could be heard laughing in the den. It made all of them feel good. Despite the horror and sadness in the world exposed that day the parade of life would always start anew and continue with high hopes. Thank goodness.

* * *

DENOUEMENT

Once it was clear Corporal Davies had been murdered Trooper Devers became the most likely remaining suspect in his death. Morty Stern had never been found but any idea he could have played an important role in the case remained very small. Even if he somehow managed to still be alive it was very unlikely he would have known, much less thought, how to try to stage a homicide to look like a suicide.

Unless he was completely unaware of someone else who was involved in a major way Nancy Devers might be a murderer. Ted decided Trooper Devers probably wasn't dead after all and he should try again to find her.

* * *

After the autopsy of Corporal Davies the Tucson police were asked to monitor her parent's and sister's homes for a second time. This time there was no difficulty finding her. She was staying at her sister's and, as the police observed her activities for a few days, she was frequently shuttled back and forth to outpatient medical visits. Just hearing she was ill Liza quickly figured out what was wrong with her. When the Tucson police investigation revealed the Trooper had recently lost a baby Liza spoke with the pediatric infectious disease specialist and a neonatologist in Burlington to try to learn about consequences of HIV during pregnancy. It was a new and troubling part of the HIV epidemic.

Ted had to go to Tucson. The medical and public health issues in the case confused him. He convinced Liza to go to Tucson with him to help interview and very likely collect Trooper Devers to return to Vermont with them. Just before the last week in August they flew out. His parents stayed with the kids.

* * *

OF THEE I SING, BABY

Air travel compresses large gulps of distance into often long but endurable hours. Three flights, going from Burlington to Tucson, consumed twelve hours but still meant arriving in Tucson in daylight, around four o'clock mountain time. A sergeant with the Arizona State Police met them at the airport. At the troop headquarters Ted offered his credentials and information was exchanged.

The Vallans were given a beat up old unmarked car for their use. The sergeant, pointedly, reassured them the AC in the vehicle was flawless and would be its most important asset. He was right. It was hot! At an intensity Liza and Ted were not at all used to.

They were given directions to northeast Tucson where the motel they were being sent to was located. The car kept them cool as they easily navigated the mostly wide and almost completely straight local roads leading to their destination. Despite their fatigue they stared intently at the landscape and marveled at the open sky and majesty of the mountains ringing the city.

They were exhausted. It was still full daylight but it was late for them. Alone, just the two of them in the room was almost awkward for them. Over a month had passed since they had spent a night at home without kids. Somehow this summer they seemed to be growing apart. The reasons were several and yet maybe there were no reasons; bickering? trust? changing personalities? They each probably were wondering or worrying what had gone wrong. Why? They both wondered why it was hard for either of them to even find words to talk to each other about what, if anything, was going on?

So they didn't. They would go out to dinner and key their actions on getting a good night's rest and doing their job in the morning. The problem was, even though it was late for them when they went to bed, it still was relatively early, Arizona time. The inevitable consequence of going early to bed was, of course, early to rise.

*   *   *

The local time was four a.m. It was still dark but they were awake. Their internal clocks said it was time to be up. They happened to wake up arm in arm; a physical distance, at least, was bridged. Eyes wide open they stared at each other. She smelled good to Ted.

For the first time in a really long time he thought he felt relaxed. He sensed the case was over. There were still some details but he guessed he was about to find out whatever else there was to know.

Then his thoughts drifted to Liza. He was uncertain about their relationship and that continued to worry him. She picked up on the worry reflected in his expression. Lying in bed, arm in arm and face to face, they spoke; in low voices just above a whisper even though no one else was in the room.

"Why that wrinkle on your face, babe?"

He stared at her, kind of knowing what he wanted to say but very unsure how or if he could say any of it. Then with a hint of a blush he spoke; slowly and softly.

"I know it's been the craziest summer and all I've thought about is Ellie's murder. But, for some reason, at the same time I have this awful feeling that we've been drifting apart for some reason." He paused, but their eyes remained fixed and he continued. "I think I feel like I might be losing you. I don't know why but I get a feeling like I'm jealous… and you're unhappy with me. And I don't really know why."

Liza's eyes drifted away from his. Her face firmed. He wondered if he saw a tear. After a time she spoke.

"Ted, all this year has been a strange time for me. I'm not sure how to describe it. I guess, in many ways, I've never felt so good about myself. I've spent a lifetime dreaming about a family and a career and working hard to have them both. All of a sudden it seems like my practice and my life in medicine has become the most important thing to me." She paused to find words she wanted. "Because I feel I'm good at it and my patients and the colleagues and the people I work with make such a fuss about me. I guess I've never felt so special.

"And, for the first time in maybe forever, I feel like I have some money that I can spend on me; just for me. So I've enjoyed buying things for myself and feeling good about how I look."

She turned her body ever so slightly. They were still arm in arm but her movement and then her words made Ted think she felt ashamed.

"I have flirted with some colleagues. Oh nothing more than some joking around with words. But somehow thinking they wanted to be after me; that other men were attracted to me, made me feel good." Another pause. "I guess I've been stupid enough to even think the way I've behaved might not be so obvious to you and, probably, others.

"And I guess maybe I've been feeling like I'm not needed as much by the kids anymore as they do more for themselves. Even you, you're in charge of your own show, solving really complex problems and still trying to be so sweet. Maybe making me angry because you're not fighting for me because, of course, you had no logical reason to think I needed to be fought over."

She turned back to him and they pulled tightly to each other and kissed, leaving their lips together. After a while their heads slowly fell apart, resting on their pillows.

It was left at that. Whatever else there might be or whatever resolution one or both of them was looking for remained unsaid, for now.

* * *

The day that followed was grim. Everything they learned about the facts were terribly sad and upsetting. First Ted and Liza met with State Troopers and then Nancy Devers together. Then Liza went off with Nancy and her sister to see a doctor at a special clinic. Ted spent time with the State Police and Tucson Police. Absolutely nothing about the day or any of the findings could be called anything but grim.

Late in the day Ted picked Liza up and they went back to their motel. They reviewed what each knew and the awful circumstances of the immediate situation. How much each had also ruminated over their early morning conversation was unclear. They both were down, likely from the accumulated weight of all of these things. But Ted decided he wanted to remain hopeful. He told Liza he was looking forward to dinner at a Mexican restaurant that had been suggested to them. He determined to keep a dialog open.

Ted decided his marriage had some complications but all was far from lost. He was disappointed to hear what Liza said. But from the way she said it he actually thought he could understand some of her feelings and actions. He had noticed changes in her and how she acted with him, but he still thought they were bonded and Liza's sense of family was too strong to ever be torn apart. He may not have realized how all consumed she was with being a doctor now. Who had any experience in how marriages mature and, likely, change over long periods of time?

At dinner he announced they should get up early in the morning (he figured that would happen anyway) and go for a hike in Sabino Canyon National Forest, which was very nearby. They struggled to stay up until it was just about dark. In bed Liza kissed and hugged Ted tightly. They made love. There was mutual interest and pleasure; involved and pleasant but not especially passionate. They each were terribly distracted and exhausted. Both quickly fell asleep as soon as they finished.

* * *

They didn't have the right gear but they were off on a trail very early. The cloudless bright blue sky wasn't sharing yet with the sun which was shielded by a mountain top. The hike was a good idea. They talked, at first about the case, then something happened that couldn't fail to direct them to themselves and family.

Not far along, all of a sudden, about twenty or thirty feet in front of them, a line of four animals crossed the trail coming out from and then back into brush. In the lead were two hairy, obese javelinas. The nocturnal pig-like animals were probably heading home. The last two in the line were much smaller. Neither Liza or Ted said a word but each knew they had just seen a family.

They talked about the kids and they talked, like parents, about a host of things that were important to them. Ted still felt there was some distance between them. At moments Liza almost seemed embarrassed. They were not inclined to disagree about anything. They strongly agreed Tucson and the west were places they wanted to take the kids to someday.

* * *

After only three days in Arizona there was no longer any reason to stay and they were to return home the next morning. Liza had spent most of her time with Nancy Devers. Her empathy and caring allowed the Trooper's family and Ted to understand Nancy's stage of illness and to respect Nancy's wishes.

That afternoon, on the phone with the kids, they each, intentionally, spoke as though they were on a relaxing vacation. To his mother, though, Ted explained how Liza had played such a critical role in helping him and the others. After they hung up Liza demurred.

"The first time you mentioned the idea of both of us coming out here I have to admit my first reaction was selfish. The thought of us getting away on the force's dime to visit this beautiful country really excited me. Then I thought some more about it and I felt ashamed I was willing to consider using such a difficult police situation for us to have a kind of vacation. So I tried to convince you to take Shawn Barry.

"But you were right, Ted. I'm really glad you stuck with it and encouraged me to come with you. This has all been so sad but I am proud to be able to help this unfortunate woman and her family. Such a terrible thing for all of them. Ted, you have been wonderful allowing me to talk with her doctors and trying to understand how this needs to be handled. You knew if I came with you you would be able to make the best decisions."

Liza had already made it clear to Ted there was no one to arrange to bring home to Vermont. Ted was conflicted but he understood. Nancy had told him everything he needed to know. They were scheduled to fly home in the morning and they began to talk about packing when the phone rang. It was very late in the afternoon and they left the room immediately.

It was less of a jolt by then when they opened the door to the blast of heat, but they felt it. The beat up Tucson police loaner continued to manage to blow out an amazing amount of cold air within only minutes of starting and they hoped it wouldn't stop. They drove nearby to her sister's house in the foothills of the Santa Catalina mountains.

Her parents and sister were in the house with Nancy so they sat on the side deck with her brother-in-law. The change of season was actually beginning to affect the heat of the day. It was probably becoming more tolerable earlier in the late afternoons now as the daily cooling from the night started sooner. As Ted and Liza looked out to the west they could see the setting sun was responsible for the change.

Ted and Liza stood to gaze at it. The house was at a modest elevation and they could look out at the city of Tucson below and the Starr Mountains ringing the western horizon beyond. The sun was an enlarging luminescent yellow egg approaching a ridge top far in the distance. The endless blue sky was being replaced in the west with streaks of clouds of brightening pastel colors filling the sky creating a brief huge ceiling for the city. All the hues intensified as the sun dropped to the ridge top and then below it. It was the same spectacular early fall sunset they knew from the Adirondacks over Lake Champlain but on a larger scale.

A day was ending; the daylight in spectacular fashion. The cooling of the evening was eagerly anticipated by most. No one spoke. The quiet was disturbed only when her father opened the door and led her mother into the now darkening sky. She was sobbing quietly. They never paused and continued to their car. Her sister stood in the doorway, her arms folded across her chest. Liza had remarked before, she was impressed how strong a woman she was.

Nancy Devers' sister understood Liza's words about transmission of the disease and was caring for her sister without any hesitation or signs of doubt. She offered Nancy her full love and comfort. The house was cool and a little dark from the sudden transition from day to night. Soft music was coming from somewhere. A bed had been set up in the dining room for Nancy.

Nancy knew she had a fatal disease. Her depression was impenetrable from losing her baby, her illness, and the loss of trust in the man she thought she loved, who had led her to this point in her life. She refused any attempts at treatment to modify her symptoms or prolong her life. Her parents had difficulty with her illness and her choices and could not manage to kiss her when they left. Some years before Nancy and her sister had parted on unfriendly terms but now had embraced each other and her sister cared for her and offered her unconditional love.

Her brother-in-law remained outside. Ted stayed at the doorway to the dining room. Liza and the sister walked to Nancy's bed and sat on it, beside Nancy. Ted could not believe the change in Nancy from only a day earlier. As pale as the sheet beneath her she was coiled in a fetal position, her hair loose and wet on her moist face. Liza reflexedly reached for a cloth by the bedside and gently dried her face while pushing strands of hair to the side. Her eyes were sunken deep in her face. Her breathing was shallow and rapid. The consequences of this disease were more than an even stalwart spirit could have battled with hope for success.

Nancy's sister gathered her up in her arms, pulled Nancy to her, and began to rock back and forth. Liza softly and slowly stroked her sister's back. Her sister gently rocked Nancy for most of an hour until the look from Liza's eyes convinced her it was over and her sister would suffer no more.

* * *

In this very darkest of moments, in a room saturated with sadness, Ted Vallan focused on the radiance of Liza through all the days of this ending. He was almost overcome with feelings of pride and how blessed he and his family were to have Liza Vallan to love and care for them.

Of thee I sing, baby…

…You're my silver lining,

You're my sky of blue.

There's a love light shining

Just because of you!

THE END